THE WAY YOU SHINE

LAWSON HILLS SERIES
BOOK 1

AMELIA CHASEN

Cover Design by Cindy Ras

Editing by Kristen Hamilton

1st edition 2024

ISBN: 979-8-9900248-0-9

ASIN: B0CT9MT2YG

CONTENT WARNING

To check content warnings for this book, please visit: https://www.ameliachasenbooks.com/content-warnings

To those who've ever felt like they're too much—
To those who've ever felt like they're not enough—
You're perfect as you are.

1

DELANEY

Last night was the worst night of my life. A series of tumultuous events that I'd never wish upon my worst enemy.

With the morning sun casting shadows on my escape, I zip up the final bag. I can't risk Josh discovering me leaving. The mere thought of crossing paths with him again is unbearable, which is why I need to get my ass and duffle bags out this penthouse door.

As I glance around the eerily silent apartment for the last time, I realize I've never felt at home here. I've been walking on eggshells for two years. Constantly in fear that I'd set something askew and piss off Josh. Watching my every word in fear that I'd pull the pin on his unpredictable verbal onslaught.

Our entire relationship felt like one gigantic nightmare, with just enough happy moments sprinkled in to make me question everything.

I grab the handle of my rolling suitcase with a shaking hand. This is happening. This is it. This is real.

Everything that means something to me fits into these four recently purchased suitcases. Should I be ashamed that one duffle is entirely full of makeup and my eight-step skincare routine? Probably. But skincare matters to me. It's consistency, it's self-care.

The rest of the stuff in this apartment? Meaningless. I thought I cared about things like crystal drinking glasses and the highest thread count sheets—but it turns out I don't.

Escaping this place alive is what matters.

With a wobbly exhale, I stick a note to the smooth stainless steel of the refrigerator door:

We're over.
Don't contact me.
Fuck off forever,
Delaney

Goodbye luxurious condo and impeccable view of the city. Goodbye heated floors and rooftop terrace.

Hello car living.

Time to start from square one.

~

"NINI, WHERE YOU GOING?" Hazel asks. Her chubby little fingers tug on the end of my shirt as she stands on top of my socked feet.

At the age of three, she hasn't gotten the hang of pronouncing Delaney. She naturally shortens it and calls me Nini. I hope the nickname sticks. The day she pronounces my name correctly is the day I'll sob uncontrollably and rant about the rapid growth rate of childhood.

I tighten her curly ponytail. "Home, baby girl."

My car is my home now, but no need to dive into the specifics. I've got it all handled—or will have it handled soon at least. "I'll take you to gymnastics tomorrow though, okay?"

Hazel whispers not so silently, "Pack me a candy. The good chocolate one I like."

"I got you, Haze." I put my finger to my lips, shushing her with a wink so my sugar conscious sister doesn't overhear from the other room.

My older sister, Jessica, walks in. "What's this I hear about candy?"

"Nothing," Hazel and I say in unison.

Looking at us suspiciously, her eyes dart between her daughter and I, as we try our best to look like the picture of innocence. She doesn't buy it for a second. Bad acting runs in our genes.

"Alright, whatever. I don't even want to know." Jessica gives up her interrogation tactic. Her husband, Todd, is gone on a twelve month long deployment with the Army. Between Jess working full-time as a nurse, and raising a rambunctious three year old, a mini-sized candy bar is the least of her worries.

When she turns her back, Hazel and I high-five and do a jumpy happy dance.

Jessica is without a doubt the responsible, mature sister out of the two of us. At a young age, she was thrust into the responsibility of raising me. Personally, I would say she did a damn fine job. Others may twitch with disagreement—expecting me to have been raised in a barn, or a Jersey shore nightclub.

No one takes me seriously. Ever. And I love that.

Who wants the responsibility of being mature when you can have fun instead? It's safer that way. Deflecting with humor or outlandish comments is a great tool for not having to be deep.

Do people want makeup advice on how to achieve the perfect siren eye? A spontaneous, drunken trip to Cabo? If yes, then I'm their girl. But no one wants major life changing discussions with the person who is impulsive and toxically optimistic.

When our mom deserted us, I had to make a choice to consciously see the silver lining in everything, or else I'd drown in sadness. The one thing I wanted to make damn sure of is that my trauma wouldn't define me. I'm stubborn and the last thing I planned on doing was to let my parents have that kind of hold on my life. I knew I was deserving of much more than the neglect and abandonment they dished out generously throughout my childhood.

So I chose happiness, again and again and again. Until one day it stuck like gum on a shoe.

Jess folds a tiny princess nightgown as she looks over at me. "So, you and Josh are really over?"

"Yep. One hundred percent over."

"Thank goodness. He seemed like a di—" she spots Hazel listening and adjusts her course of words, "meanie head. What happened?"

I sigh, not wanting to divulge too much information. I'm not sure if I can say it out loud without totally breaking down. "We grew apart. Wanted different things." He wanted to shove me into walls, and I wanted....*not* that.

"Hm." Jessica knows when I'm lying, but must sense my silent plea to not dig deeper. "Well, you have a place to stay, right? You're okay money wise without your job too?"

"Yes, *Mom*. Don't worry about me." The place is my car, but it's still technically somewhere to sleep. "But yeah, I'm okay money wise too. Though I have thought about taking pictures of my feet in mashed potatoes or selling my dirty underwear for a little extra cash."

She freezes mid-fold. "I can't tell if you're joking because that sounds like something you'd do for shits and giggles on a normal day."

"It does sound kind of fun, right?"

"Please do not squish perfectly good food between your toes. I'll give you money if it comes to that."

I wave her off. Taking handouts is not on the table for me. "Just send any hot doctors or military men my way."

"You know, I'm not sure medical school or boot-camp could prepare them for you."

I throw a ball of socks at her high ponytail. "Rude. I'm amazing, and you know it. I'd make it worth their while."

"Oh, I'm sure you would," she snickers.

"I'll choose to take that as a compliment, thank you very much."

Grabbing my purse from the console table, I corral my sister and Hazel into a tight bear hug before leaving.

My stomach is in knots as I make my way to my vehicle, with no idea where I'll park and sleep tonight. I could put down my pride, march back inside, and ask for help.

But I can't. I just can't. Because I'm already known as the unstable one. And most of all, I'm not ready for anyone to know what really happened between Josh and I.

2

COLE

My kid is the one running away from her gymnastics teacher, sneaking onto the trampoline in the far corner of the room. Her behavior is so bad that I want nothing more than to cover my eyes and ignore the entire situation. There's a sign, taped to a pole decorated in rainbow paint, reminding parents not to talk to their kids over the barrier. But surely her teacher wants me to do her a solid and tell Ava to go back with her class and listen, right?

I'm about to do just that when a blonde lady next to me starts laughing in amusement at Ava's antics —annoyingly.

It's not the sound of her laugh that grates my nerves. In fact, her laugh is infectious, full of sunshine. What irks me is that she's laughing which then eggs my daughter on since there is now an audience.

Before I can bite my tongue, I snap out, "Excuse me ma'am, but can you stop? It's not helping."

The blonde lady tries to stop her laughter, but it's still sneaking out in little spurts, like a bubbling fountain spilling over. It's then, once I turn to face her, that I realize how drop dead gorgeous she is. Her blonde hair is long and curled loosely at the ends. She's petite, but full of curves that would make any man drop to his knees. And those eyes...those fucking eyes. They flash my way, and they're full of unmistakable confidence. She doesn't give a fuck about my stern demeanor.

My dick decides to try and come alive at the sight of her. But I attempt to order it to stand down, since the waiting area of a gymnastics center is the literal worst place to get a semi.

I glare at her, as her hand cups over her mouth, as if she's physically trying to constrain her amusement. "I'm so sorry. She's adorable. Did you see her little crooked pigtails bouncing up and down with that shit eating grin?" Her face shines like a beacon of light. I don't even know her but I can already tell that positivity radiates out of her every pore.

Trying to not seem totally caught off guard by the gorgeous woman, I shake my head in response. I'm aware I'm coming across as rude, but I'm also too reserved to start a conversation with her. I've never been great with words.

Instead, I look back at the commotion on the gymnastics floor. The teacher is making her way over to my bouncing, trespassing five year old. Ava knows her little runaway spree is over and skips back to join the class, before the teacher has the chance to get to her.

"Oh, she's a smart one. Get it girl," I overhear the blonde saying beside me. Clearly referring to my daughter.

I sigh as I run a hand down my face. "For fuck's sake." I've got to get my daughter under control. But for the life of me, I feel too guilty to discipline her. The lack of authority and structure becomes obvious in group settings like this. But her life has already been difficult for someone so young. That's why I'm too easy on her.

The lady winks at me. "Don't look so worried. The wild ones are always the best."

Unsure of how to reply, I opt for glaring at this woman for a few seconds instead. A secret excuse to stare at and appreciate her for one more moment, before turning away. When I fail to respond, I see her face flicker with a brief glimpse of dejection. Then, just as quickly, it turns back to her normal mask of self-confidence.

I hate that I caused whatever feeling flashed on her face, but I can't take any chances talking to her.

Another student's dad walks up just in time, saving us from the uncomfortable situation. I'm not surprised she has a fan club. As the stocky auburn haired man talks with her, I'm pretending not to eavesdrop. But I 100 percent am.

The dumbass asks how her week has been, and if

she has any plans over the weekend. He's clearly baiting to ask her out. She responds back, cheerful and polite, letting there be zero room for misinterpretation that she's busy and doesn't want his company. 'Atta girl.

I don't know why I even care. It's not like I'm interested, or she'd be interested either.

She looks young. Too young for me. Possibly mid-twenties. Still full of life and exuberance. While I'm an old man at forty now, and the complete opposite of her—dull and grumpy. I don't have time for putting up a fake front of fucking cheerful optimism. Life is hard and I've come to terms with that.

I'm watching the chaos of Ava's class while simultaneously being hyper-aware of the animated woman beside me. The vanilla coconut smell of her shampoo or perfume. Her foot bouncing up and down as if she has so much energy she could take off running at any moment. How she keeps looking at her vibrating phone and silencing the barrage of incoming calls.

Maybe it's my imagination, but I swear her face pales every time she sees the name on the screen. Then with a quick shake of her head she regains that practiced poised expression.

It's none of my business, but who the hell is blowing up her phone? And why do I even care?

3

DELANEY

Hazel and I walk out the door of her gymnastics class, hand-in-hand. I throw her small body over my shoulder and run through the parking lot. Her delighted scream makes my heart ooze with love for this tiny human that isn't even my own child.

After running a lap around my car, I put her down with a huff and mock exhaustion.

"More!" Hazel exclaims. Her cheeks are rosy after her class and from laughing at my tomfoolery.

"Wish I could, but the pony ride is over. How about milkshakes on the way home though?"

She jumps up and down with excitement. "Strawberry!"

I buckle her into her car seat that I keep in my vehicle for the days I pick her up. Between Todd's deployment and my sister's long days at the hospital, I make an effort to help out at least once a week.

The bulky car seat feels massive in my compact SUV. But why wouldn't it, when your car also doubles as your home?

Josh used to insist on having our vehicles professionally detailed every month. Now it looks as though a bomb of bags and clothes has exploded, littering every surface. The black leather seats double as my clothing rack. Every floor space is occupied with a suitcase, bag of toiletries, or jugs of water. Cupholders shoved full with a coffee cup, tweezers, and a tangled mess of various chargers. The disarray of my vehicle mirrors the chaos within my mind.

"Why so much stuff?" Hazel asks, rubbing her eyes, clearly exhausted from her class.

I shrug, impressed by the level of observation from a three year old. "I thought my car would make a good closet. Does it?"

Hazel's eyes shine with amusement at my stupidity. "No, Nini. It doesn't."

I'm about to jab back, when the gigantic, burly man walks past my car. The ends of his dark hair peek out from beneath the edge of his turned around hat.

God help me with that hat. My first television crush, Luke Danes, ruined me at an impressionable age with a love for backward hats.

The man's arms and legs are replicas of tree trunks.

His simple outfit, jeans and a plain black T-shirt, hug his body in a way that makes it difficult not to notice. He holds his wiggling daughter in one arm with ease, and for a split second, our eyes meet. But he looks away again, so fast I wonder if I imagined it.

It's a good thing he's grumpy and standoffish, because I would climb that man like a tree if given the smallest of opportunities. Due to his eye rolls and annoyed expression at my comments during class, he clearly either hates me or has a wife at home. It's a good thing I guess, since I'm two days out of a horrible relationship. One that's called my phone thirty times today.

The last thing I need is a run in with another temperamental dick. I can still appreciate a DILF when I see one though.

ONE BRIGHT SIDE to this car living is that I'll be in the best physical shape of my life. Most nights I've parked in my twenty-four hour gym's parking lot. The sun wakes me up bright and early since, unfortunately, my Bronco doesn't come with the electric blackout blinds I've grown accustomed to.

I swim laps to clear my head every morning. Letting the tepid chlorine water rinse away the chaos of my mind. Showering with the hottest water possible to scorch the feel of Josh's fingers digging into my arms.

While I hum and wait for the intervals between my face products, people stare at me as if I'm walking around naked. Curious, yet suspicious, why there's a loud, strange woman making small talk between numerous serums every day.

I could reach out to any of my friends to crash in their guest rooms. My sister and two best friends, Madi and Ella, would help me in a heartbeat.

I've only given them snippets of my current situation. That Josh and I broke up. That I quit my job at the accounting firm. And while I told them I moved out, I made them assume I'm renting a room on the edge of town.

My pride has held me back from indulging the details. Everyone that met Josh had warned me about him. My friends. Family. Co-workers. It must have been apparent to everyone, except me, what a horrible human he is. Madi, Ella, and Jess all expressed their concerns in the early days of dating. *He's a walking red flag*, they had all said. When I moved into his fancy penthouse apartment within a month of dating him they were shocked. But they supported me, even knowing their worries fell on deaf ears. I am a grown adult after all, it's not like anyone could tell me no.

I keep reminding myself that this inconvenient little time of my life is only temporary. If one thing is guaranteed, it's that I'm a fighter. And I won't let an abusive asshole ruin my entire life.

However, more money, a job, and a place to live

wouldn't be half bad. Which is why I pull out my phone and start browsing the current job listings within a twenty mile radius.

Time to pull the scraps of my life together and turn it into something worthwhile.

4

COLE

A mist sprays me as I bolt upright in bed. "What the hell..." I'm bleary eyed from sleep, and hear a mischievous giggle from the side of the bed. Followed by consecutive rounds of water droplets soaking my face.

Ava is holding a spray bottle, inches from me, as she continues to drench me. "Ava, stop."

She sprays me one more time. "No," she says, voice full of decision, before running away, feet pattering down the long hallway. How do kids think of this stuff? And at six in the morning no less.

Looking at my clock, I see it's time to get up anyway. I'm dreading the day since it's another morning full of interviews. I didn't expect finding a nanny would be so difficult. But if the last two rounds of candidates had anything to say about it, it's that more of the women seemed interested in fucking me than caring for my daughter.

I don't see the appeal, I guess. I'm a forty year old dude, single dad, blue collar worker. I'm not charismatic, I'm not funny, I'm not a billionaire. That didn't seem to stop the eye fucking and suggestive comments though.

That aside, no one has felt good enough for the position. A part of me wonders if *anyone* will feel good enough for the role of taking care of my daughter. She's the most important thing in my life, always my top priority when I close my eyes at night and open them in the morning. I've been relying on my mother for help way too much lately and it shouldn't be that way. With the busy season for my construction company in full swing, I need to find someone fast.

The possibilities aren't looking great, but there has to be at least one decent person in this town fit for the job. Preferably one who isn't trying to harass me, and someone that can keep up with my spirited daughter. They would only be needed full-time during the summer, and switch to a part-time position once Ava starts kindergarten in the fall.

More than anything, I want to protect my child. Shield her from life's bullshit and the heartbreak she feels from an absent parent. Which is why I need a nanny who is stable and responsible. Who will help protect her from that hurt I know has already affected her.

I notice a head full of dark hair peeking out from behind the molding of the doorframe. "You up now, Dad?"

"Yep, wide awake," I mutter as I swing my feet out of bed, feeling my joints crackle as I stand—a reminder of my aging body. "What would you like for breakfast, baby girl?"

"Hm. Cookies." When I narrow my eyes at her, she pastes a smile as sweet as the sugar she's craving. "Please?"

"How about bacon and waffles? With extra syrup."

"Yes!" she shouts, as she runs down the hall like a tiny Tasmanian devil.

I make us Belgian waffles and somehow get talked into adding sprinkles into the mix. I'm fully convinced that my daughter is a future lawyer with the way she can argue her case. As she tells me story after story, I struggle to keep my eyes open due to lack of sleep. For the past five years, sleep has been a constant struggle for me. My brain remains in a perpetual state of motion, a relentless vortex that spews every doubt and worry known to man. Despite trying everything, I can't seem to shut off my thoughts.

"We have to head out soon so I can drop you off at Grandma's. How do you want me to do your hair today though?"

"Hm." She takes a big mouth full of waffle, cheeks puffed out like a chipmunk, while she ponders the question. "I want it to look like a dog holding a flower."

"A what now?" I ask.

"A dog. Holding a flower."

Fucking kids, I tell you. "I'll see what I can do."

She smiles at me from across the nearly empty table, causing a pang of guilt to hit me square in the chest, because I wish I could give her the world, and I can't.

But the pride on her face when I twist her hair into crooked "dog ear" space buns reassures me. Maybe I'm not completely failing at this parenting thing, even if the rest of my life is sorely lacking.

5

DELANEY

I walk into Little Elm Bakery, the best and only bakery in town. The baked goods and free Wi-Fi are the reasons I'm here. I don't have a ton of money to my name, but I'm almost positive that a chocolate croissant has the potential to solve all of my life's current problems.

I waltz into the bakery, saying good morning and smiling at every single person I pass. The hardest part of not being employed is not getting to be around people all day. The social side of me thrives on human contact. The more, the better.

After collecting my pastry and a paper cup of house brewed coffee, I find my place at the table next to the tall window with a view of downtown. Late spring has the tree-lined street blooming with gorgeous cherry blossoms. The light breeze blows tufts of white petals onto the sidewalks, giving the illusion of snow. People of all ages stroll downtown, enjoying the sunshine and flawless weather.

Taking a long sip of my drink, I savor the way the hot drink warms me from the inside out. The rush of caffeine courses through my veins, shaking me from my perpetually exhausted state.

A grumbling across the room draws my attention, and when it registers where the grumble originated from, I stop mid-bite.

It's the DILF from Hazel's gymnastics studio.

A middle-aged redhead woman has a disappointed pout to her lips as she stands up to leave his table.

It must be my lucky day to stumble upon this premium entertainment.

Not even five minutes later, a tall twenty-something year old enters the bakery. She looks around, head full of dark hair held high, before walking over to the man's table.

What the hell is going on? Color me intrigued. And nosey.

DILF and the random woman chat for several minutes. He leans back in his chair, arms crossed against his chest with a scowl. The raven haired lady squirms anxiously in her chair, looking caught off guard by his gruff attitude.

He seems to be asking her questions, to which she is giving very monotone answers that I can't seem to fully hear from my table. He doesn't look very impressed. In fact, he looks bored as fuck. And grumpy...but that doesn't seem like a new thing for him.

The woman leaves, the rejection causing her shoulders to slump forward as if it's physically dragging her down.

My legs move on their own accord, getting up from my table and beelining it over to DILF's table. Curiosity is eating away at me. I *have* to know what's going on. Luckily, I'm not too bashful to demand answers.

He's rubbing his face with two hands, looking stressed. When he sees me standing there in front of the metal cafe table, he freezes as if I've jumped out from a corner with the intent to startle him.

Gesturing towards the table, I ask, "What is this, some sort of weird speed dating?"

The man looks at me and says nothing. Not a word.

If he's shy, fortunately for him I know how to talk. Unfortunately for him, maybe he just doesn't like me and will possibly blow a gasket listening to me ramble on.

"You know there's apps for that? It's kind of similar to speed dating, but you swipe instead. You don't even have to talk at first which might be a good thing for you. Unless you're married then, you know...don't do it."

He crosses his arms, and looks me up and down. Probably trying to figure out who this crazy woman is that's lecturing him about the pros of dating apps at eight in the morning.

"These aren't dates."

"What are you doing then? Are you a gigolo or something?"

He shakes his head. "No, it's none of your business."

"Well obviously it isn't, but I'm invested now. If you, ya know, want to throw my curiosity a bone?" A beat of silence passes, in which it becomes clear he's not going to answer. "Okay, okay, I can take a hint." I walk away from his table, not intimidated in the slightest by his standoffish behavior.

I know his type, silent and broody. Women like me aren't generally accepted by men like him. Every man I've ever dated has said I'm *too much*. Too loud. Too unfiltered. Too opinionated.

Part of me wonders if it's true. But I don't want a lesser, watered down version of myself. I tried and suffered for two years attempting to do so with Josh. Now I'm savoring every ounce of freedom to be unapologetically authentic.

The man sits, scrolling on his phone when minutes later another woman comes in. This time she's around my age, curvy and gorgeous and without a doubt his type.

She's *everyone's* type.

Not giving up on my nosiness, I position myself exactly right at my table to watch and eavesdrop on their entire exchange. This is what living with no television will do to someone. I have to find other sources of valuable entertainment now.

The Victoria's Secret lookalike struts over to him in

four inch strappy heels like this bakery is her own personal runway. I have to commend the way he doesn't even drop his eyes to her breasts that are on display in her low cut square neck blouse. If I had boobs like that, I'd be peacocking around in a bikini everyday for everyone to appreciate the goods.

She extends her hand out in a professional, yet somehow flirtatious manner. "Are you Cole Campbell? I'm here for the nanny interview."

An interview? My ears grow ten times more attentive, because a potential job has landed right in front of me.

Sure, it's nowhere near my field of accounting, and it can't possibly pay much. But a job is a job. One that isn't rendered with a hundred different reminders of my last night with Josh.

I'm good, if not pretty damn great, at hanging out with kids. Not to mention, his daughter seems to have a wild streak I can relate to.

This can be the opportunity to get me back on my feet and out of my car.

This Cole guy doesn't know it yet, but I'm going to be his new nanny.

6

COLE

What another useless day of interviews. The first woman told me she "wasn't against" the use of corporal punishment, which got her dismissed immediately. The next two gave me the ick when they suggested they were available for overnights, insinuating they had no kids allowed intentions.

And what the hell was that bubbly blonde from gymnastics doing there? I was two seconds away from falling out of my chair when she walked up to me and started prying into my business. But damn it, I went slack jawed when I saw her walk up. Short and drop dead gorgeous, but packed with twice the personality for someone her size.

When she sauntered away I couldn't help but notice the way her jeans hugged her perfect ass. The perfect round handful. I hate myself that I'm still thinking about it too.

Daydreaming about this woman who's practically a stranger…it's not like me. Over the last few years, of course I've noticed women, but it's always fleeting. I never think about them a second time.

But that blonde is a vibrant wildfire, licking at the edges of my composure. Her words are sparks that ignite my irritation. Yet within those flames, I find an undeniable warmth that keeps me wanting more.

Which is exactly why I need her to stay far away from me.

Since the position for a nanny is still wide open, I'll have my assistant Teresa put out another ad tomorrow. The sooner I find someone to hang out with Ava, the better I'll feel on those days I pull long hours.

Eleven years ago, I started my own construction company. It had been my dream ever since my teenage years, when I helped my father hang Sheetrock during my summer breaks. When I turned eighteen, I knew I wanted to be my own boss someday. I worked hard for my degree in construction management, got some experience under my belt, then started my company.

Business has taken off, with my crew and projects growing bigger every year. I do very well for myself, the profit far exceeding my expectations from the seed of a dream over a decade ago.

When I get home from the coffee shop, Ava runs and throws herself at me as I catch her in the air. "Daddy!" Her small body thumps against mine, forcing a whoosh of air from my lungs.

"Hi, baby. Have fun with Grandma today?"

"Not really. Grandma kept trying to get me to take a nap, but I'm not a baby anymore. I don't take naps."

My mom, Susan, pops up from around the corner. She snorts out a laugh. "I asked you one time if you wanted to take a rest. You were curled up on the couch with your eyes half closed, yelling *'I'm tired'* for goodness sake."

Ava snickers, knowing she's been found out. "Did you find a nanny for me?"

"Not yet. We'll find someone soon though, don't worry."

Mom clicks her tongue. "You're being too picky. There are plenty of qualified candidates you've interviewed. What about the former daycare provider?"

"Nope. Didn't like her."

"You don't like anyone," Mom says with narrowed eyes.

Ava exclaims, "He likes me! And maybe you, Grandma, but I don't know for sure."

My mom and I exchange a look before busting up laughing. Ava sits up straight, looking proud she said something to entertain us, although she doesn't exactly understand what was so funny.

What she said is the truth after all. I'm not warm and fuzzy. I'll never be warm and fuzzy—except for when it comes to my daughter.

Ava grabs my hand to lead me into the living room to show me the art she made while I was gone. It's times like these, when she's holding my hand that my love for her is immeasurable. But it also makes me feel guilty that her mother, Isabel, isn't around. How Isabel doesn't feel that same love, that same guilt? I'll never understand it.

It's better for Ava to have stability anyway, and Isabel wouldn't be able to give that to her in a million years. She always made it known how miserable she was here in Lawson, and how difficult it was being with someone like me.

It shouldn't have come as a surprise when I caught her sleeping with my best friend four years ago, not long after Ava was born. Hell, I was more heartbroken that my best friend did that to me than I was about my girlfriend cheating on me.

To be fair, I don't think I was ever in love with Isabel, and I'm sure she felt that. She knew deep down I stayed with her because of the baby. Shitty of me? Absolutely.

I'm not mad about her cheating or leaving me. But I'm furious that she is fine living life without a relationship with her daughter.

Once her cheating was out in the open, Isabel stuck around long enough to sign away her parental rights on her way out of town. Now once a year, she reappears like a comet in our lives. The visits are there and gone so quick that you almost forget they even happened in the first place. Ava is cautiously optimistic around her mother, while I have to bite my tongue so hard it almost falls off.

If I could cut Isabel out of the picture entirely I would. The problem is I can't just think about myself, I have to do what's best for my daughter. When she's older and doesn't want to deal with the awkward random meetup with Isabel any longer then I'll support the hell out of that.

Ava holds up the picture she drew. It's of one gigantic stick figure alongside a small one, very abstractly resembling her and I. There's a brown scribbly blob that I assume is a tornado, but she informs me it is, in fact, a dog. I don't miss the way she gives me those round hopeful eyes when she emphasizes the word *dog*.

She wants one, but it's out of the question. My focus is to keep myself, my child, and my construction business alive.

That's it.

No distractions.

7

DELANEY

Exhaustion doesn't even begin to cut how I feel at the moment. I knew sleeping in my car wouldn't be fun. But I didn't expect it to be so damn uncomfortable. I'm petite, but when a car is your home, it's like my five foot three inch frame is suddenly gigantic.

Also, the noises at night...don't get me started on those. The random rush of cars or a voice of someone walking by is enough to jolt me wide awake for hours.

I'm paranoid that Josh is going to find me. I know he wouldn't break my windows or anything, he's too egotistical to draw negative attention to himself in public.

Nevertheless, after that night, I'm still on edge.

But I'm not going to let it get in my way. Because today is important. Today, I'm on a mission. Today, I will become Cole's nanny.

Which is why I'm sitting here in the Little Elm

coffee shop, waiting for my interview with him that I scheduled with his assistant through the job posting online.

Looking at the coffee cup shaped clock, I see that he's running late. And while I know almost nothing about him, it seems very unlike what I do know about his personality.

While I wait, the morning rush of customers flows around me. A soothing chatter of voices, the blender periodically whooshing, getting to chat with a few familiar faces. The chaos of it all rejuvenates me more than the coffee I've been nursing for the last twenty minutes.

I'm doodling on the notepad I brought to take notes, when the bakery door flings open. The tiny bells attached to the handle ring out with gusto at the powerful force. Cole barges in with his daughter in his arms, clinging onto him like a little monkey.

The girl's long legs and dark hair match her father's, but their expressions are total opposites. He looks serious and on edge, as if he's waiting for someone to deliver bad news. His daughter is the picture of happiness, her cheeks denting with the cutest dimples as she grins ear-to-ear. She's poking his impatient looking face, which causes her to giggle every time she touches his cheek or nose. He seems to barely even notice, which tells me this is not a new game.

Cole beelines over to a table that opened up

amongst the breakfast rush. He sets his daughter on the metal chair, as she rubs her belly.

"Daddy, I'm hungry."

"I'll get you food in a couple minutes. I just have to find..." He looks around, searching for the interview candidate he knows is in the room waiting for him. It's a good thing I'm not shy in the slightest, or else I'd be nervous to approach him. But as I walk to his table, I'm thrown off by the way my knees feel like gelatin when his eyes land on me. I can't explain why I feel this way, other than the fact that he's the most gorgeous man I've ever seen.

His hair is dark, silver sprinkled throughout like little silver stars in the dark night sky. Piercing hazel eyes framed by dark brows that furrow with a hundred questions as I stand in front of him. And his soft mouth falls open in astonishment when I hold out my hand and say, "Hi, I'm Delaney. I'm here for the nanny interview."

He's silent for a moment, but his daughter smiles up at me and I know right away that she's my kind of girl. Her energy complements my own. If I knew anything about astrology, I'd say it's because we're compatible signs or something about mercury in gatorade. Sometimes you just *know* when you'll get along with someone, and I have a good feeling about this.

I bend down to the girl's level. "Hi there, cutie. I overheard you're hungry. Would you like my banana?"

"Yes! I *love* bananas. They're my favorite fruit." Her

eyes are as golden brown as the rolling hills surrounding Lawson in the late summer, shining with excitement.

"It's all yours. As long as it's okay with your dad."

I stand up again, and he's staring at me like I just keyed his car. It takes a lot to surprise me, yet I'm thrown off when he bites out, "Absolutely not."

"Um, what?"

"This isn't going to work. Sorry. No need to interview. It's a no."

My heart sinks. "Do you mind telling me why at least? I brought a copy of my resume if you'd like to take a look at it." There's nothing related to working with kids in my prior experience, but I know everything listed on it is impressive at the very least.

No one expects someone like me to have brains. I thought it couldn't hurt my odds to flaunt my accounting degrees and previous fancy job titles.

"Daddy, I want her to be my nanny. She said I could have her banana."

Glancing down at his daughter, he assures her, "No, baby. I'll buy you your own banana. Or muffin. Anything you want."

The girl whines beside him. "But please. She's so nice. And *so* pretty like a real-life princess."

Shaking his head, he locks eyes with mine, emphasizing his point as he reiterates, "I apologize for wasting your time, but it's a firm no."

I'm not sure exactly why his rejection affects me so

much. I've been rejected in worse ways by the people who should have loved me the most. This shouldn't even be a big deal. Yet it stings being turned down by him.

Pulling myself together, I nod as I paste on a smile that I know the majority of people find charming. Somehow I don't think it works on him. "I understand. I'll leave a copy of my resume in case you change your mind." I set the paper down on the table. Then I slide my fresh banana toward the girl and wink. "For the little monkey."

She giggles and grabs the banana, raising it above her head like a first place trophy. "Banana!"

Mustering my confidence, I walk out the door of Little Elm with my head held high and shoulders back. If Cole doesn't want me that's fine. I'll make do, I'll find another job. With a masters in accounting and a CPA under my belt, it should prove easy.

I'm feeling burnt out on numbers at the moment— that stringent environment is a trigger for the night that shall not be named. A break from it all is what I need. I thought nannying would be the perfect distraction, but sometimes life decides for you what is, and is not, meant to be.

Cole

Fuck my life. My daughter has been begging for the outgoing blonde to be her nanny for the last five hours. The damn banana won her over. I never would have brought her with me in the first place, but my mom woke up sick and was unable to watch her.

After four more failed interviews this morning, I looked at Delaney's resume out of desperation. Turns out she's way overqualified. She has fancy degrees, an impressive work history—so why the hell would she want to nanny for near minimum wage? The whole situation has my guard up.

It makes me wonder what her ulterior motive is, because there's no way in hell she would want to be a nanny. She worked as an accountant at one of the biggest corporations, a billion dollar company, for the last several years. There's no way she'd be applying for a job like this when she could easily make ten times that amount somewhere else.

Maybe she was fired for doing something illegal and can't get another job in the accounting world. There has to be a reason, some huge secret, why she's not interested in a job in her field of work.

Still, I can't get over the fact I was so rude. I'm bad at talking in general. But to a drop-dead gorgeous woman like her? My mouth shutters up and my brain scrambles like an egg in a hot pan. I didn't mean to be an ass, but it definitely came across that way.

There's no chance I can have her here. Without a doubt, Ava would adore her. But most of all, I don't want to be the old creep ogling the nanny. And there's no way I *can't* not look at her if she's here everyday. She has that talent that puts a spell on anyone in her presence. Like a burst of sun beaming through dark clouds.

All I know, with every bone in my body, is that it's a bad idea to have her around.

Because I know what she'll do to me.

And I can't take that risk.

8

DELANEY

The interview did not go as planned. More like it went to absolute shit. But I'm not going to let it get me down.

Even amongst the shambles of my life, I feel at peace. I know I got away before it was too late, before things got much, much worse. I'm proud of the way I've played my cards over the last two weeks.

I could have turned a blind eye and pretended everything was fine. But that's not me. Of course, I'm not going to be silent.

When I found out Josh was embezzling from the tech company we both worked for, JunoTec, I had two options. Sweep it under the rug, or tell someone. Unfortunately for Josh, I've always been a tattletale.

I brought it up to him privately first, which was my initial mistake. Those final pieces of his facade splintered away with the news. He was not happy, and didn't show an ounce of guilt. Josh was just mad that he got caught. Then that anger zeroed in on me.

The way his face twisted in shock and then rage. How his fists curled up into tight balls like he was ready to fight. The spit misting the air as he screamed how it was all my fault so he could afford our current lifestyle. I can still feel the hard thump of my back hitting the wall. The thought makes my blood run cold as ice.

In an effort to distract myself, I dedicate the weekend to spending time with Ella, who is visiting from Washington, and Madi. We indulge in mani-pedis at the fancy salon that offers free mimosas and leg massages. Later, we enjoy dinner at a family-owned Italian restaurant that has been our go-to for years. Of course, the reason it is our favorite is for the dessert cart of heavenly baked goods—always selecting one of each dessert as soon as it graces our table.

Our waiter loves us so much he brings out free drinks and appetizers, which I'm over-the-top thrilled about. Watching the number in my bank account drop daily is depressing. Every digit lower brings me closer to the trauma of my neglectful childhood, which I prefer to ignore.

I shamelessly flirt with the hot tattooed waiter all night, because he saved me a lot of money. I'll admit that low key pimping myself out for appetizers hasn't been my high point.

Ella wiggles her eyebrows at me from across the

table after he walks away. "That waiter definitely wants to bang you."

I roll my eyes. "Well he isn't getting any. I've sworn off men and have decided to attempt celibacy."

Madi snorts with laughter. "You could never, you're the horniest person I know. But I'm interested in watching this swearing off men phase go down, so go for it girl."

I see Ella begin to say something, but she hesitates and then decides against it. Closing her mouth and not meeting my eye.

"What is it, El?"

She shakes her head, her ponytail swaying with the motion. "Nothing."

Ella is the cautious, tentative one of the bunch. A feeling in the bottom of my gut knows what she wants to ask. And while I don't exactly want to indulge every question about the cause of my breakup, I also don't want to appear weak.

I'm not weak.

At least not what I show to the world.

"It's okay. You can ask me. You know I'm an open book."

Madi's silent, listening intently to us and sipping on her Chardonnay, as she assesses me for bullshit. Finally, Ella meets my eye and sighs out her question, her face full of concern. "What did Josh do to make you want to swear off men?"

My heart drops at the question, because I know the

honest answer. It's still too soon, too raw, to tell the unfiltered version out loud. My brain does me a solid and steam rolls ahead with a good, generic response. "He's just an ass. Turns out you two bitches were right about him. Walking red flag."

They both nod in agreement, mulling it over as I cross my freshly manicured fingers that they'll buy it.

A subject change in the form of my phone vibrating against the table with an incoming call saves me. I don't recognize the number at first glance, but it could be one of the jobs I recently applied to today. Although it's odd they'd call at 8 p.m.

"Got to take this, sorry." I quickly stand from the table and hurry out the exit.

I take a seat on the empty bench outside the restaurant and accept the incoming call. "Hi, this is Delaney."

A man clears his voice. "Uh, hey. This is Cole. From the nanny interview. Are you busy right now?"

I can't help but cackle. It's not very cute, but he is the very last person on earth I ever expected to call me. "Huh. You know I don't exactly remember there being an interview. In fact, I may or may not remember you telling me that there was no need to interview because it was a *firm* no."

He sighs, "Look, I apologize for that. I was an ass. Would you still be interested in the position though?"

I'm thrown by the fact that he apologized and admitted he was an ass. Josh would have never. But my body is struck with a jolt of excitement at the job offer.

"Yes, definitely. I'm still very interested. As long as your sassy attitude doesn't come out anymore that is."

There's a beat of silence. I can practically hear him grinding his molars through the phone as he replies, "Sure. Um, sassiness to a minimum. Got it."

"So when do I start?"

"Tomorrow morning, 7 a.m."

"Text me the address. See you tomorrow morning, boss."

I hang up, feeling elated about the new job. Staring at the bubbling fountain beside me, I try to ignore the fact how enthused I am to have the world's finest DILF as my employer too.

Small victories. Starting with hot bosses.

9

COLE

Weak.

That's exactly what I am, weak.

My mom is still sick with the flu, and Ava hasn't shut up about the "pretty lady that has bananas in her purse." I can't call in sick for another day, so desperate times called for desperate measures.

Delaney is a risk, but she's also the best choice for the position to care for my daughter. Not one other candidate could keep up with Ava, but there's a wild energy about Delaney that makes me certain she'll do just fine. I can't say I trust her, but I don't not trust her either. It's more like I don't trust myself around her, which I can suck up and get over. I hope.

I'm still itching to get to the bottom of why she would apply for a position that she's overqualified for. But I keep reminding myself that it's none of my business. I still plan to do a quick background check on her this morning, and talk about the logistics of the day, which truthfully isn't complicated. Then I can head to work and stress out the whole time about if I made the right decision, and what they're doing at home.

The doorbell rings, breaking me from the trance of anxiety and my cup of lukewarm coffee. I run my hand through my hair, trying to fix any loose strands so I don't look completely rough around the edges.

As I open the door, there's nothing that could have prepared me for the sight of her standing on my front porch. The only word to describe her is unreal. Delaney Emerson is 100 percent unreal, and about to step foot into my house.

"Good morning!" she exclaims in a voice too energetic for the early hour.

I gesture for her to come inside. "Morning."

She's looking around, taking it all in, not shy in the slightest to inspect my house from top to bottom. I built this place right after Isabel left. I needed a new space, one without the memories tarnished by deceit.

The rustic mountain ranch home I built was a therapeutic project. One that took a lot of blood, sweat, and tears over the course of two years. But I'm happy with the results. Ava and I have been very comfortable in this space, and I plan to live here until I'm dead. The craftsman details on the exterior, with floor-to-ceiling windows featuring a nice view of the sprawling hills have always been the eye catching element to guests. I've grown used to it now, but her astounded reaction makes me realize maybe I should appreciate it a little more from time to time.

With cheeks pink from the chill morning breeze, her full lips fall open in amazement. "Holy shit. This house is amazing. Did you build it yourself?"

"Sure did. With a little help, of course." I'd be a goddamn liar if I didn't say I was proud that she's impressed by the house. I'm not sure if she's bullshitting me or if she's genuinely impressed. As far as I can tell, Delaney comes from a life much fancier than this.

"Well, it's gorgeous. It looks like it could be the featured house on one of those dream home giveaways. Would it be weird if I took pictures of it? My friends are going to shit their pants when they see where I get to work."

"Go for it. And speaking of work, why do you want this job? You're clearly overqualified."

The question takes her by surprise. Her body tenses and face pales as she reaches for her phone. Then she's right back to normal, nonchalant and happy. "I'm burnt out with the whole accounting world. I needed a break. And I enjoy hanging out with kids. So why not?"

"How long do you plan on sticking around? I'm not looking for someone who's looking for a *break* and is going to run away as soon as they're bored. My daughter needs consistency."

"Of course, I understand that. I can't promise I'll be here forever. But I can give my word I'll stay for at least the summer—three months."

I nod. "Okay." Three months isn't ideal, but it gives me time to find a replacement who can be permanent once Ava starts kindergarten in the fall.

Delaney snaps a few pictures on her phone and I can't help but watch her every movement. How she tucks her long, honey blonde hair behind her ear. The dainty bracelets that jingle on her wrist. Her simple outfit of light-washed jeans and a fitted black shirt, that's modest yet extenuate every knuckle-biting curve of her body. The way she furrows her brows as she concentrates, then smirks while admiring her snapshot. It's sexy, and overwhelming, and I need to get out of here before she's disgusted by the middle-aged creep watching her.

"Okay, follow me. I need some information for a background check, and then I'll go wake up Ava so you can meet again before I leave."

She gives me a small salute and follows me to the kitchen. "Yes sir, boss." I think she's mocking me.

"Don't call me that. Just call me Cole."

She smirks. "Yes sir, Cole."

I shake my head before getting a few personal details for the background check. She hands me her drivers license, and I'm not surprised how beautiful she is in her picture. Everyone knows how horrible those pictures turn out, like they purposely try to capture the moment right when you're about to sneeze. Somehow Delaney makes it look like a modeling headshot.

As I enter her birthdate into the online form, I'm

relieved she's older than I initially thought. Thirty; still too young for me, but at least she's not a kid fresh out of college.

Making herself right at home, she begins to search in the cabinets as I finish filling out the form. "Looking for something?"

"Yeah, a mug. For coffee, if you don't mind."

"You didn't seem to care if I minded or not a few seconds ago. Top cabinet to your left though."

I hear her mutter, "Thanks, asshole."

My mouth quirks up at her words. She's right, I am an ass. One who feels guilty for my snide remark now. At least she calls me out on it, I like that.

After taking a big sip of the mug full of coffee, she runs to the sink and spits it out. "Oh my god, what the hell did I drink? Tar?" She wipes her mouth with the back of her hand, grimacing in disgust.

I can't help but smile at the debacle. "I double run it. It's a little strong."

"Strong would be an understatement."

"Sorry, that it's not up to your standards, sweetheart."

She narrows her eyes at me. I lean against the kitchen island and narrow my eyes right back.

"Don't call me that. Just call me Delaney," she says, mimicking my words from earlier. Little flits of taunting edging her words.

"Background check is done. No lengthy criminal history, much to my surprise." I know I'm being a dick.

But something about bantering with her makes me feel alive, for the first time in years.

She rolls her eyes as she walks past me. The scent of her perfume, hints of floral and clean linen, trail behind her. It makes me lose my train of thought, because all I can think about now is how I want to run my mouth along her neck and jaw. I want to breathe her in and memorize every detail about it.

Ava pops in at that very moment, rubbing the sleep from her eyes, her dark hair sticking up in ten different directions.

"Come on in here, let me introduce you again to Delaney," I say.

My daughter's big brown eyes dart between Delaney and me before she shouts, "Banana lady! You're here."

She runs and jumps into Delaney's arms, not shy in the slightest. And here I thought my daughter would need time to warm up before I left. I should've known my social butterfly of a child wouldn't be nervous in the slightest. Especially around someone like Delaney, who's all smiles and warmth and good vibes.

Twirling her around a few times, Delaney sets down a giggling Ava, and tells her, "I have a surprise for you."

From her large purse, she pulls out a banana and holds it out to my daughter like she's presenting her with an award. Delaney's wide smile makes me want to smile too. Almost.

Ava jumps up and down, full of excitement and fresh morning energy. "A banana!"

"Yep. A banana for the little monkey."

Ava grabs the banana and does her best monkey impression, which has Delaney throwing her head back with a laugh.

If an outsider was looking in, they'd assume these two have known each other for years. They click—an instant connection. It puts my mind at ease that Ava will be in good, and hopefully responsible, company while I'm gone for up to twelve hours a day, five days a week.

"Leave, Daddy. I want to play now. You're in our way."

I shake my head at the cheeky comment, as they both giggle with amusement behind my back. Then I see Ava slip her small hand into Delaney's also small one, telling her she'll show her around the house. I realize at the sight of their conjoined hands that I made the right decision. Delaney is without a doubt the right decision for my daughter.

But for me? I'm fucked.

10

DELANEY

Ava and I spend the next week getting to know each other. We pick little yellow wildflowers in the field behind the house, making flower crowns like true flower princesses do. We catch ladybug pupa attached to long blades of grass, and check them daily in a big habitat to watch their transformation into an adult. We swim in the large in-ground pool, eating dripping popsicles while sitting in lounge chairs on the sun shelf.

She's cut from the same cloth as me. We're both fiercely independent, witty, outgoing. We understand each other. Being her nanny doesn't feel like a job I'm dragging myself out of bed to go to everyday. I don't wake up dreading the mindless projects, numbers, and frantic deadlines. I don't have to put on my fake professional smile and demeanor over a paper cup of coffee in the break room. I don't have to pretend like I care what

Gary is saying during our weekly progress report meetings.

Instead it feels like I get to go hang out with my miniature best friend five days a week.

Since my first day, I've looked around the masculine, sleek-lined house for pictures of Ava's mother. There aren't any. Only candid shots of Ava kissing her dad's cheek. Or a closeup of Ava's goofy grin. And Ava alongside her grandma, bear hugging each other in the snow. Each adorable picture threatens to melt my heart as quickly as the drippy popsicles we devour nearly every afternoon.

I'm not sure what happened with her mom, but it's obvious from the lack of pictures and mentions of her that she's not around much. I know all too well the pain that's tied to having an absent parent. My father left when he found out my mom was pregnant with me—the second girl.

Apparently he wanted a son and was gravely disappointed when the sonographer told them a second daughter was on the way. As if my mother could control the situation and genitalia. I've never met him, but from the hazy memories Jessica has, he was a toxic douche.

My mother leaving had hurt the most. She chose to stick around for my childhood and most of my teenage years. Looking back, she was always detached and apathetic; at the time I chalked it up to the stress of a single mother raising two children. But it was once she decided motherly life wasn't for her that I learned differently.

Not only was she overwhelmed, but she was also uninterested. She told a nineteen year old Jessica that she had struggled long enough to raise us. That it was time to 'pass the torch of responsibility.'

One day she left for Cincinnati with her alcoholic boyfriend, left an envelope of cash with enough for two months rent, and a note scribbled on top saying *love you, good luck*.

Perhaps I don't know what true love is, but I do know that ain't it.

In what I'm assuming is a guilty gesture, she attempts to call us once or twice a year. Being the cold hearted bitch that I am, I ignore her calls. I want nothing to do with her.

While Jessica, the kinder sister, will answer on occasion.

Abandonment issues are the cherry on top of my fucked up history.

Life is unpredictable. But one thing I am certain of is that my boss hates me—and the feeling is mutual.

Every morning I arrive, fresh off a horrible night sleep in my Bronco, Cole can barely even stomach to look at me. When he does glance my way from under the brim of his worn hat, it's full of disdain. I can feel the annoyance dripping off him like he's saturated to the bone with it.

It doesn't stop me from smiling and saying good

morning every time he answers the door. I'm overly cheerful, purely out of spite now.

All I get in return is a nod. A damn *nod*. Then he's dragging himself out the door, only to return hours later, looking exhausted and even more tan from a long day in the sun. I usually say goodbye to Ava and sneak out while he reheats the plate of dinner I leave for him.

Everything about this house feels comfortable to me. Until he gets home and I become acutely aware of how I don't actually belong here.

Not with them. Not in a family. I'm merely a fraud, hiding from her real life. The understanding of being inept crawls under my skin, not wanting to leave.

By five o'clock, it becomes so hot that you can hear the cement sing. The crickets are already chirping in the sprawling hills, as the breeze whips through the long willow branches. The perfect summer soundtrack.

Ava and I swim in the refreshing water, practicing her straight arms on matching rainbow kickboards. The look of pure joy on her face, fogged up goggles, and happy screams balance the chaos of the world. Everything feels right when you're reminded that life isn't only full of assholes and deadlines.

Right as we stick our faces into the water to blow bubbles at the end of our lesson, I hear the heavy footsteps of steel toe work boots on the wooden deck. I look up to see Cole standing at the pool's edge. He's watching his daughter and I play in the water, and not one emotion is displayed on his face.

His hazel eyes sparkle with the reflection of the water, fine lines crinkling near the edges as he squints against the sun.

Thankfully, I'm in a modest swimsuit, an olive colored square neck one piece, or else I'd feel naked around him. His eyes on me for the first time in days have me wriggling under the weight of his stare.

Ava runs up the pool stairs, her bulky life vest causing her to waddle. "Dad, did you see me swimming?"

He picks her up, soaking his own clothes to hug her close. "I did, I was very impressed. I missed you, baby."

She climbs her father's tall body, hoisting herself up and onto his broad shoulders as her life jacket bangs into his head. With the way the second hand pool water drenches him, it causes the dark fabric of his shirt to cling to his abdomen. It's distracting. Because now I know my boss is not only downright sexy, but also ripped.

I swim to the pool's edge. "Sorry dinner isn't ready yet, I wasn't expecting you home so early. I was going to start it after we swam."

Cole doesn't say anything at first, he just keeps on looking at me while Ava ruffles his hair. Annoyance creeps up on me, the gentle simmer growing into a full on boil. Even if he doesn't like me, he still needs to fucking respond back when I talk to him. I don't want Ava to notice the bad blood between her father and I. It's not her responsibility to worry about us getting along. She's an intuitive child so I know she'll catch on eventually.

It's that motivation alone that propels me out of the pool. Swiping at the mascara that most likely is smudged beneath my eyes, and wrapping the fluffy towel around my body. "Well, anyways, I'll go get started on it. I had fun swimming with you, banana. Good job blowing bubbles in the water today."

She smiles, mischievously. "The bubbles looked like a fart under the water."

He shakes his head with a sigh, while I burst out in laughter, holding up my fist for Ava to bump.

I turn to head back into the main house, when I hear his steps behind me. "You don't have to cook anything."

I glance back over my shoulder at him. "I know. But I'm still going to."

Ava pipes in, "Dad, she is a *way* better cook than you. Her food is so good."

I don't hear his grumbling response back, but her compliment is like dropping an ice cube into a pot of boiling water. My near bubbling-over annoyance at her father is subdued.

I love her, and I do appreciate Cole giving me this job.

On the bright side, cooking for him also means I won't have to go back to my home that consists of four doors and a bumper. Every evening it's either reading in my car, or trying to weasel my way into my friend's plans.

Dinner tonight is nothing fancy—chicken thighs, roasted potatoes, and carrots. Cooking is surprisingly fun when it's done in a kitchen like this. The space is expansive and open, featuring lengthy L-shaped stainless steel countertops complemented by a butcher block island. Naturally, Cole has stocked it with an extensive array of kitchen tools, including ones I never knew existed until this week—like microplanes.

I'm chopping parsley, fresh from the garden, when I look over and jump, almost dropping the knife in surprise when I see Cole standing in the kitchen.

He's freshly showered, hair still damp, wearing well-worn jeans and a flannel. I don't know what it is about a flannel shirt, but they do it for me, okay? And holy shit, is he doing it for me right now. It's a good thing I don't like him as a person.

"Jesus, you scared me. I need to put a bell on you, like a cat, so I know when you're walking up."

Crossing his arms, he stares at me. His biceps look bigger than my torso and I'm not going to lie, it turns me on.

"Need any help?" he asks, surprising me.

"No, don't worry about it. Go spend time with Ava, or do what you need to do."

He nods and walks away, not saying another word which is what I've come to expect from him.

Minutes later, Ava runs in and is bouncing up and

down, her little hands clasped to her chest in anticipation. "Can you stay for dinner? Please, please, please."

Glancing toward the family room, I try to spot where Cole is and anticipate how horrified he'll be by his daughter's request. I doubt he'll want to spend one more minute around me.

"I'd love to, banana. But I'm not sure if I can. I'll have to ask your dad in case he wants some time alone with you."

She grins from ear-to-ear from the use of the fitting nickname I've been calling her. "It was his idea. He said to come ask you. So can you? Stay?"

I'm doused with shock that it was his idea to invite me to stay for dinner. There's a thread of uncertainty in my decision. But the big brown eyes tinged with hopefulness do me in. "Um, *yeah*. Of course I'd love to eat dinner with you then."

She dashes away, her excitement echoing through the lofty ceilings and exposed beams. It's rare for me to dread being around someone. But the thought of Cole's contemptuous gaze makes me want to bolt, all the way back to the safety of my vehicle.

11

COLE

Our arrangement was that Delaney watches Ava, and to cook lunch and dinner, Monday through Friday. Thing is, they've always eaten dinner before I'm home. This awkward little run in has never been a problem. For over a week, I've been doing a damn fine job at keeping my head down and eyes off her.

What was I thinking when I invited her to stay for dinner? It's too long to be near her. Too long to stand in front of her like the nervous, tongue tied idiot that I am. I know she feels it every time she's near me, how awkward and standoffish I am. She's bubbly and personable, while I'm on the opposite end of that spectrum. The way, way opposite end.

The three of us sit around the long farmhouse table that I built years ago. It always feels oversized with Ava and I. Having Delaney sitting here now, chatting animatedly with Ava between bites feels surreal. I'm the one who feels out of place between the two of them, as they talk a hundred miles a minute about some video that has cats and pickles. I have no idea what they're talking about, but I do love watching them together. They radiate a warmth that outshines the dawn itself, their genuine connection blooming like the first light of morning.

It's too late to do anything about it, but seeing how much they've bonded in one week worries me. How is Ava going to feel when Delaney leaves in a few months?

Deep down, I already know the answer. And it wrecks me.

She doesn't have a mother in her life. Of course she'll get attached to the sunny woman who freely gives all the affection and undivided attention that she has craved for nearly her whole life.

I'm a fool if I think any of us will get out of this unscathed.

Ava taps my arm. "Dad, remember that video game we played? What's it called again?"

"Mario Kart."

"Oh yeah. Can we play it? I want to show Delaney how good I am at it."

I look over at Delaney, who's staring at me with her round blue eyes. Like she can see straight through my gruff exterior to all the insecurities buried inside. "Oh, uh. I don't know. I'm sure she has somewhere she wants to be. Or has to get home to her boyfriend or something."

Ava snickers like I'm a dumbass. "She doesn't have a boyfriend. We dance to the "Single Ladies" song like every day."

Delaney's eyes bug out, before hesitantly meeting mine. "Hope she's allowed to listen to that. Because if not...too late."

"It's fine."

Relieved, she turns back to Ava. "If it's okay with your dad, I'd love to play Mario Kart with you."

"I'm going to go set it up before he says no!" Ava dashes to the sink, giving her hands a quick rinse before rushing to the family room to set up the game.

I rise, grabbing the dirty dishes from the table. "Look, you don't have to stay if you don't want to. I know you've hung out with her all day already."

Grabbing the cups and scooting in chairs, she replies, "No, it's fine. Is it weird if I say Ava is one of my friends? I really do enjoy spending time with her."

I give her a disbelieving look, which only makes her smile at my stupidity. My heart jumps alive at the sight of it.

She tilts her head, mirroring my face and dishing it right back. "You don't have to pay me to stay longer or anything too, if that's what you're worried about. I like being here. And I don't have any plans."

"I don't believe that. It's Friday night and you're young."

"I'm not *that* young. Plus, I save all my clubbing and heavy drinking for Saturdays," she teases, winking at me.

I nod once, ignoring that pulse low in my stomach, and instead pretend to focus on washing the dishes. What I'm actually picturing is some guy all over her on a drunken Saturday night, and I don't like it. I can't explain why, but I don't.

"Don't have a heart attack on me now. I'm kidding. Kind of. It's only minimal dancing and rare cocktails nowadays."

"You're allowed to do whatever you want on your weekends off."

She smirks, reading me too well already. "That's not what your face said about twenty seconds ago."

I shrug, at a loss for what to say.

"So what do *you* do on the weekends? What's your version of letting loose look like?" She leans her curved hip against the counter. "Ax throwing? Strip clubs? Cigars?"

"I don't."

"Don't what?"

I keep my focus on rinsing the dishes and loading them into the dishwasher. "Let loose."

"Oh. Well, why not?"

"Because I'm a single father. I can't do that."

Furrowing her brow, she tries to understand. "Well, you can, but you choose not to. Letting loose doesn't have to consist of questionable activities, by the way. Just something to... you know, blow off steam and relax for a couple of hours once in a blue moon? Self-care. Treat yourself and all that."

Her voice softens to a near whisper, "Just because you're a single father doesn't mean you can't relax or have fun ever again. It's good for you to get a break occasionally too. And work isn't a break by the way."

I don't want to admit it, but she's absolutely right. Lately I've felt like a dried up version of myself. A human crouton. I don't know who I am besides a father and business owner. And as much as I love my daughter, I do crave time to myself. I've never wanted to leave Ava unless it was absolutely necessary, strictly for work purposes. She only has one parent so I strive to go above and beyond for her.

My mom and Ava have begged for sleepovers together in the past. I've always turned the idea down because pawning my kid off on someone else rubs me the wrong way. It's my fault after all for choosing the wrong person to have a child with. Which is why it feels like solely my responsibility to care for her with minimal help. To give double of myself to make up for the void of her absent mother.

But not once in the last five years have I done something for my own enjoyment. I hate that Delaney knows that about me now. It feels too personal, too vulnerable. And I'm the opposite of that—avoidant and closed off.

Walking right up to me, she rests her elbows on the countertop and leans forward. "Let's say Ava was with a sitter. And work didn't need you for the day—"

"Work always needs me. I'm the one running things."

She smiles before rolling her eyes at my interjection. "Okay, mister busy pants. We're pretending here, okay? Roll with it."

"Mister busy pants? Really?"

The sound of her laugh fills the room with the melodic sound. "Yes. Because that's what you are. A very busy man in pants." She clears her throat, continuing her point. "Tell me what a perfect, fun, relaxing day would look like to you."

I'm silent for so long that she probably thinks I'm ignoring her. But she keeps on staring at me, waiting. Not backing down.

The truth is, I don't know what I like anymore. I don't know what makes me happy besides my daughter and work.

She angles her head, still watching me as if I'm primetime news.

I avert my gaze back to the farmhouse sink. "Quit staring at me like that."

"I asked you a question. I'm waiting for a response. I'm trying to figure out what's going on inside that head of yours."

I'm thinking about fucking you on that counter doesn't seem like an appropriate response. But out of the corner of my eye, I can't help but keep glancing at her rounded ass that's sticking out when she's leaning forward like that. If I could bite every curve on her gorgeous body I'd be happy every damn day of my life.

A small smile tugs on her lips as if she knows exactly what I'm thinking. "I think I guessed it...what you do to relax."

I turn off the running water and turn to face her. Crossing my arms against my chest and looming over her like a tall building. "Enlighten me."

"You—ya know." Her small fist moves back and forth. "Masturbate. Jerk off. Whatever you want to call it."

To her, this is merely a joke. But to someone with social anxiety the size of a small army, I'm stunned speechless. And turned on hearing those words come out of her pretty little mouth.

I can feel the tips of my ears turn pink as I fight off a boner. "Is that what you think I spend all my time doing? Fisting my cock?"

"Well, do you?" she crosses her arms, mirroring my own body language.

I drag a hand down my face. "For fucksake. I can't tell you that. It's inappropriate."

"It's only inappropriate if you whip your dick out right now to do it. Even then...I wouldn't be too mad about it."

"You're killing me," I groan. "But yes. I jerk off sometimes. Happy?"

A triumphant smile spreads across her heart shaped face. "I'm glad you have some way to relieve all that tension."

I look at her and she looks right back at me, neither of us breaking eye contact. The air between us feels thicker. Like the oxygen is denser, charged with magnetism and the excitement that only comes with the risk of crossing a well drawn out line.

The sweetheart neckline of her shirt draws my attention to the smooth skin of the swells of her breasts. Either I'm seeing things or Delaney's chest is rising and falling quicker than it was before—feeling that same wavelength I'm on.

Shit. What am I doing? I'm one small step away from losing my composure and doing something I'll regret.

She lets out a gentle hum in response, thinking about what I said. "Well, damn. Now I kind of want to know what you imagine when you do it. But I guess that'd be crossing a line?"

You. I think about how it would feel to be inside of you, or your exhale on my dick right before you go down on me.

But before I say anything Ava's voice yells from the other side of the house, telling us the game is set up.

Delaney and I jump, breaking out of whatever lewd spell we were just under that would make us have that delusional conversation.

Then the last thing I expect her to say, as we walk side-by-side down the hall, is, "Come out with my friends and I tomorrow night."

It's a terrible idea. One I actually consider, and then surprise myself by agreeing to.

12

DELANEY

The nights have been getting too hot. I've gotten lucky to be at Cole's during the peak of the sweltering heat on most days. But it's the beginning of summer and the nights are growing more uncomfortably warm and sticky now. The temperature also doesn't give a shit about how much gas it takes to run my car air conditioning. The leather of my seats sticking to my skin while I turn in my sleep will forever be imprinted in my brain.

Car living is getting less and less glamorous. Well, it was never quite glamorous in the first place, but it was better than nothing—an adventure in a screwed up way.

Certainly better than living with that piece of narcissistic shit, Josh. With a couple thousand to my name, there isn't much I can do. Most apartments and rooms run at least two thousand a month here, requiring a minimum of first and last months amount of rent as a deposit.

The apartment Josh and I lived in was in his name. He convinced me to pay all the bills since I got to live in his fancy apartment—which didn't cost him a dime since his rich family gifted it to him.

At the time, I was eager to oblige because I was ecstatic to belong somewhere and to be wanted by someone. In hindsight, I can see where I fucked up. Where I was too willing, too determined to make our relationship work. Giving up all these tiny pieces of myself in exchange for someone to accept me. But he took those pieces and would throw them back in my face. Tell me how to change "for the better."

Never again.

I've been determined to put a positive spin on all of this though. I have to. The day is only as good as you make it. All these sleepless nights have me plotting, formulating a perfect plan to put everything in the universe back to normal. To go back to a comfortable living space. To make sure Josh stays the hell away from me. To get my job back after quitting on a whim and pissing off too many people.

It won't happen overnight, it will take planning and forethought—which can be hard work for a spur of the moment person like myself.

For now, I need to focus on the task at hand—a perfect distraction: Operation Help My Boss Unwind.

I'm shocked he agreed to my invitation. It was a suggestion I devised without even thinking of how he'd feel about it. I could see the pained look on his face as he mulled it over. He must *really* need to relax if he's willing to do it with the one person he seems to hate.

He has no idea what the plans are for the night. I don't either, which is half the fun. I'm torn between giving him the wildest night of his life, a la *The Hangover* movie style—blacking out and waking up with no shoes or ID's.

Or doing a simple night out, drinking a couple beers, eating greasy hot dogs from the vendor out front.

As tempting as a rowdy night of taking vodka shots off each other's body is, I think it will scare him. The goal is to help him relax, not to be thrown into a state of absolute shell shock.

I invite Madi, her fiancé Noah, and her brother Jude. Being alone with Cole seems like a bad idea—wrong in some way. There's no explanation why it would be bad, I just get the feeling we both aren't ready to experience that yet. My friends will be excellent buffers, with the possibility of Cole making a new friend amongst the men too.

It's now after 9 p.m., and I'm standing outside the bar waiting for Cole to arrive. He's late and I'm beginning to think maybe he decided this was a crazy idea and has ditched me entirely. My friends are inside holding down a table at The Depot while I wait.

A converted granary and furniture warehouse, now

an eclectic bar, sits about fifteen minutes down the road from Lawson. It's a little hidden gem among the bars, filled with quirky decor and taxidermy animals inside.

Ten more minutes pass, as I sit scrolling on my phone. I don't want him to feel lost when he arrives which is why I've insisted on waiting outside for him. I'm about to give up when I see his massive form approaching. He's a head taller and foot wider than anyone else here—wearing a nice pair of jeans, boots, and a fitted gray shirt that stretches across his chest and arms.

I don't get nervous, ever. It's not in my DNA. But my heart rate quickens, and stomach flips, every step closer he gets.

When he's almost to me, I say, "Well, well, look who decided to show up."

He looks past my shoulder, inspecting the bar. "Sorry, I'm late."

"I'm just glad you showed up. I was ninety percent sure you'd bail."

"Trust me, I thought about it. Usually I'm asleep by now."

I elbow him, my joint hitting a wall of solid muscle. "Don't look too excited to hang out with me now."

He shakes his head without a word, proving my point. As we walk inside he holds the door open for me and then trails behind. Close, but not too close.

The bar is busy when we enter, and we have to push

and weave through the hipster crowd blocking the entrance. It's full for a Saturday night, with a wall of bodies pushing, laughing, drinking. A grunge band plays nearby, filling the bar with notes of an electric guitar and a slightly off-key singer. The place smells of stale beer with hints of tobacco and cheap men's body spray.

I look back to make sure he's still following me, and catch him with his eyes glued to my ass. I don't want to gloat, but I can't help it. Him looking makes me get a big head.

"Like what you see, boss?"

He freezes when he realizes he's been busted. "What, no."

"It's a nice butt. It's okay if you look. All those hours on the stair climber have to be for *something*."

His cheeks tinge pink. "I wasn't looking."

"It's okay, I've looked at your ass before too."

With a choking, coughing noise escaping him, I try to hide my laugh. Teasing him is too easy. I grab his wrist, pulling him along as we weave through the drunk, clueless crowd. My hand can't even wrap fully around the cords of his muscular forearm. Huh. Who knew forearms could be ripped?

I try to ignore the way touching him makes me feel. My fingers tingle with lust that zaps straight to my core. It's my natural reflex to want to drop his arm like a hot pan, but it would be too obvious. I'm not looking his way so he can't read my face and see whatever I'm feeling toward him. It's a well known fact that every single emotion I feel is displayed for all to see in my expressions.

I tug on him harder, maneuvering our way through a rowdy bachelorette party. All the women are wearing pink cowboy hats and drinking Manhattans. Swaying offbeat to the live music. Every single one of the women aren't shy about the way they eye-fuck Cole. I hear one in a high-pitched voice yell, "Goddamn, he's fine."

I'm tempted to high-five her in agreement, but Cole might bolt right back out the door. The best part is he's completely oblivious to the herd of catcalls directed his way.

We round a dark corner leading to a room of green leather booths and scratched up tables. I drop his arm and stand at the front of the booth looking at my friends, waiting for the lull in the conversation to introduce him to everyone. "Everyone, this is Cole. Cole, these are my friends—Madi, her fiancé, Noah, and her brother, Jude."

Everyone says hello as we sit down, scooting our way across the sticky vinyl. Noah passes Cole a glass and a pitcher of dark beer they ordered some time ago. Madi scoots down the now watered down rum and cola I asked her to order for me. It's apparent in their loud and boisterous body language that Cole and I are already behind on the spectrum of tipsiness.

Madi leans over, whispering quietly in my ear, "You never told us your boss was gorgeous."

"Yeah, well I forgot to mention it, okay? All I've been able to focus on is how much the man loathes me."

Madi's eyes glance over at Cole, who is sitting to my left, back as straight as a board. "From where I'm sitting, the man does not hate you."

"You're right, I'm not that special. He probably hates everyone and everything."

"That's the spirit." Madi pats my leg before turning back to her conversation with Jude.

Cole sits next to me, quiet and stone faced, as he sips on his beer. He looks miserable, like he's about to take a sick pet to be put down. I feel responsible for dragging him here and almost accept defeat that I can't force him to have fun. If anyone is annoying and persistent though, it's me. I'm determined. He *will* have a good time by the end of the night.

I touch his arm again, and he tenses, so I pull away as fast as I can, trying not to draw attention to it. "Hey, how was Ava today? Did she do okay going to your mom's house?"

"Yeah, better than expected."

"That's good news, right?"

"It is. When I dropped her off, I think her exact words were *'you can leave now.'*"

I laugh, and the corner of his mouth tips up ever so slightly. The closest I've seen him to smiling. It's a start.

Despite his grumpy demeanor, he's a fantastic

father. It's endearing. If I had a dad like him, maybe my life would be different. Maybe I wouldn't be so damaged and living in my car as a means to get away from yet another troubled relationship.

He shrugs and takes a sip of his drink. "You know, sometimes I wonder if she loves me or not."

"She does. Trust me. She talks about you all day long, and how good you are at everything. You're a hero in her eyes."

"Yeah?" The shine in his expression tells me he's eating this up.

"Oh yeah. She's told me how you know how to build or fix anything, how you can always beat Bowser on the first try, *and* apparently you play basketball really well?"

Taking another long sip of his beer, he bobs his head, as if acknowledging, *yeah, okay, it's true, I do all that.*

Noah's friend, Peter, that I've seen in passing comes over to join us. As everyone scoots down to make room for him, I'm pushed into Cole. Our arms make contact, and my bare knee bumps his jeaned one. There's nothing soft about him, he's solid and I can tell by the way he's unwavering when I'm pushed up against him. My heart pounds at the proximity, which tells me I need to get laid if this is what does it for me now. I'm holding my breath to see if he shifts his knee away. Because I damn well am not moving. Touching him, even a simple touch like this, makes my veins blaze fiery. Our legs stay glued together, my leg looking comically small next to his tree trunk limbs.

As I chat across the table with my friends, I'm actually living in an alternate reality where Cole and I get along and touch legs like it's no big deal. I convince myself he must not notice the contact, and don't make a move to scoot away from him. We both don't glance at each other, instead it's our legs beneath the table connecting us.

I wonder if the contact is grounding for him too.

Out of the corner of my eye, I see a woman in her mid-thirties shamelessly checking him out. I bump his knee with my own, and nod toward the woman. "Hey, that lady is checking you out if you want to go for it."

"What? No, she's not."

I lean forward to peer around his broad shoulder. The gorgeous platinum blonde woman is staring straight at him, waiting to make eye contact. "Look over there. She's staring right at you and biting that cocktail cherry off the stem. If that doesn't scream 'I want to have sex with you,' I don't know what does."

His head stays perfectly in place, but I notice his eyes dart to his left to see what I'm talking about. When he makes eye contact with the woman, she gives him a little wave.

"She most definitely is. Look at her looking at you like you're her next meal. Oh my god! She even licked her lips."

He glances at the woman briefly and looks back at me. "She probably thinks I look familiar or something."

"Cole. She wants to fuck you. Just accept it. You're really hot, I'm sure you get it all the time."

When the word *hot* flies out of my mouth, he chokes on a sip of his beer. I almost regret my lack of filter, but an intuition nags at me that he needs to hear this. That he needs to know people find him attractive and want him for more than swinging his hammer at work. *Swinging his hammer* is a damn good metaphor though. I'll have to try and work that into our conversation someday.

His hands spin his half empty glass of beer. "You don't have a filter, do you?"

"Nope, not really. Want to dance?"

The live band stopped playing several minutes ago and upbeat dance music with good bass has begun to play. An array of couples, friends, and solos have made their way to the dance floor. It's crowded and rowdy and looks like fun.

"I think I'd rather die."

"So dramatic. C'mon, we're dancing. I'm supposed to show you a good time tonight, remember?"

I begin to rise from the bench of the booth and nudge him to scoot down and let me free. He reluctantly stands as I climb out behind him. The music is set to such a high volume that there's no way we could argue over the noise now. As I slide past him, I start in the direction of the plank dance floor. Pausing, I turn back to see if he is behind me. But his boots are still planted to the floor near our booth with his hands shoved into his front pockets. He looks...nervous. And really damn handsome.

With the bass in my chest, I walk back to him and outstretch my hand.

It shouldn't, but it feels vulnerable. Waiting to see if he'll accept or reject me.

Two beats pass before he finally grabs it. His skin is warm and mine is freezing. I hold on tight, soaking up every ounce of his warmth that I can as I lead us hand-in-hand to the dance floor.

He stands there, a head taller than the rest of the crowd. His face borders on annoyed and grumpy. And it makes me smile up at him bigger—because only he could stand out here looking unimpressed and as motionless as a boulder.

I start dancing along to the music. The highs and lows of the song guiding my body as I make a total fool of myself in front of my employer, and not caring. His eyes are on me, on my hands and the way my hips sway back and forth. If I was a smidge less bold he'd make me nervous. But I love it. I love the way his eyes burn a trail along my skin as if he was actually touching me.

"You want to dance with me?" I yell over the music.

Not hearing over the tall speaker positioned next to us, he shouts back, "What?"

I step into his zone, going up on my tiptoes and bracing my hands on his shoulders. He's as steady and sturdy as a brick wall. A fantastic smelling brick wall with dark brown hair that curls at the very ends.

"I said dance with me!"

He leans into me, his hands still tucked into the safety of his pockets. "I don't dance." His breath tickles my ear, igniting a spark in my abdomen.

I pull back and give him a skeptical look before leaning in again. "*One* dance. Please. I'll help you."

He stares down at me as I grab his wrists, untucking them from the pockets of his dark jeans. Then I spin around, my back to his chest, and place his hands on my hips. Behind me, he is stiff as if placing his hands on me has frozen him to ice. With my hands still atop of his, I rock my hips back and forth. I'm not the best dancer in the world, but a number of nights spent at raves and clubs have taught me a thing or two.

I crane my head to look behind me, and Cole's gaze locks with mine. I'm sucked into his vortex. And if it wasn't for the occasional drunken person bumping into us, no one would exist in this crowded bar beside him and I. I'm not even tipsy, yet I feel drunk from the feeling of him touching me. That spark in my belly turns into a full on wildfire as his fingers press into my skin with more pressure.

I give him a reassuring smile. "Just like this."

As I press my back into his pelvis, his eyes darken. The motion prompts him to lean down over me like a shield. Together, we sway to the music, my ass pressing into him, our hips moving as fluid as liquid. He says he can't dance, but obviously he's lying, or a natural.

Feeling brave enough to test the waters, I drag his palms up my body and back down as a means to let him know he can touch me wherever he'd like out on this dance floor.

I'm not sure what I'm getting out of this moment. And I'm definitely not sure how I plan to face him on Monday morning. But currently I'm reveling in the way his pelvis presses into mine, an unmistakable length growing harder by the minute.

He may be my boss, but there's nothing professional between us right now. As we continue to dance, those large hands begin to explore my body all on their own. Traveling from my hips, trailing up and over the expanse of my ribs, to right underneath my breasts. His fingers brush the underside of my tits, and the touch starved shake of his hands only makes me want more.

He's touching and exploring me like I'm a fascinating unknown specimen. We're in a whole other dimension—flowing and breathless and craving.

I can sense it like my own thoughts. He wants and needs this as much as I do. The urgent want to be desired, and the hungry touch of another human.

The song comes to an end, causing Cole to pull his hands away as if he was caught stealing. It snaps me back to the present—wondering what the hell kind of impulsive hole I dug myself into...yet feeling lighter and more content than I have in years.

Not ready to turn around and see the regret on his face, I glance around the packed bar. It's all a blur of faces and sweaty drinks in mason jars. That is until I make eye contact with the one person I never wanted to see again.

Josh.

He found me.

My ears ring, panic flooding me as the smug bastard crosses the bar to me.

He looks the same. Buzz cut blonde hair, preppy clothes. It's now that I've seen the other side of him that I notice the empty look residing in his eyes. No life, no soul, no feeling. Was it always like that and I didn't notice until now? Until I got the fuck away and saw it from a different vantage point?

As my ex makes his way toward me, he doesn't spare anyone else a glance. His cold eyes are only on me, like a puppeteer that's finally found its prop again.

I'm paralyzed with fear—that night rushing back to all my senses.

Muscle memory.

Josh throws his finger in my direction and I jump. "I need to talk to you."

This was supposed to be a fun night. Not one that I ruin with Josh, again, for every one.

I'm surprised to see Cole looking right at me, assessing me with a look of...something. I can't interpret it. But his face brings me back to the moment. His eyes search mine, looking for an answer. *Are you good?* is what I think he's attempting to convey. It's what gives me the strength to nod, scoot past Cole, and go outside to speak with my ex and clear the air once and for all.

Even if my soul does leave my body as I follow Josh out the exit.

And even if every alarm in my brain is blaring like a five-alarm fire.

13

COLE

I don't like the look of the asshole who dragged Delaney away, demanding to speak with her. I'm not sure who he is to her, but the guy has bad vibes. He looks like one of those entitled finance bros that think they're better than everyone else, when all they really have is soft hands that have never seen tough work, and an unhealthy dose of petulance.

The terror I saw in her eyes made me want to grab the guy by his Armani collar and throw him out the door. Delaney is a lot of things, but she's not fearful. At least not until she saw that man.

I make my way back to the booth. Everyone is staring at me with wide eyes and I'm not sure if it's because of my reckless decision of dancing and losing myself in Delaney, or the jerk that she followed out the door.

Her friend Madi, looks around the table, biting her thumb nail in worry. "What should we do? I shouldn't let her go alone with him."

"Who was that?" I ask, before even thinking twice about it.

"Josh. Her ex-boyfriend. He's...not a good guy."

"How so?" I bite out. I'm not annoyed at them, only desperate to know. All I can hear is my heartbeat in my ears.

"We've always hated him. You know how Delaney is, full of life and outgoing. Well, Josh...he brings her down. *Drags* her down. Talks down to her, manipulates everyone each second he can." She pauses, looking at Noah for a second, while twisting her ring on her finger. "She never told us how or why it ended. Normally she tells us everything—she's an open book. I'm assuming it didn't end well and she's not ready to talk about it."

Noah squeezes Madi's hand and rises, "I'll go check on her."

My legs have me standing again before I realize what I'm doing. "I'll go."

The group stares at me as if I've just volunteered to go to war for them as I retreat to the exit, taking steps twice as long as normal.

When I reach the door, I pause and consider how she will feel about me bursting through the door to come to her rescue. We're not friends. We hardly know each other. She also doesn't seem like the type that would want rescuing. But after everything her friends said about this asshole, I need to do something or else the worry will consume me. I'd never be able to forgive myself if something happened to her.

I slide through the door, the noises of the bar escaping outside until the door closes again. It's a warm night, the kind that doesn't belong once the sun sets. A few bikers smoking cigarettes side eye me, unsure of my motives of being in their tobacco clouded presence.

Catching the harsh tones of her ex and Delaney's gentle pleas, make me break into a sprint. My resolve solidifies as a protective fire ignites within me.

When I round the side of the warehouse building, it's worse than I could have imagined. I'm only seeing a snapshot, but that snapshot is all it takes for me to see red. Josh's face is twisted in anger as he snarls at her through gritted teeth, "Come back home. Or you'll regret it."

"I'm not going back with you." Her voice sounds smaller than normal, yet a thousand times over decisive, holding her ground.

"I wasn't asking," he hisses. "Get your stuff. We're leaving."

I've heard enough. No one deserves to be talked to like this. Especially by a man who's three times her size and stepping closer to get in her face.

Rounding the corner, her ex sees me before she does. His eyes bug out of his head when he registers I'm coming right for him. He attempts to put on a casual smile that doesn't fool me for a second. I know guys like him, who try to play it cool while internally they're bastards with blazing anger problems.

Noticing the odd look on her ex's face, Delaney turns to see what he's reacting to. The relief and the way she steps closer to me, to put distance between herself and this asshole, reassures me that I made the right decision to come out here.

I'm a big guy, but I stand up straighter to make myself appear as intimidating as possible when I approach him. "Back the fuck up and get away from her."

The small grin on his face irks me, as he spreads his arms wide, welcoming me to bring it on. He wants me to throw the first punch, so he can play victim, press charges, cry wolf. This is a game to him, and we're all his pawns.

She takes small steps closer to my side, until her shoulder makes contact with my arm. If it wasn't for this idiot harassing her and standing five feet away, I'd be consumed by the contact. I wonder if she feels it too. How a simple touch between us can drown out the chaos of the world.

She takes a deep breath, steadying herself. "Go, Josh. Please. Don't contact me again or else I'll call the cops."

Josh is not dumb. Delaney leaning into me is not

lost on him. I can see it in the way his eyes glint with disdain.

He's about to open his mouth to make another smart ass comment, but I cut him off. "You heard what she said. Get the fuck out of here and never come near her again."

His nostrils flare with rage, as he stands there thinking it over. He's calculated all the possible scenarios and knows there's no logical way to force her to go with him without causing a scene.

He turns on his heel and heads for the parking lot. Not before grumbling, "Fuck you, slut."

If Delaney wasn't here, I'd sock him in the face so his jaw would be wired shut and that phrase wouldn't be able to come out of his mouth for months. As I'm about to yell at him instead for his utter disrespect, Delaney's shaky exhale brings me back to what's important. Refusing to meet my gaze, she keeps her eyes downcast, and I notice they're filling with tears. The sight hits me like a punch to the gut.

I lean down so we're eye level. "Hey, look at me. You're safe, okay? I've got you."

She nods up and down at such a fast speed that I'm certain it matches the panic swirling inside her brain. I want to comfort her. I want to make everything right in her world again. But I just met her and don't know what she needs at this moment. Would a hug be too much? Does she prefer distance?

She deserves an Academy Award though. Because where I once saw tears, I now find mischief. "Of course I'm okay." She winks, in a graceful attempt to play off the tears that were once there. "Ready for a round of body shots now?" It's a diversion. She wants me to forget everything that happened tonight. So I switch gears, or at least pretend to. Making an effort as we walk back inside, to act like I'm relaxed, when it's a well known fact that I never do that.

Especially not right now.

The flash of relief tells me it is enough for her, and that's all that matters to me right now.

MY HANDS FEEL shaky the rest of the night. Not because of the one beer I've been working on for the last two hours. Because of the adrenaline rush from the confrontation with Josh. The possibility of what may have happened if she was alone with him for five more minutes.

I make it a point to not care about people. My focus is fully on my daughter and I. Delaney is the only one who threatens that. I don't want to care, but I do. I don't want to worry about her, but I know I won't stop now.

As we head back inside, she goes straight to the restroom with her best friend. They're gone for about fifteen minutes while I make mind-numbing small talk with the guys. Everyone is nice and makes an effort to include me. But I don't exactly enjoy talking about things that don't matter.

Once Delaney and her friend come back, they order tequila shots for the table. I pass on the drink, opting for water instead. Wanting to be ready if her ex comes back, since his body language told me he isn't done with her.

I'm not a violent man in the slightest. But the thought of someone harming her—this woman I just met—makes me want to defend her with every bone in my body.

She has a smile on her face, and is throwing jokes left and right. But I know the truth. I can see the note of distress in her eyes. Feel the desperation for safety as we sit side-by-side in the booth, with her one trembling arm or leg always touching mine.

The whole situation has soured my stomach with concern. But I'm not going to lie that I relish the feeling that rises in my chest when she knows she's safe with me. I like it too damn much.

Which is why it's time for me to separate myself from her and get out of here.

As I close out my tab at the bar, she follows me over, a whole foot shorter in her heels. "Come here, I want to show you something."

My mind turns dirty for a half a second before switching off that part of my brain. She leads me to the back of the bar down a long, half-lit hallway. Her heels click and echo on the dingy hardwood floor. There's a whole other area of the bar I didn't even know about. It's a smaller, quieter section. With a taxidermy polar bear enclosed in a glass case, his arms wide as if he's about to attack. An old school jukebox sits in the corner, alongside a smaller bar, with old bearded men hunched over on bar stools.

We stare at the polar bear, my hands in my pockets to keep myself from touching her.

"Look, I wanted to apologize for earlier." Her voice is barely a whisper and she won't meet my eyes.

"Why are you apologizing? It's not your fault."

She looks at me now, her free spirit replaced with timidity, "But it kind of is. I chose to date him."

"Still not your fault. He's in charge of himself, you can't predict or control how someone else acts. That's on them."

"Okay."

I can tell she isn't buying it.

As she continues to look at the creepy polar bear, a playful smile crosses her face. "Think we should name this bear Josh? Kind of looks like him, don't you think?"

Not expecting that reply, I husk out a real laugh. "Very fitting."

She beams. "I've never seen you smile until now. You have *dimples*." She grabs my cheeks, her face only inches from mine. "Smile again."

I shake my head no, like I'm resisting her request. But she's too cute, just saying whatever comes to her mind. I feel my mouth crooking up without my consent.

"Oh my god, there they are again. They're adorable. You should smile more so you can show these off to the world." She's standing on her toes, inspecting them up close, poking each of my stubbled cheeks with her fingers. "Seriously, women would be dropping their panties left and right if they got the chance to see these."

Maybe it's her comment, or the proximity. Maybe it's because I haven't been this close to a woman in years until tonight. But I can't control it when my eyes drop to her mouth. And as if right on queue, she bites down on her full bottom lip, nibbling at that plushness with her white teeth.

Every noise is drowned out, every molecule of oxygen thickened with the tension. Her own eyes trail down to my lips, as if she's thinking the same thing as me. I want to kiss her more than I've ever wanted anything in my life, and it's never been a worse idea.

She's my daughter's nanny, she's a decade younger than me, and I'm a complete idiot.

The rational side of my brain kicks in as I realize nothing good could come of this. It has to be the last thing she wants tonight—her boss trying to come on to her right after her ex harassed her.

That's what has me stepping a whole stride back, out of her reach. "I better get going."

I'm positive she knows what's going through my head. She's skilled at reading a room, and knowing everything about everyone in one glance. "Tell Ava I can't wait to see her Monday morning."

To make sure she's safe, I walk her back to her group of friends in silence. Then I take off before I fuck myself over anymore tonight.

There will be no kissing my nanny.

Even if I've never wanted anything more than to feel her lips pressed against mine.

14

DELANEY

My heart is in my throat when I knock on the door Monday morning. The fun night I was supposed to give Cole went so sideways it turned upside down.

I still can't believe fucking Josh showed up and tried to intimidate me back into returning to the condo. One of his buddies must have spotted me and told him where I was.

The *night that shall not be named* changed something for both Josh and I, but in different ways. It was that night that the lurking ugly monster in him decided to fully reveal itself.

In the past, I had only seen bits and pieces—his short temper over everything, wanting to control what I wore and what I spent my money on.

Maybe it was the vase shattering beside my head that evoked my change. But that night I looked the devil in the eyes and thought *never again*. I'm proud I've stood up to him—twice now.

It doesn't mean I'm not terrified. Every night I close my eyes, worried I'll be woken by the sight of him standing outside my vehicle. I tuck my pepper spray between the seat and center console in case my nightmares do come true.

If Cole hadn't come to check on me outside the bar, I don't even want to know what Josh would have done. He's capable of more damage than I ever thought possible.

For the rest of the night, Cole sat straight as a board with a dark storm brewing in his eyes. It was only when his eyes dipped to my lips that the clouds parted in him. Only for him to shutter right back up and retreat when the same thought crossed my mind.

The door opens, and instead of my boss I'm surprised to find a kind looking older woman. "Hi, sweetie. It's so nice to meet you. I'm Susan, Cole's mom."

"Oh my gosh, hi. It's so nice to meet you too." I step inside and open my arms to hug her immediately. With the way Ava talks about her grandma, it seems as if I know her already. Susan embraces me back in that soft way only moms and grandma know how to hug.

"I've heard a lot about you. It's nice to put a beautiful face to a name," she smiles warmly at me.

I'm elated. Maybe I am lucky after all. I don't have to see Cole after the awkward night out *and* I finally get to meet this famous grandma I always hear about. "You're too nice. And I hope I don't make this awkward, but Susan...you're hot."

The tall, slender woman grabs my shoulder and doubles over in laughter. "You're bullshitting me now, girl."

I'm not bullshitting her though. Susan has long, smooth black hair that reaches her mid back. She either has a magical skincare line or sold her soul to a sea witch, looking much too young to have a granddaughter. Her stylish outfit screams she's in her Sofia Richie era.

Hottest grandma I've ever seen, that's for sure.

"I'd never bullshit you, I promise. Only stating the facts," I reply.

Susan's eyes gleam like she's found out a fantastic secret. "I can see why they like you."

"Not so sure that your son would agree. I think he may find me a tad annoying. But so do a lot of people, so I can't hold it against him."

She shakes her head in a way that makes me think she's not surprised by his attitude. "Don't let him fool you. He's got a tough shell to crack."

I want to keep asking, force her to tell me, maybe pry her brain open a smidge so I can peek in and know if he has mentioned me. "Speaking of Cole, where is he?"

"He had a work emergency, and had to leave earlier than normal this morning. He shouldn't be any later than normal coming home though. I'll wake Ava up and then I'll be out of your hair." She begins to walk toward the hallway when she stops short. "Oh! One more thing, he told me to tell you to look next to the coffee pot."

I make my way to the counter, expecting to find another pot of the coffee so strong it tastes like mud. Instead, I find a sticky note attached to a bag of light roast macadamia nut coffee—the fancy locally roasted brand that's only sold at Little Elm Bakery.

> *Thanks for the other night.*
> *Thought you'd prefer this blend over my double run dark roast.*
> *-C*

He's *thanking* me for the other night? It's obviously a lie, but the coffee...the coffee throws me for a loop. It's a simple gesture, but I can't stop smiling over it the whole day.

Before he gets home, I tear a scrap of paper off a sheet of junk mail, not able to find a sticky note. I scribble back:

> *Don't lie. That night was atrocious.*
> *P.S - Thank you for the coffee. My tastebuds are relieved.*
> *-A*

Cole comes and goes again, quiet as a sinner in church. Only looking at me from under the brim of his hat as he walks past with a nod and *have a goodnight.* I'm certain the night at the bar was too much, in one way or another, which explains why he can't even bear to look at me now.

The next morning, my brain is telling me not to expect another note, while my heart holds out hope.

My eyes scan the room, looking for it as soon as I step foot onto the cold kitchen tile. My chest feels light as I see and race to it, plucking it up to read his scratchy writing:

> Glad you like it.
> Also, my mom said you told her she was "hot"? Now she's got a big head.
> -C

He never talks like this with me in person. His responses typically range from one to two words with zero humor. That's when it dawns on me...is he shy? I've assumed he doesn't say more because he doesn't want to talk to me. What if he wasn't sure what else to say when we're face-to-face?

Ava walks into the kitchen, sleepy eyed and looking adorable in mismatched pajamas. "What are you smiling at?" she asks.

Feeling too sacred to throw away, I tuck the note

into my back pocket. Even if it is only one small yellow square with three chicken scratch sentences. "Nothing, just a note. What can I get you for breakfast, you little banana?"

We conjure the idea of a cereal buffet. In one bowl, we combine multiple different sugary cereals. She thinks it's the wildest thing she's ever done, but I beg to differ. I saw the girl lick a snail's shell last week, which in my book is pretty damn wild.

As the days pass, he still barely looks at me in the mornings and evenings. But the notes continue on for the next week:

Have you seen your mother?
Is she single? I'd date her.
-D

~

She's widowed, and too old for you.
-C

~

You know, I was thinking she's almost too young for me. I like 'em old.

-D

~

I have no words…
-C

~

What else is new? Kidding.
-D

~

You're not kidding.
We're ordering pizza tonight if you want
to join us.

~

THE NOTES between us feel like little secret slices of him. A conversation that's in purgatory, never being said aloud, yet still existing. I look forward to them every morning, crossing my fingers that he hasn't decided to stop the routine. One sentence from him, paired with the freshly brewed pot of light roast coffee he has waiting for me in the mornings now, is like getting a glimpse of him.

The *real* Cole.

Today, Ava and I are planting pumpkin seeds in the garden boxes out in the sprawling yard. The sun on our backs, and dirt under our fingernails, channels our energy into something serene.

She is throwing handfuls of seeds into the holes we dug. "Laney, when will these turn into pumpkins?"

"In the fall, just in time for Halloween."

It suddenly hits me that I won't be here to watch her harvest the big orange pumpkins. She'll do that with her dad or a new nanny. I ignore the way it makes me feel, because it shows I'm getting attached. Attached is never good, because nothing lasts forever.

"Oh. That's a long time," she remarks.

"It is, but it will go by fast. Plus we'll get to watch them grow which will be fun." I finish covering the holes with dirt, and grab the hose to water the soil.

Grabbing the nozzle, I help her press in the lever. She glances up at me, and we exchange a smile that tugs on my heart. Two wild girls in their element.

Turning back to watering the garden, her little muddy hand rests atop mine. "Did you know I don't have a mom? Well, I kinda do, I guess. She doesn't want to see me though."

Her comment makes me want to freeze or cry, but for her sake I can't. I want her to be able to tell me anything, without an overreaction. She states it so simply, like it's a known fact. My petty side wants to tell her that her mom's a bitch and she's better off without a shitty parent like that—but I don't think Cole would appreciate my choice of words.

I put down the hose, and kneel down to her level. "That's her loss, because you're the most amazing kid I know. I feel so lucky I get to be your friend."

Her big brown eyes search mine, seeking an answer to something she's clearly wondered before. "Everyone else I know has two parents. I don't."

Grabbing her hand, I tell her, "You know, there are many ways to be a family. Some families have a mom and a dad. Some families have two moms or two dads. Some have one mom, or one dad. Some families have another grownup, like a grandma or aunt. It doesn't mean one family is more special than another. They're different, but the love is still as special in each one's own unique way."

She throws her body into mine, as her arms wrap around my neck. "Okay. I love you so, so much."

"I love you too, banana."

I hope it's not too much to tell her that I love her. I'm not sure how Cole will feel about it. My heart is worn on my sleeve though, and every word I told her is true.

My body flinches when I see him standing a few yards off, watching us with that always serious look on his face. I wonder how much he's heard.

"Daddy, you're home!" She jumps off me and runs into her father's arms.

His face is set with his normal perfectly neutral expression as he lifts his daughter up. Reading a bomb defusing manual would be easier than trying to decipher what the hell is going on inside his head. But when his eyes lock onto mine, I freeze. He never makes eye contact and now he won't look away. It makes my stomach swirl with questions I may never get the answer to.

We head inside, Ava following me as we wash the caked-in dirt from our fingers. Cole waits at the table with enough pizza to feed a small army.

He scratches the stubble on his jaw. "Are you planning on staying for dinner?"

The way he asks, I'm uncertain if he wants me here or not. With note-Cole, I feel confident he likes me. With in-person-Cole, his body language reads like he'd rather have a sinkhole swallow him up rather than talk to me.

"I'd love to, if the offer still stands."

While opening and inspecting the various pizza boxes, Ava shouts, "Please stay. We could have a mermaid movie pizza party!"

Her father groans from across the table. "We've seen that movie *at least* thirty times. Maybe we should give another one a try."

She gives him the stink eye, her five year old way of

saying *hell no, we're watching the fucking mermaid movie, or else.*

With an evil smile, I say, "I'd *love* to watch this mermaid movie."

He glares in my direction as if I've stabbed him in the back. Ava claps her hands, thrilled to have won.

An hour and two pizzas later, the three of us curl up on the gray sectional couch. I'm on one end, Cole on the other, with Ava outstretched between us. Before the end of the first song, she falls into a deep sleep. Her tired head rests on her father's arm, while her unicorn slippered feet are in my lap. The blue light of the TV dances around the room as neither of us make a move to turn off the movie.

Trying not to be too obvious, I look at him. Checking him out while he stares straight ahead at the movie he despises, yet watches time and time again, for his daughter.

He's oblivious and gorgeous and stern. That head full of wavy dark hair, unshaven stubble, strong line of his jaw. I'm certain he has absolutely no clue how attractive he is, and it only makes him even more so.

He turns to find me staring. "What?"

I smirk. "I think you secretly like the mermaid movie."

"That's a hard no."

"At least admit the songs are catchy. I can already tell I'll be singing them all week. Don't worry, I'll teach them to Ava too. Though I'm sure she already has them memorized."

He runs a hand down his tired face. "I think you like torturing me."

"Maybe a little. You make it too fun."

My pulse quickens, as we look at each other from opposite ends of the couch. He's observing me as if I'm a puzzle he's trying to solve. I wish he'd ask me every question that's running through his head right now. I'm as open and blunt as one can get, never scared to tell the truth. I feel myself drawn to wanting him to ask me something, anything. Maybe it's because if he asks, it means he's curious, and if he's curious—he cares.

In some tiny form, it's caring.

He turns away to switch off the television before gently moving Ava's head from his legs. With care, he lifts her tired body from the couch, his hand brushing against my thigh as he reaches for her. As soon as his touch is gone, my body longs for it, craving it as if it's the only thing that can sustain me.

"I'll be right back," he whispers, as he carries her tiny snoring body to her room.

The impending aloneness with him has me fidgeting a thousand different ways until he returns. I know I need to tell him what Ava said about her mother. Telling him doesn't serve a dual purpose, I'm not trying to pry into their family business. It's just that if I were her parent, I'd want to know.

He walks back into the room and sighs with the force of an eighty year old.

With only the two of us in here now, I'm hyper aware of his presence. I can't shake it. It's like standing in the fog—my surroundings are the same, but everything looks and feels different.

"Hey, I need to talk to you about something Ava said today."

Worry instantly consumes his face. "Shit, this can't be good. What'd she say?"

I recount everything she said about her mother not wanting to see her, along with my responses. The subtle shifts in his expression, as he hyper-focuses on my every word, indicate that this isn't an easy topic for him.

When I'm finished, he sighs. "Thank you for telling me. Your response was good, I think. Definitely better than anything I'd ever come up with."

He leans onto the counter, head turned down, fingers gripping the stainless steel like it's his lifeline. The pain etched across his face feels like a weight on my chest, threatening to tear at my psyche. "Cole?"

"Yeah?"

"You're doing a good job with her. You're an amazing father."

A beat of silence passes. I'm certain he doesn't plan on replying, until he lets out an exhale with a shake of his head. Like he's clearing the cobwebs of insecurity. "It doesn't always feel like I am, but I try."

"That's all that matters. You trying is already miles better than a lot of parents."

I don't know his ex. I don't know the situation. But I don't like the fact that a little girl thinks her mom doesn't want to see her. It breaks and withers a piece of me, that no matter what I do, I can't fix this for them. Perhaps it hurts more because I've been dealt a similar hand, and I know the significance and potential impact of neglectful parents.

But she has one parent that cares. One parent that consistently goes above and beyond, putting in more effort than anyone else I've ever known.

With arms still braced on the counter, he searches the surface like he'll find the answer within its depths. I need to get out of here before I decide to say *fuck it* and interrogate him until he gives up his deepest secrets and greatest traumas. We all have them.

I grab my purse from the wingback chair. "I better get going."

His head pops up. "Oh. Yeah, of course. Let me walk you out."

"You don't have to do that. It's not like there are any bears or criminals out here in the country to get me."

As he walks me to the front door, he pauses. "There are actually. Bears that is."

I stop halfway through exiting the door. "You're fucking with me, right?"

"There are one hundred percent bears out here. I don't fuck around."

The teenager in me can't help it. I'm nearly bursting at the seams with a laugh. "Well maybe you should start...Fucking around." I swear he has a stroke—momentarily freezing from my outlandish advice.

Proud of having shocked him, I begin to stroll over to my Bronco. The sound of boots crunching in the gravel follows me as I take long strides. His long legs are no match for my short ones. I open the door of my SUV, ready to find a cozy parking lot to snuggle up in.

But when I turn to say goodnight, his eyes aren't on me. Fresh horror sinks in as I follow his eyeline, a puzzled look blooming on his face. One of my secrets unraveling before my eyes.

Through my windows he's looking at the piles of belongings inside. It's impossible to miss with the way the overhead lighting casts them in a spotlight against the dark of night. Mismatched luggage stacked on top of one another. My neatly folded blankets with the pillow on top. A laundry bag, nearly full and ready to take to the laundromat this weekend.

"Are you..." His eyes dart from me to my belongings. There's no good way to explain this. I could try to weasel myself out of the question, but I know he won't buy it—he's too smart and knows bullshit when he sees it.

"On my way to a friend's house for the weekend. I don't pack light as you can see." Panic multiplies in my chest as I wait to see if he takes the bait.

After a brief pause, he replies, "Okay." His hesitation says a thousand words I'm glad are not said out loud.

He doesn't believe me, and I don't want pity.

I move to close my car door when he stops it with one hand.

"If you find yourself not comfortable at your friend's place," he says, *friends* with an emphasis implying he knows it's a flat out lie, "then you come take your pick of a guest room here. Any day, any time, okay?"

"Don't need it, but thanks for the offer. Have a good weekend."

I drive off into the night, as my breath comes faster and faster. My head is dizzy and stomach sour from the fact that he is onto me.

That I'm a mess. My whole damn life is a mess. And that the crumbs I've assembled of a new beginning are so fragile they could be knocked down by a light breeze.

Yet, in their fragility, they're mine.

A patchwork of hope in the midst of my messy reality.

15

COLE

She lives in her car. Delaney Emerson lives in her fucking car and I've been such a fool I didn't notice it until now.

The thought of her alone in a random parking lot keeps me awake for two nights. Tossing and turning, mind reeling with the worst-case possibilities.

What if something was to happen to her? She's a young attractive woman, sleeping in the middle of god knows where, with a psychotic ex out there. If anything happens to her, I will feel responsible.

My house is big, too big for Ava and I. For the early mornings she nannies, it makes more sense to have her already here. I should've offered this option to her when she first started. But I was oblivious to her situation, too hyper focused on keeping it professional between the two of us.

Screw professionalism at this point. I don't give a

shit about professional boundaries right now. What I care about is her having a safe place to live, where she doesn't have to look over her shoulder every five minutes. With a fucking bed and running water at the very least.

A heavy weight sits in my stomach over the forty-eight hours she's gone. I'm constantly thinking about her, where she's at, what she's doing. I have to actively resist the urge to drive around town to look for her vehicle. If I found her, I'd only want to throw her over my shoulder and carry her back to my house, where I know she'd be comfortable and safe. It's two days too many, not knowing if she is okay.

Monday morning, I'm up an hour earlier than I need to be. Can't sleep for shit anyways. Looking out the floor-to-ceiling window at the front of my property, I sip on my cup of macadamia nut coffee that I now find myself looking forward to.

I lie to myself that I'm watching the sunrise peeking over the small grove of olive trees out front. But in reality my eyes are searching the gravel road leading to the house, for any sign of a certain blue Bronco.

Fifteen agonizing minutes later, I see her vehicle roll into view. Two days of worry dissolves as relief floods in. I can finally breathe again, she's safe.

When she knocks on the door, I wait a few seconds so as to not seem obvious that I was waiting for her.

Opening the door, I brace myself for the sight of her.

Every morning she comes over, she takes my breath away. Today's no different.

Pushing her way in, not shy, she catches me murmuring a gravelly good morning. In a delicate yellow sundress, she embodies sunshine; so bright that everyone notices, glowing more than anything else you've ever laid eyes on.

From under the brim of my hat, I assess her for any signs of damage. Aside from the circles under her eyes, you'd never know she lives in her car. The only possible tell is that she's tired. But hell, I'm tired and didn't have to sleep in my car all goddamn night.

I force myself to shake my nerves and talk. "There's a box of pastries and a fresh pot of coffee, if you're interested."

Her eyes light up. Something so simple like danishes and coffee make her happy. I get off on making her smile like that. It's because she thinks I'm an asshole, but really I just have no clue on how to talk to a gorgeous woman like her. When I do something nice, she's taken aback and I hate that it has to be like this.

It's best if I keep up my ruse of annoyance though, because the alternative is too risky.

"Thank god, I'm starving." When she walks past, she casually squeezes my forearm. "Thank you."

I'm left dazed and confused. My skin tingles where she touched me, wanting more. That damn yellow dress has me trying to shake myself from the trance I'm in.

Seeing me stare at her dress, she rolls her eyes and tugs on the lightweight fabric, a cherry pastry in her opposite hand. "It's 5 a.m., and already too hot for pants. This is as professional as it gets."

She's on the defense, thinking I don't approve. That's the last thing I want her to assume. "I like it. You look nice."

Surprised by the compliment, she pauses mid-bite. "I think that's the first compliment you've ever given me. Thanks, boss."

"Stop calling me that. Just use my name."

"Okay, boss...I mean, Cole." She smirks. She meant to do that.

I grumble, although it's fake. "Alright, well, see you later. Be careful with the heat out there."

With her arms held out wide, she relishes the cool air drafting from the vents. "We get to be in the AC or pool all day. It's going to be a great day. *You* be safe."

At work, as the day heats up, it's like stepping into hell. I keep a close eye on my crews, making sure they take plenty of breaks in the shade with water to prevent a wave of heat-related issues.

Despite the unrelenting temperature and extra precautions, all I obsess about is how I can't let Delaney leave my house—how she can't spend one more night sleeping in her car.

Embarrassing her is the last thing I intend to do. But she needs a safe space and all I want is to give her that.

WHEN I ARRIVE at the house that evening, I find Ava running through the sprinkler in the large patch of grass out back. Stretching across the horizon, the vast green hills transform into a richer golden shade under the summer sun. It's a beautiful view. But it doesn't even come close to rivaling the sight of my daughter and Delaney doubled over and belly laughing together.

They don't see me as I watch them from the kitchen window. But Delaney holds the hose, periodically spraying Ava as she runs past, giggling like a maniac.

"Again!" Ava shouts, drenched from head-to-toe.

Delaney continues her playful antics, catching Ava off guard with sprays of water. My daughter's laughter rings through the air as she sprints towards Delaney, pure joy evident in every step. Leaping into Delaney's arms, they tumble together into the soft grass. Delaney excitedly points to something in the sky and Ava nods in agreement, looking at her nanny with all the love in her heart. My own heart clenches watching them together. It's almost physically too much.

Choosing not to interrupt their fun, I head to the shower to wash away the day's sweat and dirt.

Several minutes later, as I'm getting dinner ready, they both push through the back door holding hands and teasing each other over who screamed the loudest at a passing wasp.

"Hi, Dad!" Ava runs to me, and hugs my leg. Squeezing with all her might.

"I missed you. But it looks like you didn't miss me much, huh?" I smile at her beaming face. "Go change your drippy clothes and wash up for dinner. I need to ask Delaney something."

I feel Delaney's eyes snap over to me. She's nervous about what I'm about to bring up. *I'm* nervous myself, but I'm doing what needs to be done. Someone needs to protect her, and I'm not sure why I feel responsible for doing so, but I do.

"Everything okay?" she asks, once Ava skips away down the hall.

"I was wondering if you'd be able to stay the night tonight? It might be for a while if you could manage. I have some early mornings coming up for work with the heat wave and I don't want to bug my mom to come over while it's still dark out. I'd compensate you, of course."

She doesn't answer right away and instead focuses on adjusting her dress—which I'm trying to ignore with every ounce of strength I have, because she's drenched. And the way the fabric clings to her body makes me want to peel it off her and run my hands along her cool, smooth skin.

The wheels are turning in her head. I'm holding my breath, waiting for her answer. Anxious she'll say no and I'll have to hold her here against her will. I wouldn't actually do that, but fuck me, I'd be willing to beg and cry.

"Okay," she finally says.

"Yeah?" I exhale, relieved.

"Yeah. But you don't have to pay me extra. I already feel like I'm swindling you since this doesn't feel like working. I get to hang out with my friend in a baller house with free food, five days a week. It's a good deal."

"I'm going to pay you. It's what you deserve. I don't want to take advantage of you."

"Oh, you could take advantage of me any day," she teases.

I stiffen…in more than one place. Her eyes soften when she notices me tensing up. "Okay now, don't have a heart attack. I'm kidding. I know you only tolerate me."

I shake my head because that's as far from the truth as she could get. "You're fine."

"Wow, *fine*. Don't be too enthusiastic now." With a tilt of her head she smiles, trying to catch my eye to drive her joke home. But I'm trying to look everywhere but her. The air conditioning has kicked on, causing her nipples to pebble under the thin fabric of her dress. If it was only us two here right now, I'm not sure how much willpower I'd have.

Not that she'd ever go for me. But if she did…I'd fucking ruin her. One touch and I'd be high off of her forever.

"You okay? Regretting asking me to stay yet?"

"No, I'm good. Sorry, long day."

What the hell am I getting myself into? I'm not regretting asking her to live here the way she thinks I am. I hadn't thought this far ahead, however. I'm relieved she's safe now, and that I'm the one to help her.

But it feels an awful lot like walking straight into a fire. Alarms are blaring in my brain, I know danger is up ahead, yet I'm sprinting right toward it.

16

DELANEY

I pretend to leave and get my belongings, only to drive around for forty minutes to keep up the ruse. There's a good chance Cole noticed my bedding and luggage the other day, and came to his own conclusion. Still, I'm too prideful to ever admit the truth to anyone quite yet.

With every passing night beginning to grow hotter, stickier, and more tortuous—I'm thankful to be in a real bed tonight.

Now I unpack my suitcase, folding my clothes neatly into the oak dresser. My life's been a rollercoaster over the last month, and tonight feels like I can take a deep breath again for the first time in weeks.

The guest room is modern and simple. The white walls, curtains, and bedding set a clean backdrop. The dark textured throw blanket at the foot of the bed, paired with the abstract wall art and potted tree in the corner, elevate the aesthetic of the room. It's a serene haven that I'm half humiliated, half relieved I get to live in for the week.

Ava is sitting on the bed, passing me shirts to put away. Cole said he needs me for more than a night, so I'm taking the liberty of getting cozy here. Also if I have to dig to the bottom of my suitcase looking for a particular outfit *one* more time, I will lose it.

"This is going to be like a sleepover every night. I'm so excited," Ava says, bouncing on the king size bed.

I whisper conspiratorially over my shoulder. "How many times do you think your dad will let us watch the mermaid movie before he says no?"

"Probably *so* many. My dad never tells me no."

Cole pops his head in the room causing Ava and I to clutch our chests and scream.

"Oh my god, you scared the shit out of us," I yell, panting like I've seen a ghost.

Ava stares up at me with big puppy dog eyes and a giant smile. It dawns on me I just cussed in front of her, a poor innocent five year old. She totally knows too, I can see it in the way her eyes twinkle in the midst of my slip-up.

"I mean...*shoot*?"

I look at Cole to see how pissed he is. To my relief, he's not. Instead, he's trying to not crack a smile, but the corners of his mouth tip up against his will.

"It's okay, she's heard me say it a thousand times before."

Ava nods. "Oh yeah, definitely. Dad says shit *all* the time."

Cole swipes a hand down his face, trying to keep himself together, while I collapse into a puddle of laughter.

"Hey, Ava, *you* can't say shit. It's a grown up word," he says.

"So when I'm old like you I can say shit?"

"Oh for fu—" he pinches the bridge of his nose. "Yes, when you're my age you can say it."

"Wow, I'm going to have to wait a *long* time then. Like really long."

"Yes, we all know I'm very ancient. Now say goodnight and go climb into bed. I'll be in soon."

As I say good night to Ava, I scoop her up, gently cradling and swinging her as if she were a newborn. Her laughter fills the room, making me feel like the most entertaining person alive. Kids are great ego boosts.

When she dashes out, Cole remains lingering near the doorway. Not once has he stepped foot in the guest room since I moved in. He acts as if there's a force field preventing him from entering.

He leans against the door frame, and holy shit. I see why women find that attractive. The arm holding him up flexes, his dark hair pulled back beneath his favorite hat. His quiet confidence exudes an effortlessly sexy aura, causing my stomach to flutter.

Behind that hat, he thinks he's concealed, but I

sense it's his way of keeping a distance from the world —a shield in the form of a hat.

His eyes flit around the room, zeroing in on my scattered belongings. "You okay? Have everything you need?"

"I'm good. More than good. I feel like I'm staying at a fancy hotel tonight. All I'm missing is my margarita by the pool. Guess I'll have to survive," I tease.

Nodding, he backs away from the door jamb. "Good. Well, let me know if you need anything."

Then he's off to tuck Ava into bed, while I finish settling in.

Twenty minutes later, I hear the metal blades of a blender whirring to life. Being exceedingly nosey, I tiptoe out of my room and down the long hall to investigate. His back is turned to me as he pours the contents of a pitcher into a pink acrylic cup.

Silently, my bare feet glide across the wood floors as I approach him from behind, leaning in to peek over his shoulder. Standing only inches away, I feel the warmth radiating from his skin. How would he react if I pressed my body to his? If I ran my hands along the contours of his firm muscles?

"What's that?" I suddenly ask, causing him to jump.

"Fuck. You can't sneak up on me like that," he huffs.

He turns around and we're close. Too close. I can smell the cedarwood scent of his body wash, and see every fine line on his face. There's a crease between his brows from the hours spent frowning, that I find myself wanting to run my finger along. To smooth out his scowl and force him to show me his dimples again.

"Have a hankering for a smoothie at 8 p.m.?"

"No, it's for you. The margarita you wanted."

"Wait, really? I was teasing. You didn't have to do that."

"You said you wanted one, and I had the stuff. No big deal." He hands me a glass. "Pool's warm if you still want to drink it poolside too."

I stand in the kitchen, holding the margarita, completely dumbfounded. If a blank stare resides in my eyes, it's because it feels like he has short-wired my brain.

Maybe I was wrong about him. Maybe he is a big old softie under that hard, intimidating exterior.

I examine the pink cup. "I never would have expected you to have pink margarita cups. I love it."

"I'm a girl dad. Of course I have pink cups."

"Where's your drink?" I say, as I take a large gulp of the icy strawberry liquid.

He gives me a wry look, before pouring a second drink for himself.

Extending my cup in his direction, I say, "Okay, now we have to cheers while maintaining eye contact."

I can tell I've lost him, based on the look he's giving me, as if I've grown two heads.

"It's a whole thing. It will bring us seven years of bad luck if we don't. I've already had that four times over, so I'm not taking any chances."

He reluctantly extends his cup to mine as I step toward him. When our plastic glasses make contact, a dull celebratory clink cuts through the air like a brief spark. Locked in each other's gaze, a surge of electricity courses through my body, awakening every nerve and muscle.

His eyes are deep and piercing, pinning me in place as if he's peering straight into my soul. I have to remind myself to breathe as I struggle to hold back from saying or doing anything irreversible. Restraint is a lot of work for a chronic word vomiter like myself.

Breaking eye contact first, he takes a few steps back. "I'll leave you to it."

"Cole?"

Those hazel eyes meet mine for a fraction of a second before snapping away again. He rubs the back of his neck, his corded muscle popping with the action. "Hm?"

"Want to join me? For swimming?"

He reacts like I just asked him if the earth is flat. He struggles to find the right words. "I'm sure you'd rather be alone."

"I hate being alone...despise it. It's okay though, I know you probably need to get to bed."

Hesitating for what feels like an eternity, I'm sure he's grappling with how to decline. "I'll meet you there in a minute," he eventually responds.

I'm shocked, and simultaneously throwing a rager

of a party in my mind. Not wanting to scare him off, I put on my best nonchalant attitude. "See you in a bit."

When I change, I choose a skimpy black two piece. I try to tell myself it's because it's more comfortable. But who am I kidding? It's entirely for the purpose of gaining his attention.

Am I wrong to want him to look at me? Wanting to see if he'll lose control, especially when it comes to this? Us.

But I push those thoughts to the back of my brain as I practically run to the sleek rectangular pool, only stopping to grab my margarita on the way and setting it on the black coping that edges the pool.

Looking into the water's lit depths, I inhale and plunge in. A very elegant cannonball.

When I emerge, Cole is walking out, his swim trunks hanging low on his tall body.

And damn, he is a whole ass meal. His body glows tan, muscles defined by hours of hard work and lifting heavy objects. Strength that wasn't made in a gym, but formed by real-life athleticism due to the nature of his job.

I'm completely gawking, my eyes glued to the lines of his abs. There's no denying it; he knows I'm looking, and I'm not even attempting to hide it at this point.

"Uh, okay, wow. Look at you mister Calvin Klein underwear model."

Either he doesn't hear what I say or he chooses to ignore me. Although if the tips of his ears turning pink are any indicator, then I can bet good money he's heard me loud and clear.

Reminding myself to play it cool, so as not to embarrass the poor man further, I blurt out, "You're lucky to have a pool. I always dreamed of having one as a kid."

Walking down the steps, he wades into the water with his drink in hand. "I'm surprised you didn't have one."

"Why's that?"

"I don't know, I guess I assumed. You give off the impression of having had the stereotypical, well-off upbringing."

"Is that your way of implying that I'm fancy?"

He shrugs, as I swim closer. The pool water at night gleams like liquid sapphire, reflecting the soft glow of string lights suspended from above.

"We actually grew up dirt poor. Top ramen most nights for dinner, a brief bout of homelessness—the whole nine yards."

His expression shifts to a mix of surprise and guilt, his gaze now framed by a different perspective. "Shit. I'm sorry. I feel like an ass now."

"There's nothing for you to be sorry for. It is what it is. It's a part of my story. Just because the past was shitty doesn't mean the future will be."

"You're very positive, huh?"

I snort, "Yeah, that's kind of my downfall."

"How's that a bad thing?"

"Because sometimes I fail to notice the red flags

since I'm too busy looking at the silver lining. You've met my ex. Obviously I make bad decisions."

He cracks a timid smile. "The crazy polar bear. How could I forget him?"

"Can I ask you a question?" I'm treading water, inching closer.

Looking me up and down, he counters, "Only if I can ask you one back."

His stare feels as if he's running his hands along every inch of my skin, and I'm eating up every crumb of his attention.

"Little game of truth for a truth. I like that, though I think you may come to regret it. I'm pretty nosey, you know."

He runs a wet hand through his hair. "What's your question?"

"What's the deal with Ava's mom?"

The way his jaw ticks tells me it's not a pretty story.

"She's not in the picture. Ran off when Ava was a baby. Seen her maybe three or four times since."

The desire to bridge the gap and wrap my arms around him hits me. The pain he and his daughter share strikes a familiar chord, resonating with my own parental abandonment. The empath in me wants to soak up every drop of pain from them, absorb it like a sponge to lessen their hurt.

"She sounds...horrible." My eyes begin to fill with tears that I don't want him to see, so I dunk my head beneath the water.

When I come up, he's still standing a few feet from me. A mixture of curiosity and hurt in his expression. "Won't say you're wrong about that."

While I don't know the full story or both sides, I do know that this is the aspect of life that's difficult to stomach. When a parent can abandon their child without even glancing back at their path of devastation.

Attempting to change the subject, I tell him, "Your turn, ask me anything you want. I'm an open book."

He pauses, a moment of hesitation evident in his voice as he finally asks, "Were you sleeping in your car?"

"Yep. I was." A chip of my pride crumbles at my admission. I don't want his pity. It's not his job to fix me or my chaotic situation.

His eyebrows shoot up, clearly surprised at my blunt and honest answer. "How come?"

"Mm, one truth a day. Come back tomorrow and I'll tell you."

My heart pounds as I step out of the pool. It's easier to run away than answer more questions. I'm a coward, but at least I'm an honest coward.

My cheeky swim bottoms hug my ass as I walk up the tile steps. I don't make a move to adjust them, wanting his eyes on me.

He remains in the pool, silent and watchful. When I glance back to smile, his eyes mirror the dark night sky above, drinking me in with both intensity and a dash of apprehension.

Beneath the wooden gazebo, I dry myself off with one of the towels lying on a chair. Taking my sweet time by dutifully going over the swells of my breasts and ass. I'm putting on a show for him, because no one's ever looked at me the way he does.

So hungry that his meticulous self-control may snap like a brittle branch at any moment.

"Night, boss," I tell him, as I walk back inside. Leaving him in the pool as he surely questions why the hell he let me in his house.

All I know is that I need to get back into the safety of my room, because I want to suck my boss's dick and I think he might want that too.

17

COLE

I leave before the sun is up the next morning. The house is quiet—too damn quiet—with Delaney and Ava still asleep.

My mind keeps drifting to last night. The way I followed her into the pool like a schoolboy with a crush. How she might as well have been naked, with the way her bikini barely covered her round ass.

There was no fucking way I could get out of the pool first, seeing as I was hard as a rock under the water. The need to jack myself off when I went inside was overwhelming. Her perfect face flashing in my mind was the only thing I could picture while I came. I've never felt so guilty and wrong about rubbing one out.

Our little game of truth for a truth turned depressing very fast. With me telling her about Isabel, and her admitting she was living out of her car.

My chest nearly collapsed when the words came out of her mouth. I already was almost positive that was the case. But to hear her tell me, confirming it...it tore me apart.

I wanted to tell her she's always got a home here, but it could've had her packing and running as far away as possible. Too intense, too soon.

Something about her tells me she's unpredictable. It puts me on edge, because I'm the most predictable person alive. Which is one of the many reasons why Isabel left. Numerous times she told me, *You don't have an exciting bone in your body. Everything about you is bland and predictable.*

Delaney isn't anything like Isabel.

But I can't help but think that the one thing they surely have in common is finding me dull and unexciting.

DELANEY:

Would it be ok if my sister and niece came over to swim later today?

COLE:

Of course, it's fine.

DELANEY:

Thanks, just wanted to double check.

COLE:

I'll pick up dinner for everyone on my way home.

DELANEY:

Thank you! I could get used to this.

COLE:

Good. Did you sleep okay last night?

DELANEY:

I'm going to need to steal that magical mattress when I leave, because it was the best sleep I've ever got.

COLE:

Well, now you've gone and admitted your future crime in writing.

DELANEY:

Forget this conversation ever happened. Hey, side note, what's your phone password? I'm definitely not going to be erasing any evidence later...

COLE:

1, 2, 3, 4

DELANEY:

Wait...is that really it? Did you actually give me your confidential login credentials? (Not to mention, the most basic one ever)

COLE:

You're going to tease me over my easy password when you're the one potentially committing a crime here?

DELANEY:

Pleading the fifth.

COLE:

What am I going to do with you?

DELANEY:

Well, there's a lot of things I can think of... :)

COLE:

Delaney.

WHEN I ARRIVE HOME, I hear the splashing and squeals of laughter as soon as I step through the front door. As I set down the paper bags full of takeout boxes on the table, my gaze catches on my daughter and Delaney's niece trying to climb on top of the unicorn floaties. Their attempts are thwarted by their bulky life jackets, causing them to splash back into the water and scream with laughter.

Delaney and the woman who must be her sister, swim near the girls supervising their hectic game. Her sister is listening and nodding, while Delaney speaks animatedly with her hands.

Through the window, Delaney spots me and waves with so much excitement that I question if she's waving to the correct person. Only Ava, my own flesh and blood, has been thrilled to see me like that.

Maybe I'm a fool and she is ecstatic for the takeout I brought home. Whatever the reason, it pierces me like an arrow to the heart. My legs move on their own accord, spellbound by the gorgeous blonde who acts as if I'm from the Publishers Clearing House arriving with her sweepstakes earnings.

Drawing closer to the poolside, I offer an awkward wave to her sister—who's an apparent contrast to Delaney in every way. While their appearance shares similarities, their resemblance ends there; her sister exudes a quiet, poised demeanor, while Delaney is more or less similar to a loose cannon.

Motioning toward her sister and niece, Delaney introduces us, "This is my sister, Jessica, and adorable niece, Hazel. This is Cole, my boss."

"Nice to meet you." I try my best to smile and be polite, finding myself wanting to make a good impression.

"Thanks for letting us come over. Your house is gorgeous. My sister wasn't lying," Jessica replies.

"You're welcome anytime. Dinner's inside when you're ready for it. Tacos for the adults and cheese quesadillas for the kids."

"You don't have to tell me twice. C'mon girls, let's go get taco'd up." Delaney guides the floatie the kids are sitting on to the pool's edge, and hoists them onto the shaded cement. She wraps large neon pink swim towels around their small bodies as they shiver.

I take hold of Ava's hand, while Hazel links arms with her mother and aunt. Upon entering, I grab a stack of paper plates, while Delaney digs through the fridge to find juice boxes for the girls.

As she walks past, still in her swim top paired with a tiny pair of unbuttoned denim shorts, she gently places her hand on my bicep.

"Hey, thank you for dinner. You didn't have to do that, but it was a really nice gesture."

I struggle to form the words I want to say in response, my gaze fixed on her features—those captivating big blue eyes, the elegant slope of her nose, and those bee-stung lips. "Of course," is all I manage to say. It comes out strangled and awkward.

Her gaze drifts down to her hand resting on my arm. A brief touch that seems to stretch into eternity, elongated by the sudden halt of my racing heart in response to her contact. Abruptly, she tightens her grip on my bicep with a confident squeeze.

She nods, more to herself than me, and squeezes again. "Wow, you're jacked. Impressive."

There are honestly no words I can say right now because I'm stunned speechless and want to show her what else is hard and impressive about me.

Luckily, her sister swoops in to save me from embarrassing myself. "Stop groping your boss and come eat already. I taught you better than that, so leave the poor man alone."

"Sorry, *Mom*," she teases. Then she smiles up at me before giving my bicep a final squeeze.

At this point, I know I'm so far fucked. So entirely out of my depth with her.

I need to make an immediate plan to get over my crush on the nanny—fast.

I'm just worried it won't be fast enough.

LATER THAT NIGHT, I see Delaney in the kitchen grabbing a lemonade from the refrigerator, wearing black athletic pants that hug her every curve. I lied to myself that I needed something from this side of the house. I'm *not* over in the kitchen because I heard her awake.

Between sips, she asks, "Is Ava down for the night?"

"Out like a light."

"Good, because now you can come outside with me. We have a game to continue." She heads to the back door, pausing to look over her shoulder to see if I'm coming too.

I sigh and follow her. A dead man walking.

We get to the pool's edge, and she plops down onto the cement and dips her feet into the shallow sun shelf.

We're both fully clothed. The warm evening air carries a cool breeze that makes relaxing outdoors enjoyable, yet a tad too chilly for swimming.

Sitting a safe distance away, I mimic her, taking a seat on the edge and submerging my feet. She is looking up at me, a subtle smile curving on her lips—a quiet triumph, acknowledging that I followed her suggestion and joined her outside.

Her feet gracefully dance through the water, in a perpetual state of motion and sway. Meanwhile, mine dangle stagnantly, akin to anchors immersed in water. A stark contrast, reflecting not only our feet, but also our distinct personalities.

"How about we start tonight with a couple easy questions to break the ice?" she suggests. "I'll ask first. Favorite color?"

"I'm forty. I don't have a favorite color."

She quirks an eyebrow up at me disbelievingly, patiently waiting for my answer.

"Fine. Blue," I relent, the words slipping out casually. Yet deep down, I'm aware it's her sapphire eyes that inspired my choice.

"Excellent pick." She nudges me with her shoulder, "Now your turn."

Blanking on what to ask, I copy her. "What's your favorite color?"

"You're supposed to come up with a new question. But I'll still tell you—sparkly gold. And do *not* tell me that's not an acceptable color. It's beautiful, and I'm sticking to it."

"I'd expect nothing less from you—I like it."

Caught by surprise, her head quirks in my direction as a proud smile tugs at her glossy, full lips.

I find myself wanting to know more—a completely new feeling for me. Typically, I don't give a shit about someone's likes or dislikes. But with Delaney, I want to know every intricacy of her. I want to know how she ticks, and what makes her so magnetic.

"What's your biggest fear?" I ask.

"Mmm, going deep now."

A smile escapes despite my best efforts to keep a straight face. "That's what she said."

With her head tilted to the dark night sky, she bursts into laughter. "You dirty, filthy man," she teases, her gaze snapping towards me, eyebrows wiggling mischievously. "Are you trying to hint that you like going deep?"

"I like it a lot of ways."

Neither of us break eye contact as we stare, locked and loaded into each other's gaze. A beat passes, a palpable connection forming by the second. Perhaps it's entirely one sided, but with her, it's more than a spark —it's an undeniable blaze.

Breaking the tension, she clears her throat. "The non-intense answer—wasps. Fucking hate them with a passion." Her joyful expression falters, turning hesitant.

"But the thing I'm *most* scared of in life? It would have to be never experiencing being loved to my very core. I've never had that, and I'm terrified I never will."

My heart slams into my ribs at her confession. I want nothing more than to pull her into my lap and hug her. Make her feel cherished, and worshiped, and important. "You deserve that. And you'll get it."

She hums in silent disagreement before looking up at me. "Okay, you can ask me now."

"Ask you what?"

"The question from last night."

"Oh, yeah. That. You don't have to tell me. It's none of my business."

"I know it's not. But it's fun and I have one more question for you. You'll be doing me a favor."

Leaning back on my hands, I reply, "Fine. Why were you living in your car?"

As much as she said she was ready for the question, I see her mask slip for a millisecond. Pain hidden beneath her sunny exterior.

"I lived with Josh. It...didn't work out. I left suddenly." She blows a raspberry between her lips, forcing herself to say the words out loud. "Didn't have much money to my name, didn't want to bother my family or friends or have them suspect how bad things were. Living in my car seemed like the quickest and easiest solution at the time."

I'm not exactly sure what Josh did, but I do know that I want to pummel him.

"I'm sorry."

"Don't be. You've helped me so much. Took a chance on hiring me, letting me stay here with you two for the week."

"Yeah, about that. You're not leaving at the end of the week. You're welcome to stay for the entire summer."

"I can't do that to you."

"You're staying. For as long as you need to." My voice is final, leaving no room for argument. I'm not letting her sleep in her car again—I can't.

Her lips twitch with amusement and I glance at them for a moment too long. "Fine, I'll stay. But only for the summer, until I'm back on my feet again. Thank you."

"Of course."

"Your turn to answer a question now. How wild should I make it? On a scale of one to ten? I'm thinking an eleven."

I groan like she's killing me, but I'm enjoying the hell out of this. "Just get it over with."

She kicks water in my direction, purposefully splashing me. I glare at her like I'm annoyed, but I'm eating up every crumb of attention from her.

Looking me dead in the eyes, she asks, "Are you happy? Like really, truly happy?"

"Happy? Yeah, I guess so."

"You don't exactly sound confident about that."

"I have everything I need in life. My daughter, a nice

house, good job." I don't want to admit that something does feel like it's missing; that some days I'm so goddamn lonely my skin crawls.

"You can have everything you want on paper, and still not feel happy."

She's right, but admitting it out loud feels selfish. Despite a couple bumps in the road, I'm fortunate. I have an easy life.

But happy? That's a little more foreign to me. Especially when I see people like Delaney, who ooze contentment from their every pore over something simple as a cute dog or a fresh pot of coffee—it makes me hyper aware that I don't have that level of happiness residing within me.

"When's the last time you did something fun, just for you?" she asks.

"You know, the whole bar thing a couple weeks ago."

"That night was *not* fun. In fact, it was so bad that I need to make it up to you. Let me help you find your happiness. We could...make a bucket list or something?"

I don't want her thinking she needs to help out the grumpy old man out of obligation. I'm not depressed or anything. But there are times where I feel deficient. "I'm not your project, don't worry about me."

Delaney stands from the pool's edge, water trickling down her legs, as she walks over to me and holds out her hand. I stare at her nails that are painted a bright cherry red. "C'mon, up you go. We're going to do something."

I don't take her hand, because I shouldn't touch her. A man only has so much restraint. "What are we going to do?" I ask, skeptically.

"Don't leave me hanging. Grab my hand."

Reluctantly, I give in and take her hand. She pretends to pull me up by my arm, straining with a moan.

"Good god, you're enormous. Follow me." She keeps her hand tucked into mine as we walk the cement path to the long side of the pool.

It dawns on me, I don't want her to let go. I want to tell her what would make me the happiest man in the world would be to simply hold her hand for the rest of the night.

We stand side-by-side in the pitch black of night, hands intertwined, looking into the water lapping at the sides of the pool.

She squeezes my hand. "Ready to jump in?"

"What are you talking about?"

Her eyes sparkle. "We're going to jump in now."

"We're still fully clothed," I gripe.

"I know. That's the fun, spontaneous part of it."

"Delaney, no."

"Ready, set, go!" she yells, releasing my hand and jumping in.

"Goddamnit," I mutter to myself, jumping in after her.

The water, though lukewarm, still shell shocks me, soaking me to the bone. Her warm laughter echoes around me as I resurface. I emerge, surprised to find myself feeling...different. Lighter, in a way I can't quite pinpoint.

"I can't believe you did that," she says as she floats over to me, her hair flowing and fanned out in the water behind her.

I push my wet hair back from my face. "That makes two of us."

She's so close that I can see the tiny freckles dusting her nose. I'm staring, unable to tear my eyes away from her. What shocks and thrills me is that I find her doing the same.

Her eyes are big round moons, as she takes in all the details of my face. "So, how do you feel?"

I smile, unable to stop it this time. Warmth spreading across my chest, because I've never had someone care so fucking much if I'm happy or not. But here's wild Delaney, asking me how I feel, and making me participate in spontaneous shit, like jumping fully clothed into the pool in the dead of night.

With an amused laugh, she grabs my cheeks with the palms of her hands. "There's those dimples again. God, you're so cute when you smile."

"I don't think I've ever been called *cute*. I'm too old to be cute."

She rolls her eyes. "You're not even old."

"I am. I'm forty." *Ten years older than her,* I remind myself, as her nails trail down my neck. My resistance slipping with every inch lower she drags them.

To keep herself afloat, she grabs onto my shoulders. With my height I can stand at this depth, but for her she has to tread water. "Wow, okay, never mind. I take back what I said, you *are* old."

Too goddamn cheeky for her own good. "I should make you pay for that," I growl, as I grab her by the waist.

I chalk it up to helping her not work so hard to swim, but my brain is looking for any excuse, any opportunity, to touch her. Her shirt floats up, and I'm touching her bare skin, my hands nearly wrapping around the entirety of her waist. Thank god I'm submerged in this water, or else she'd see the effect she has on me.

"Make me pay then." Her eyes are assessing me, challenging me to call my bluff.

I throw her over my shoulder as she shrieks, her laughter bursting out in a staccato of sharp inhales and exhales. Without a plan or inkling of what to do next, I find myself simply going along with the moment, embracing spontaneity for perhaps the first time in years.

From behind my back, I hear her say, "I've accepted my fate, whatever it may be."

As I walk out of the water, my clothes hang wet,

clinging to my body. A swift smack on my ass draws my attention however. "Did you...."

"Just smack your ass? Yeah, I did," she says, matter-of-a-factly.

I sit her down on an Adirondack chair several feet away. I'm leaning down, arms braced on either side of her. Our faces are inches apart, sharing the same breath. "What am I going to do with you?" my voice rasps.

Her eyes drop to my lips, and I wonder if I'm imagining things. Conjuring them to real life, entirely made up from my intense want for her.

"Anything you want." She licks her lips, and breathes in deeply. It's the type of inhale you make before you plunge into something that takes courage.

My brain slams on its brakes, sending warning signals, blaring loud and rude as if my life is in danger. *What the fuck am I doing? This would never last. She would never want someone like me.*

"I'll get us towels." I stand up, abandoning the moment like a coward, leaving her breathless in the chair. Walking to the pool deck to get us towels before I say good night, I try to get myself in line. Who the hell do I think I am? Flirting with my nanny? Flirting with someone a decade younger than me?

I'm crazy to think she'd even look at me like that.

She has a bright future ahead of her. One that doesn't consist of a cranky single dad that would bore her to death.

But fuck, the feel of her skin against me, that tiny inhale—it's all I can think about when I wrap my hand around my cock again that night.

18

DELANEY

ELLA:

How's the new job going?

MADI:

Did you and your boss kill each
other yet?

DELANEY:

It's going great! Got him buried in the
backyard last night.

ELLA:

You're joking, right? RIGHT?!

MADI:

The way I'd be flabbergasted, but also
not really.

DELANEY:

> Did I say buried? I meant harried. But thank you? I think? For believing I'm capable…even if it is for such a heinous act.

I'm in a conundrum. I should come with a big ass sign across my forehead with that catchphrase. Because what else is new? My whole life is one huge conundrum.

The looming decision of what I should do tonight is throwing me off. I have a plan to get my accounting job back. I'd like to say it's going according to my haphazardly thrown together strategy, but when I emailed my slimy supervisor yesterday to request a meeting—he told me to meet him for drinks instead.

Drinks.

Code word for *maybe we can fuck later.*

Sure. I'll meet Kenneth for drinks. But I'll be suspicious of his intentions all night. Ready to poke holes in his slutty little plan, if need be.

As much as people want to label me as the ditzy blonde, I'm not. Kenneth always did want to put me in that box. At JunoTec, he would question my intelligence to take on projects for our big accounts. *You sit there and look pretty, we'll leave it to someone else,* he'd joke. It wasn't funny. But Josh told me I was overreacting whenever I'd come close to speaking up about it.

I loathe that I need to beg Kenneth for my job back now. Quitting abruptly wasn't the wisest move, but I was desperate to sever ties with Josh swiftly and completely. I'd have willingly devoured a whole box of nails rather than endure an office space brimming with haunting memories of his fist slamming into the drywall next to my head.

Survival won over logical thinking.

After Josh-madgedon happened, my brain was like a tornado. On edge, terrified, spiraling. The only way to stop the tornado dead in its tracks was to remove the eye of the storm—Josh.

Every single trace of Josh.

Then I could breathe. I could think. I could be at peace.

My job was one of those pieces I stripped away in my frantic purge. I wasn't the one who was caught embezzling. But it sure felt like I was guilty by association.

The thought of the whispers in the break room, or side eyes as I walk through the office. *How could she not have known? I bet she was in on it.*

I wasn't in the head space to deal with it.

Now, I feel myself ramping back up. Feeling more confident and ready to kick hypothetical ass. I can't mooch off Cole's generosity forever, even though I love it here. So this is what needs to happen as much as I'm going to dread every second of it.

My Uber pulls up to the sophisticated lounge bar I'm meeting Kenneth at. I don't want to worry about my car if I decide to have a drink, even one drink makes me tipsy—a disadvantage of being miniature size.

As I step through the polished wood door, the overpowering smell of Kenneth's cologne hits me. He's already waiting for me, making a point to look at his oversized silver watch like I'm late, even though I'm right on time. Kenneth is attractive in that same preppy way Josh is. Long, lean, perfectly gelled hair, Rolex watch, with the arrogant attitude to match.

He's wearing a gray designer dress shirt, perfectly fitted dress pants, and Italian leather shoes that cost more than my monthly car payment. If I was any less confident, perhaps I'd feel inferior in my bodycon TJ Maxx dress. Luckily for me, I don't give a shit about guys like Kenneth and their opinions on designer fashion.

"Hi, Kenneth. Nice to see you again." It's not actually, but I've got a job to win back.

He places his hand on the small of my back. "Delaney, a pleasure as always."

It's nice to see we're both lying through our teeth. I've always gotten the sense that Kenneth has disliked me. My only potential saving grace is that he dislikes Josh more.

Kenneth leads me through the low-lit vintage chic

bar ushering me straight into an empty barstool. From floor-to-ceiling the bar is decked out in polished dark wood. A glass wall with glittering rocks and flames dancing in the reflection make this my personal version of a fancy hell. Kenneth waves down the bartender and proceeds to throw down a hundred dollar bill on the lit bar top.

Another reason why I hate Kenneth. He's flashy, likes people to know he has money, thinking it will make him look cool. But it just makes him look like a douche.

The silver haired bartender sees the hundred and hustles over. "What would you two like to drink tonight?"

I order an Old Fashioned, Kenneth orders top shelf scotch on the rocks.

When the bartender leaves, Kenneth leans in. "Are you sure you don't want something else? Fruitier?"

"Yes, I'm sure." My annoyance flares because it's a move Josh would pull. Trying to persuade me to choose something else they think is more fitting. More ladylike.

I brush it off for the sake of politeness. "Thanks for meeting me. I know I left JunoTec abruptly, and I thoroughly apologize for that. I can admit it wasn't my finest hour."

Kenneth eyes me as he takes a large gulp of his drink. "Wasn't a great look, that's for sure. What did you want to discuss?"

Swiveling my barstool to face him, I strive for a

professional, confident demeanor. "I messed up quitting like that. But I would like the opportunity to come back, if possible."

He waves his hand dismissively. "We've already got someone in backgrounds for your position. Why should we hire you back anyways? You quit via email with not even two weeks' notice."

Damn, he's cutting straight to the chase. "Because I'm good at my job. Because you know you can trust me. And you won't have to train someone new."

"*Are* you trustworthy though? Your boyfriend was caught embezzling thousands of dollars from the company. That seems like something you would have been aware of."

I grind my teeth, frustrated. The accusations I foresaw coming, punching me straight in the gut. "*Ex*-boyfriend. And do I need to remind you who reported Josh?"

Kenneth glares at me, eyeing me up and down. "I'll think about it."

I'll take it. It's not a straight up yes, but it's also not a firm no. I can work with a *I'll think about it.*

"Thank you," I say, relieved.

He places his arm on the back of my barstool, stopping my nervous swiveling. "So what have you been up to since you quit?"

"I've been nannying for a family actually. It's been a nice change of pace."

"Wow. No wonder you're begging for your job back," he says, huffing out a laugh.

I'm pleading with myself to keep my mouth shut. *Do not reply back, Delaney. Do not reply back.* It goes against every fiber of my being to shut my mouth. My first instinct is to tell him to fuck off because it's ten times more satisfying than preparing financial statements. Probably not the best move when I'm attempting to win my job back though.

I go in for a long, *long* sip through the tiny black straw instead. Can't talk if I have a mouth full of liquor.

The bartender places a fresh Old Fashioned before me right as I finish my current glass. Either he must know I'm in terrible company, or it's Kenneth's hundred dollar bill doing me a solid.

Feeling more relaxed from the rush of alcohol, I turn back to Kenneth. "So how has work been? Anything new?"

He narrows his eyes, disdain lining his every feature. "I'm going through a divorce."

Shocked he's telling me this, I freeze mid sip. He's never told me one personal detail in all the years I've worked under him. If it wasn't for the ring he previously sported I wouldn't have even known he was married. "I'm sorry to hear that. Hopefully it's for the better?"

"Lot less bitching, that's for sure."

I'm internally applauding his ex, hoping she gets a lot of money in the settlement for having to deal with this prick for so long.

My phone buzzes in my clutch with an incoming text. Perfect timing to check it amidst the awkward small talk.

COLE:

Sorry to bug you, but have you seen Ava's bunny?

DELANEY:

On the couch, probably under a pillow. She had it "napping" there earlier.

COLE:

Found it. Thanks.

DELANEY:

What would you do without me?

COLE:

Don't get a big head now.

DELANEY:

Too late, already big. Always has been since birth.

COLE:

That explains a lot.

Dropping Ava at my mom's for a sleepover. Getting Indian food on the way back. Want some?

DELANEY:

I'd kill for some chicken vindaloo right now. But I'm not sure when I'll be home.

COLE:

Ok. No worries.

KENNETH CLEARS his throat beside me. "Hello? Are you almost done there?"

"Sorry, yeah. It's my boss," I say, tucking my phone back into my purse.

"Ah yes. I'm sure there's a very pressing issue regarding snacks and bedtime." He doesn't say it in a teasing manner. His tone is straight up condescending, and I'm on my last nerve with him.

It was about a fucking stuffed bunny Kenneth, get it right.

When he sees I'm ignoring his statement he continues to drive his point home. "Shouldn't you be a little more focused on me right now, so you can win back your job?"

"You'll either take me back or not. There's no *winning* it."

"You sure about that? There may be one way to *win* it." Kenneth places his hand on my bare knee, causing me to flinch with surprise. "Come back to my apartment and show me how much you want it."

There it is. The curveball I saw coming from a mile away. It's still a slap in the face that he really thinks I'd go along with it. "No way. I don't want my job back *that* bad."

Kenneth leans in, the breath of his whisper humid in my ear, and the grip on my leg too tight. "If you're smart then you would. No one's going to want to hire you with your ex drama and the way you left JunoTec. If you come back with me though, then maybe you'll have a chance."

"I'm flattered," I deadpan. "But there's no way in hell I'd ever suck your dick."

I throw my own lump of cash down on the bar, trying not to wince that it's deducting from the money I desperately need. But I have a point to prove, damn it.

Standing from the barstool, I grab my purse and down the rest of my drink before placing it back down on the glowing bar with purpose.

Kenneth seethes, "Stop throwing a fit because I want to have sex with you. Take it as a damn compliment. Sit back down."

Yep, no way in hell I'll ever do that. Nice Delaney is finished with this conversation. "Thank you for your time. Now go fuck yourself, Kenneth."

I flip him off for good measure, mentally taking a picture of his stunned face before I turn around and leave. It's probably the first time someone has talked back to him like that. Glad I have the privilege of being the first.

Bursting through the doors to wait out front, I attempt to get an Uber. But it's just my luck that there are no available cars left in this small town tonight. And walking isn't feasible since it's dark and fifteen minutes down the highway.

As I scroll through my contacts, there's only one name I find myself searching for. Only one person I know will come save me, despite his prickly exterior.

Cole drives up in his gigantic, shiny pickup truck, looking like he's straight out of the show Yellowstone. When I say this truck is huge, it is in fact monstrous. The tires crunch on the asphalt as he pulls up to the curb near me. He leans over to open the door from within, as I peer up comically into his vehicle, wondering how the hell I'm supposed to get in while wearing the tightest dress known to mankind. I can barely sit in this thing, let alone climb into a truck without flashing the entire bar my vagina.

"Um, we have a problem." I lean into the truck's interior, looking up at him.

"What's the problem?" His soft mouth is turned down, pouty and grumpy. No dimples in sight.

"I need you to lift me inside. I can't get into the truck without showing everyone out here my goods. Even though I am wearing my cute panties tonight so it wouldn't be all that bad."

I hear him let out an exasperated sigh. "Good lord, Emerson."

He gets out of the truck and walks around the back of the vehicle in long strides, not even batting an eye when he sees me dressed up like this.

I'm not ashamed to admit that I was hopeful to see that hungry look in his eyes. But instead, he barely glances at me, just shakes his head as he grabs my waist to lift me up into the cab.

"Ready?" His breath on my ear makes me shiver, and I hope he doesn't notice. I'd wither of embarrassment from the unrequited attraction.

"Lift me up, big boy." Big boy? Where the hell did that come from? I blame it on the way his fingers curl into my waist as he lifts me up, as if I'm as light as a feather.

My ass is definitely level with his eyes right now. "It's okay if you take a peek while you're down there. Can't let my good panties go to waste after all."

"I'm not looking," he huffs out, slamming the car door behind me.

Cole is the first person to ever actively dislike me. It drives me insane, because I want everyone to like me. At times, like the other night in the pool, I'm hopeful that he enjoys my company. Tonight he's making it clear that's not the case.

He climbs back into the truck, and after making sure we're both buckled in, begins to drive. I find myself captivated, unable to look away from his focused gaze, illuminated by the dancing shadows from the passing road lights. His stern yet handsome demeanor intrigues me, and the urge to run my fingers along his stubbled jaw is almost irresistible. Despite the sensible voice in my head, two drinks have amplified my innate lack of a filter.

It's quiet in here, too quiet, as just the sounds of the vehicle on the highway rush around us.

"You know what they say about guys with big trucks, right?"

"Are you trying to imply that I have a small penis?" He keeps his eyes trained on the road.

"Of course not." I'm totally busted. "You said it, not me."

He shakes his head at my absurdity, his face looking grumpier than ever.

"I would flat out ask, but I don't think that's socially acceptable nowadays," I tease.

"It sounds an awful lot like you're still asking though."

"No, of course not. You're my boss. But I mean, I wouldn't be offended if you told me. Every man I meet, I secretly wonder what he's packing."

"For fucks sake, Delaney." He grips the steering wheel until his knuckles turn white.

"Forget I said anything." I turn a slight degree to stare out the window. I give up. Nothing will ever make this man like me, so there's no use in trying. Although talking about penis size probably isn't the right way to go about things.

I reach over the console to turn up the stereo. The radio is turned to a classic rock station, playing some band that I probably have a shirt of.

I'm curious if he feels as uncomfortable as I do.

Probably not. Cole seems like he gives zero shits about anyone or anything, other than his daughter. I respect his ability to not care if people like him. I will bend over backwards, and do a little song and dance, to win even a scrap of affection.

It's something I'll have to get used to—not being liked by this man with the hard shell that I find insanely attractive.

19

COLE

The whole ride home is horrible. I'm fighting a constant boner after touching her, terrified she'll see and be repulsed. Who am I, that touching a woman's clothed waist turns me on?

When I came to get her, I was flustered the whole drive over. She was at a bar, probably on a date. It's none of my business, I know that. Yet, the jealousy that floods me takes me by surprise.

That damn dress caught me off guard. It left nothing to the imagination. The black fabric clung to every curve of her. Her perfect ass was right in my face, and I had to actively try and not bite it.

I feel like a complete asshole for the situation. Obviously her night hasn't been great—she had to call me for a ride after all. From the second her name flashed on my phone with an incoming call, I've been stressing over if her date hurt her somehow. I'll break every one of his fingers with a hammer if he so much as laid a hand on her.

Protectiveness surges through me and I don't want to reflect on why I feel the way I do.

Now to top it all off, she has to endure the next fifteen minutes next to the grumpy old man who wishes he could touch her again.

I turn down the music. "Did you eat already?"

Delaney glances over to me, surprised I'm finally speaking. "No, not yet. Never got time."

"Too busy with your date?" I hate that it comes out of my mouth. The ability to bite my tongue is lost at the moment, overridden by the need to know before my head explodes.

Curiosity crosses her features as a smile blossoms on her gorgeous face. "Why, would you be jealous if I was?"

One hundred percent yes. "Of course not."

"Interesting. Very interesting." Her eyes are gleaming with realization and I'm certain I'm caught. Terrified she knows what's running through my head.

"Our relationship is strictly professional. You're my daughter's nanny. You can do what you want."

"So it would be inappropriate to tell you that I was trying to get my accounting job back? But then my former supervisor wanted me to have sex with him to show him how much I wanted it." She taps her chin, thinking. "Is that okay to tell my boss, or does that cross a professional line between us?"

We're driving on a deserted country road, when I slam on my brakes, our bodies and her purse catapulting forward.

Pulling over to the shoulder of the road and putting my truck into park, I turn to face her. Gripping the center console with so much force it may crack in half. "He did *what*?"

"Wanted me to suck his pretentious dick. I didn't, of course."

Rage makes my blood run hot. I'm not a violent man, but to protect her I would be. "I'm gonna kill him," I mutter.

She eyes me with amusement. "I'd like to see that, but Ava needs her father not in prison."

I assess every square inch of her to make sure she's unharmed. Regret washes over me for acting like a jerk earlier, oblivious to the fact that she was dealing with another man's harassment tonight. "Are you okay?" I ask.

"I'm fine. I told him to go fuck himself and walked out."

Relieved, I exhale. "That's my girl."

She beams, proud of herself. "Now what's a girl gotta do to get some chicken vindaloo?"

Not thinking twice, I say, "Is it too soon if I make a joke about what you *could* do for it?"

Beside me, she slaps my arm before doubling over with giggles. "Cole! I *was not* expecting that from you."

She wipes the happy tears from beneath her eyes. "I *knew* you could be funny."

"You made it too easy by setting yourself up for that one." I put my truck into drive again, flipping a u-turn to head back into town towards the Indian restaurant. "Now let's go get you some food. No dick sucking required."

Looking at the blur of passing streetlights from her window, she murmurs, "There's a big difference between you and Kenneth."

I want to ask her what that statement means. But I think I already have an idea and don't want to dig myself deeper into a hole. One that's impossible to refill.

In the quiet of our drive, I can't resist stealing glances at her. The moonlight paints her in a breath-taking glow—big blue eyes, long blonde hair cascading over her shoulder. Her knees curled up on the leather seat to get more comfortable, as if she's ridden in my truck hundreds of times. My heart threatens to beat out of my chest at the thought of anyone trying to take advantage of her. "I'd be more than happy to go beat up that bastard for you."

"No it's okay, he's not worth it." She meets my eyes for a split second before I look back to the road. "I'm surprised you'd want to do that for me though. I thought you hated me."

My hands grip the steering wheel. "You think I hate you?"

She shrugs, indicating that yeah, she thinks I don't like her.

We pull up to a red stoplight, and I turn to her. "Look at me. I don't hate you. Not even close. I'm just an idiot around you sometimes. But I'd do anything to protect you, okay?"

My arm rests on the center console when I feel her slender fingers slide into mine. She tucks her small cold hand into my large, warm one and gives it a grateful squeeze. "Thank you."

"There's nothing to thank me for."

As I continue to drive, we both stare straight ahead, hands still clasped tight. She doesn't move her hand away, and neither do I. We're locked together at that central point, and it grounds me like a gravitational pull to the center of the earth.

We don't talk about it. We don't draw a speck of attention to it. All I try to do is ignore the electric current running through my body, and the way my thumb brushes back and forth against the smooth skin of her hand. I ignore that it's been several minutes and I still have no plans to let her go.

We exist, sitting there, hand-in-hand, acting like this is completely normal for us.

And that's the scariest part. It does feel too normal.

Too tangible.

Too right.

Hey, thank you for the ride last night. You didn't have to rescue me, but you did.

Also you've created a monster—I've thought about chicken vindaloo at least thirty times within the last eight hours.

-D

~

I would say any time, but I don't want you to have to deal with asshole men again.

-C

~

You did get pretty jealous last night, huh?

P.S. You're one of the good ones. Not an asshole, I mean.

-D

~

I'm going to ignore that question.

And don't you think I'm an asshole that hates you?

-C

~

Maybe not an asshole. Just a hole. It's the equivalent to not a complete ass.

You vindicated yourself with the ride and bomb food.

-D

~

The chicken vindaloo was a game changer.

-C

~

We're going to the Summer Fest this weekend.

Ava and I decided. Sorry, it's two against one.

-D

THEY DRAG me to Lawson's annual downtown Summer Fest. It's the biggest event of the year in town and also the one I loathe the most. Every year it's too hot, too many people, too overwhelming. Ava begged me to go last summer, and I was able to persuade her out of it with an ice cream and arcade date instead.

This year though, Delaney is here. And she has upturned our lives. Ava is thrilled to have a like-minded person on her side, which is why as soon as I park my truck, they're flying out the door, racing hand-in-hand to go explore the rides and booths.

The usually dull and worn-out cookie-cutter park has undergone a stunning transformation. Rows of vendors line the expansive grassy area, adorned with fluttering banners and twinkling lights that infuse the space with a vintage, whimsical charm. Several enormous inflatable bounce houses and obstacle courses are on the far end of the land, their vibrant colors standing out against the landscape. Herds of children run amuck, laughing and yelling, sticky-fingered and red-faced from the sun.

My stomach turns at the sight of the cheap looking carnival rides nearby, aka my own personal hell. There is no way those things can be safe with the rate they're assembled and disassembled. You have to know they missed a screw or bolt somewhere. Somehow I already know I'll be roped into riding them.

When I finally catch up to the girls, they are in line to buy funnel cake from one of the booths. It's no shock that their first stop involves something sweet. They're practically hummingbirds, thriving off of sugar, water, and zipping about. Delaney, despite her small stature, holds Ava effortlessly in her arms. The sight of them together evokes a bittersweet pang deep within my chest. A mixture of overwhelming affection with a tinge of apprehension for what lies ahead—for when Delaney leaves.

This whole arrangement is temporary—already a third of the way through. Ava is undeniably attached, always drawn to Delaney like a moth captivated by a flame. I'm not quite sure what we'll do, or how we'll feel, once she leaves.

After we finish three plates of oily sweet funnel cake, Ava beelines it for the bounce house area. But as we draw closer, she slows down. Her eyes widen as she takes in the frenzied sight before her. Kids shouting, running, pushing. Limbs colliding with the sides of the nylon walls before crashing into one another. I'm worried once I see a kid get lowkey trampled in one, and I myself have reservations about letting my daughter go into this chaos.

My daughter is fearless, but every person has their limits. Pretty sure she just found hers. Perhaps she does have a bit of me in her.

I kneel beside her. "Everything okay?"

Ava's gaze shifts back and forth between me and the

brightly colored bounce houses. "I don't know if I want to go on actually." Hesitancy is written all over her face.

"You don't have to do anything you don't want to do. It's your decision," I tell her.

"I do *want* to. But I'm scared I'll get jumped on," she counters. "I wish you could go in with me."

Delaney crouches on the grass beside her so that they're eye level. "I'll go with you if you want. I'll keep you extra safe. Totally up to you though, girl."

Ava's face lights up. "Would you really? Do they let grown-ups on?"

Pointing to one of the kids jumping, she replies, "That boy is nearly the size of me. I'm sure we can persuade the nice workers. C'mon, let's go find out."

They walk up to the bored looking college kid running the bouncing section. The guy's dark eyes bug out of his head when he sees Delaney approaching him. If he wasn't so young I'd want to flick him upside the head for the way I see him staring at her tan legs in those tiny denim shorts. He's not listening to a damn word she says—just nodding along, mesmerized by the charming smile purposefully plastered on her face.

Get in line, kid. I know the feeling.

They give me an excited thumbs up as they're let inside the jumping area; clearly achieving their mission thanks to the lovestruck teen.

They beeline toward the bounce house slide, sprinting up the stairs that squish beneath their every step. At the top of the inflatable, they hold hands and slide down like two bats out of hell, shrieking with unbridled excitement. Ava's apprehension completely evaporates, replaced by an exhilarating rush as she glides down the twelve foot slide.

I'm marveling how Delaney can turn any situation that's flipped on its head, and make it right side up again. Some people are like me, cursed and ruining everything with one touch despite their best intentions.

Then there's a rare species of people, who turn everything into pure fucking magic, even when they don't intend to. It's *in* them, naturally, without even trying.

Delaney has that.

Walking closer to the structure to gain a better view, I position myself behind a couple of familiar faces from town, women I remember from high school. Over the years, they've always been friendly, and judging by their children's ages, it's likely I'll be seeing more of them when the school year begins.

As I focus on observing Ava and Delaney enjoying themselves, striking wild new poses while sliding down, I inadvertently overhear the two women, leaning in towards each other and snickering loudly. Amidst the sounds of the fun-filled chaos around us, one of the brunettes lets out an exaggerated sigh that catches my attention.

The woman I recognize as Lisa, rolls her eyes and remarks, "Probably trying to put on a show for her new employer." She gestures toward the slide. "And can she put on some clothes? The whole ensemble screams desperate nanny whore."

It takes me a minute to grasp that they're pointing and talking about Delaney.

When it clicks, I'm livid. Pure rage, molten as lava, trickles down my spine.

There's only so much tongue biting I can do while they stand there tearing down another woman. An innocent woman that I've never heard badmouth a soul.

The other woman, Pamela, scoffs, "Seriously. It reeks of desperation."

"Look at her trying to show off for all the men here. She needs to find some self-respect, if I say so myself."

I step around them, into view. "Sure better than standing around gossiping."

When their eyes meet mine, their faces pale as they recognize who I am. "Oh hi, Cole."

I glare at them, unable to hide my dislike. "Do me a favor and don't talk about my nanny like that. She'd never do the same to you, so have some fucking respect."

As I stride toward the inflatable, leaving the two women gaping like startled fish, Delaney and Ava are reaching the top steps. My heart races from the earlier exchange, the bitter taste of cruelty lingering in the air.

In this harsh world, the act of tearing each other down only adds to the weight we all carry. An overwhelming sense of protection hits me. Because without a second thought, I would give up every piece of my carefully constructed armor in order to shield Delaney from damage. I've only felt that way with my own daughter, so I'm not quite sure how to process it.

Fishing my phone out of my pocket, I cup my hands over my mouth and yell, "I want to get a picture of the two of you. Smile."

Of course, never listening to a damn word I say, both the girls do the opposite of what I request. Instead of smiling, they paste on the biggest frowns I've seen while I take the picture.

As I walk away, I glance at Lisa and Pamela for a final time. Their gazes swiftly evade mine as I pass by, their sudden silence signaling a realization that discussing Delaney in a negative light is off-limits in my presence.

All I know is that it doesn't get much better than this. Watching my daughter having the time of her life, while holding the hand of the woman that I never expected to flip my life upside down.

"MILK. THE. COW. MILK. THE. COW." Delaney and Ava chant together as they stand on the rungs of a metal safety barrier.

They've teamed up against me all day making me ride the nauseating, worn down spinning rides that have seen better days. Now they've roped me into some ridiculous fake cow milking contest. Delaney convinced

Ava I'm the only one qualified since she found out I grew up on a farm for most of my life.

Unfortunately, I'm doing it because I'm physically incapable of saying no to them. Which is why I'm now seated on a stool five sizes too small for a grown man in front of a fake, hand-painted, double-sided cow.

"Go, Daddy!" I hear Ava's small voice yell as I give her a small wave back.

A crowd of people have gathered to watch the contest. I hate being the center of attention, and I already recognize a few of the guys and their families from work. I'll never hear the end of this.

But damn it, my heart loves seeing Delaney smile at me like she is now. Pure fucking sunshine. She thinks she's wrangled me into doing this, but really I'd jump off the tallest cliff if I knew it'd impress her. It's some ancient, primal caveman instinct buried deep inside me.

The horn blares as my cue to start milking. Grabbing the udders with my thumb and forefinger, I squeeze and pull down on the plastic teat, like my father showed me decades ago. Artificial milk sprays in white spurts into the silver bucket as I get the hang of my rhythm.

If I'm going to milk a fake cow, I'm making sure I at least milk the hell out of it.

Go big or go home, right?

After a few minutes of hustling, white liquid crosses

the red line drawn within the bucket, as I raise my arm up. "Finished!"

A judge strides over to review my work, and announces that I'm the winner.

Amidst the otherwise calm crowd, Ava and Delaney are jumping up and down with uncontainable excitement. Whooping, and hollering, and high-fiving.

Why do I feel like I've won the Super Bowl?

The judge hands me a small cow print trophy and a certificate for a free milkshake at the local diner, as Ava jumps into my arms. "You did it! I knew you could," she says, hugging my neck tightly.

"Look what they gave me too. It's all yours." I hand her the prize as she admires it with pride. You'd think I won the Olympics by her reaction.

Delaney is standing a couple yards away, hands in her back pockets, and smiling up at me like she's seeing me for the first time. "Congratulations, boss."

I nod in response, finding myself at a loss for words. Because the knot in my chest is growing bigger every second I'm around her. It's as if I'm experiencing life anew after years of stagnation—and she may be the one to thank for that. With the way my daughter is on cloud nine staring up at me like a cow milking hero, I'd say I'm at least doing something right for once.

20

DELANEY

We drop Ava off at her grandma's house after our celebratory strawberry milkshakes. When Susan opens the front door, and sees her granddaughter in the middle of Cole and I, holding each of our hands, her smile grows tenfold.

She waves the three of us inside her rustic farmhouse. "It's hotter than a two-dollar pistol on the Fourth of July. Come on, and get your asses in here."

Cole sighs. "Mom, language."

"Campbell's are born with a mouthful of colorful language. I'm pretty sure you were dropping F-bombs like a pro at her age," she retorts.

Susan's house is both homey and gorgeous, a small two-story adorned with natural wood accents and a tall stone fireplace. Black metal picture frames of various sizes hang on every wall, prompting me to begin snooping as I peruse the photos on display. Some are creased, black-and-white snapshots from decades past, while others capture more recent moments, like the image of Ava blowing out the candles on her fifth birthday cake.

As someone with no family pictures, I'm extremely fascinated by them. And when I happen across a picture of elementary school Cole, I can't help but grin.

He's no older than twelve, his hair neatly parted on the side and gelled so heavily it resembles a helmet. The expression on his face mirrors his present-day look —tired of everyone's bullshit.

Susan comes up behind me, her eyes gleaming with pride as she gazes at the picture. "Wasn't he handsome?"

"He was. And still is," I reply, glancing over my shoulder at him. The tips of his ears turn pink as he pretends not to listen to his mother and me.

"Takes after his father. Just as much of a lovable asshole as him too," Susan remarks, her gaze shifting between her son and me. Then she leans in and whispers, "But one thing about these Campbell men is that they'll love you with an unshakeable force until their last dying breath."

She pulls back and looks at me with an unmistakable look of perception, while I stand there, smiling and nodding like a speechless idiot.

Finally, I manage to mutter, "That so?"

"Yep. And with that said, go have a drink or two and

have some fun. Together." Susan winks at me suggestively, as Cole has a coughing fit from several feet away.

"Allergic to the cats?" his mom asks him, as we watch Ava pet a black kitty nestled into the pillow of the couch.

"We better head out. Before Mom decides to whip out my yearbook and every single embarrassing story she has of me."

"You know there are quite a few. But if you haven't driven her away yet, then she probably won't mind the head gear."

"Okay, that's our cue. Bye, Mom. Bye, Ava girl."

He hugs his daughter, before we slip away into the dark cab of his truck. Tonight, I've convinced him to go to The Tavern, a popular hole-in-the-wall bar in town. With how quiet he is, combined with the amount of scowling he directs my way, I was certain he'd decline and lock himself away in his room all night. That's his status quo most evenings after Ava is asleep.

I swim laps, while he shutters himself away like the beast in a princess movie. If I'm lucky, he'll hang out on the couch feigning disinterest in the true crime docs I get sucked into. Although I have a strong suspicion that he secretly likes them too.

He insists on driving, refusing my offer to be the designated driver. Truth be told, I want to see him let loose after a few drinks, to metaphorically let his hair down. Perhaps he'd even dance on the bar top and let me take a vodka shot from the lines of his abs—I've seen him shirtless, I know they exist.

The drive over is uneventful, silent with the exception of the nineties rap I have blasting and am attempting to sing along with. I test him, trying to see when he'll put his foot down and tell me to shut the hell up and calm down.

My entire life I've been like that tiny silver ball inside a pinball machine—bouncing around, wrecking havoc, annoying the shit out of people.

With Josh, he'd constantly tell me how he expected me to act in social situations. *Don't say anything weird. Calm the fuck down. Can you not do that?* If I sang out loud at a grocery store, he'd whisper that I was embarrassing him and ditch me mid-aisle. At fancy work dinners he'd request me to not open my mouth unless absolutely necessary.

Eventually out of habit, I toned down for him. Fitting the lackluster mold of expectations he set forth.

Looking back, I see the red flags, the errors in allowing him to exert control over me. But dwelling on it won't change the past. All I can do is rediscover that unrestrained side of myself. Open the door of my cage, and coax myself forward; remind myself I'm free again.

Cole opens the door of the bar for me, his hand lightly grazing the small of my back for all of two seconds. It's gone before I fully process its presence, but I wish he hadn't moved it. I wish he still had his hand on my back, connecting us together.

The bar is old and dingy, but full of spirit. The floors are nearly as scratched up as the bar top. A glowing neon sign reading *Cocktails* is so old it has to be considered vintage, hangs on the red brick wall. But everyone here is in a good mood, the happy chatter is a soothing white noise.

As we sit at the bar, the top sticky from spilt drinks, Cole appears like a tightly wound spring. His discomfort is palpable, casting a shadow over the air like an impending storm on a summer's day.

I wish I could take a scoop of his anxiety from his mental load. The best I can do is try to make him laugh instead.

"Think they give discounts to winners of fake cow milking contests?" I ask him with a nudge.

"Unfortunately, I'm gonna go with no."

"I can't believe how well you knew how to milk that cow. Seriously, I was impressed. You're very skilled with your hands. That could come in handy...if you know what I mean." I smile up at him suggestively, and his cheekbones turn pink from my comment.

"Delaney." He says my name like a warning.

"What? Just stating the obvious."

"Sounds like another one of your sexual innuendos to me."

Making my eyes wide with innocence, I reply, "Wow. You sure have a dirty mind. I was talking about how it'd come in handy for your *construction* job." I totally meant sex. We both know that. "What did you think I meant?"

He swipes a hand down his face like he can wipe his flushed skin back to tan. "You know…"

"No I don't know. Tell me. Go ahead and say it out loud for the whole class to hear."

Grabbing the edges of my bar stool, he surprises me by scooting me right up next to him. Our knees collide and neither of us make an effort to move. Then he leans down, his lips pressed to the side of my hair as he whispers, "Sex. You think I'd be good at sex. Specifically, playing with nipples and fingering pussy. Is that what you want to hear me say?"

His gravelly words. His breath on my ear. His arms caging me in on either side of my stool. The combination of it all turns me on, making me press my thighs together to relieve the dull ache below.

"That's more like it." I pretend to be unaffected by him, as I peruse the handwritten menu hanging on the back wall. He removes his hands from my chair and swivels back to face the bar top. His intense gaze is back on me again, attempting to discern how his words have made me feel. Perhaps he's worried he went too far.

But I don't show him my hand, I keep my cards close to my chest. Even though the only feeling I currently have in my chest is an overwhelming want of his touch back on my body.

I knock the top of the scratched up wooden bar with my knuckles. "So, should we put a little twist on tonight and only order milk based drinks?"

"That…sounds nauseating. I'm getting a beer."

"You better load up on more than a beer. I'm signing us up for karaoke at 10 p.m."

His head jerks over to my direction, scared to death. "I hope you're joking."

"I am, for you. But I want to do karaoke, so I'm signing myself up. Unless you'll be too embarrassed to be seen with a fantastic singer like myself, of course."

Josh would have begged me not to sing, claiming I'd embarrass him and myself in the process. I'm not a horrible singer, but I'm not great either.

Under his gaze, my skin burns as he looks me up and down slowly. "I'd never be embarrassed to be seen with you." He rolls up the long sleeves of his flannel shirt, cords of muscle in his forearms making a very welcomed appearance. "Do whatever makes you happy, as long as I can sit on this stool and sip my beer while I watch you have fun."

Hm. Look at that. He doesn't even seem phased by the possibility of my drunk singing. However, the sensation stirring low in my belly from the mere prospect of his focused attention, entirely derails my train of thought.

We order drinks, and I force him to cheers with eye contact before downing my shot of vodka. A poor excuse to look into his stunning hazel eyes.

As I fill the silence with mindless conversation, he nods or offers a sporadic sentence or two. Gradually, his shoulders ease as he begins to get more comfortable amid the noisy atmosphere.

Maybe it's my two shots I've consumed back-to-back, but everything about him is distracting. The way his navy shirt stretches across his broad, muscular shoulders. The dark stubble on his face contrasted by his greenish brown eyes. His long fingers wrapping around his frosty beer glass. The same ones that held my hand in his truck the other night. The ones I fantasize dipping inside of me if we both ever lose control.

I'm not the only one checking out Cole. It's impossible not to notice the half dozen or so women eating him up all around the room. As I leave for the restroom, having him sit out there alone feels a lot like throwing a steak dinner to the wolves.

When I return from the bathroom, a beautiful, curvy woman is leaning on the bar top, her cleavage on full display for Cole to take a look at. She pushes his shoulder with an over the top laugh. Either he got a whole lot funnier in the last four minutes, or this woman is trying to flirt with him. He leans back, as far as possible in his stool to create distance between them —never looking her directly in the eye as if she's a Medusa incarnate.

As I walk over, jealousy sparks inside me like flint against steel. Maybe he does want her or another woman's attention in this bar. Why wouldn't he? He's an attractive, single man. As far as I know, he's not celibate. There's plenty of gorgeous women here that he could take his pick from, and they'd give themselves up on a silver platter.

The idea of playing wing woman for him sends a wave of panic through me. While I'd go along with it, the underlying cause of my discomfort eats away at me. The reason behind that, I'm not ready to confront. All I know is that I don't share, but he isn't even mine in the first place.

When I sit back down in my seat, relief courses through me as I see the silent plea for help in his eyes as he glances in my direction. His face is waving a flag, screaming *SOS, save me please.*

This is going to be fun. "Hey, babe. Thanks for saving my seat," I say, as I touch his tense thigh.

His eyes snap to mine, shocked at how I'm going about saving him. I squeeze his leg, hard, with my fingers, trying to convey my message. *Play along, okay?* Understanding crosses his face, and he reaches his arm across the backrest of my stool.

The dark haired woman scowls at me, before pasting a tight smile on her face. "Oh, uh, hi there. And who are you?"

She wants to pull my gold claw clip out and stab me with it, I know it.

I lean into Cole, resting my head on his shoulder, as the woman struggles to make sense of who I am to him. "I'm Delaney. Nice to meet you."

Disregarding me, the woman turns to him, not even bothering to respond back to me. "I wasn't aware that you were no longer single."

He shrugs. *Shrugs.* And doesn't say a single word

back. It's become glaringly obvious that he's of no help right now, potentially for the best since I suspect he's a terrible liar.

Luck is on our side though, because acting was my ten year old dream ever since I was a tree in my elementary school musical. I've got this shit in the bag.

"We haven't put a label on it. We're having fun. You know how it is," I answer suggestively, running my fingers through the ends of his thick hair at the nape of his neck. Good god, what kind of product does he use? His hair is silky smooth.

My touch elicits a reaction from him, causing his eyes to flutter shut and then snap open again. I thought he would freeze up with the way I'm touching him. But he seems to be...enjoying it?

"Well then, technically he is single if you're his fuck buddy..." the woman counters, not backing down.

I yelp with surprise as he scoops me up from my bar stool and places me in his lap. I feel so small and soft against his massive form.

Holding me against him, he wraps one arm around my waist. "I'm taken." His tone is final. Leaving no room for any slutty possibilities.

Defeated, the woman with balls of steel rolls her eyes and pushes off the bar. Finally giving up on her man prowl.

I snicker, my inner bitch coming out, because I won and he is mine. Not really *mine*, but a girl can pretend for a millisecond.

Still sitting in his lap, I throw my arms around his neck and turn to look at him. "I had a feeling it'd be dangerous taking you out to a bar. You're too handsome for your own good."

"Now I know you're full of it." His eyes are fixed on mine, twinkling with amusement. His attention hits me in the chest as I become hyper aware of every little movement between us.

"That lady was ready to fight me for you. Then what would we have done?"

"I'd never let her, or any one for that matter, lay a finger on you." His voice goes soft. "You're always safe with me, okay?"

Maybe it's the alcohol or the fact that I do feel completely protected when I'm with him. But I let myself be weak, just this one time, as I wrap my arms around his torso and bury my head into his chest. I breathe him in—his pine cologne—hear the sound of his heart racing in his chest, and feel both of his arms slowly wrapping around me, hugging me back. He rests his head on top of mine, never letting me go.

The jokes on us now, sitting in a bar, clinging onto one another like we're each other's life rafts. We no longer need to pretend that we're a couple. Yet here we are, both acting like this is necessary to ward off advances—while truthfully all we want is to touch.

If no one believed we were a couple before, they'd be fully convinced now. The line is even beginning to blur itself for me too. That is until he scoots me off his lap and places me back in my own respective chair.

He clears his throat and stands, adjusting his pant leg, and motioning toward the restroom.

Maybe I freaked him out and came on a little too strong. Typical.

I'm growing antsy with every minute he is gone, wondering if I messed up the inklings of a friendship we've begun to form. I drink two more shots, turn down one man's advances, and am on stage for karaoke by the time he comes back out. It feels like a lifetime when you're buzzed.

"Mr. Brightside" by The Killers starts playing and sweat breaks out on my back as I see Cole take a seat on his barstool. He looks so serious, so intense. Completely fixated on me, and me alone, that I can't help but grin —like a flower unfurling its petals to relish the sunlight.

I'm drunk and emotional, but the first line of the song hits too close to home. The crowd sings along because who can *not* sing to this song? It's the reason I chose it. Less pressure and more opportunity to make a fool of myself with tipsy dancing and shout-singing

I'm not shy, but I'm more nervous than I anticipated with Cole's eyes on me. The corner of his mouth tips up into something resembling happiness as he watches me. It eggs me on, which only makes his smile grow.

When the song ends, the packed bar erupts in a flurry of cheers and applause. I take a dramatic bow, nearly falling over with the action thanks to the alcohol coursing through my blood.

As I walk back over to him, I'm nervous he'll react how my ex would. *I'm glad that's over*, Josh would've said —complete with an eyeroll and dismissive tone.

But as soon as I'm within reach, Cole wraps a brawny arm around my shoulders and pulls me flush against his body. Leaning down, he whispers, "That was so fucking sexy."

His breath tickles my neck, causing me to squirm against him. "*You* think *that* was sexy?"

He shrugs and nods, never letting me go from his tight grip around me.

I tilt my head, laughing with amazement. It surprises me that he finds that attractive, especially after years of being told that embracing my true self was embarrassing. It's a huge relief to consider that maybe I'm not the one who's broken—perhaps it was my ex all along.

"Please let me show you how sexy I can actually be. I have to redeem myself."

"No."

"No?"

"I already know how sexy you are," he murmurs, voice low and gravelly.

I feign shock. "Are you? Complimenting me? Did you just imply I'm sexy sometimes?"

"Not sometimes. Always."

I crane my head up high to be able to look at his

face, to ensure I'm hearing this right. I elbow him, "You're going to make me get a big head."

"You don't know the effect you have on people, do you?"

"Annoying the shit out of them? I'm well aware."

He delicately grasps my chin, directing my gaze towards his. "You're the sun, Delaney," he replies, softly. "And anyone who has the privilege to be in your presence basks in the way you shine."

Every molecule of oxygen is sucked out of my lungs. I'm speechless for perhaps the first time in my life.

My eyes drop to his lips, as he searches my face. And damn it, I want to kiss Cole.

My grumpy boss. The absolute last person I ever expected to be telling me that I'm the sun.

Before I have the chance to act on kissing him, he releases me and turns back to the bar, making quick work to close out our tab.

"Ready?" he asks, as he tucks his worn leather wallet into his back pocket. He won't meet my eyes anymore, and I'd sing a thousand more horrible karaoke songs to know what's going through his head right now.

"Ready."

He leads me through the packed bar, his firm chest a protective wall against my back as we weave our way through to the exit.

The car ride is silent and awkward, palpable with tension. The type of tension I'm still attempting to decipher. My brain spins with a million questions that are determined to burst from me. Does he see me as more than his annoying nanny? Is he only being nice since we have to live together? Does he regret what he said? Did he want to kiss me?

The touching. The compliments. The silence.

It's enough to make me believe he could want more.

Followed by a dash of doubt to make me think I've imagined it all.

Back at home, he barrels straight for the bar tucked into a nook of the family room. He pops open a bottle of whiskey with the intensity of someone that's been stranded in the desert for days, in desperate need of a drink.

I can't help but follow him. I'm watching and observing, like he's a National Geographic special. Trying to make sense of what's going on with him. He's talking even less than normal, which is saying something for Cole—the quietest person I've ever met. The swell of his shoulders are so tense that they seem bound to his ears, and he won't meet my eye.

He pushes a dark strand of hair out of his eyes and pours himself three fingers of whiskey, gulping it down without flinching.

Something is definitely up with him, and it goes against every cell in my body to be quiet. "Okay, you're freaking me out. What's wrong?"

Rubbing at the back of his neck, he stares at the lines of grout on the floor. "Nothing."

"It's not nothing. I feel like you can't even look at me all of a sudden. Did I piss you off?"

His eyes snap to mine. "No."

I want to shake him to see if it'll help spill the words from his brain. "I thought we were finally making progress tonight. I don't know what I did wrong."

"You didn't do anything wrong. It's all me."

"Just fucking tell me. This whole trying to guess what you're thinking game is making me on edge."

He strides across the room, his steps purposeful and confident. As he towers over me, standing so close that I can smell the whiskey on his breath, I can't help but notice the steady rise and fall of his chest. "Trust me, you don't want to know what I'm thinking."

"But I do," I whisper.

"Fine." He stares at me for a beat, and I swear he can see straight through my tough facade. "I can't stop thinking about how much I want to kiss you every second of every day. I want to know what you'd feel like if I bent you over this counter and fucked you until you couldn't walk the next day. I want to know what sounds you'd make if you came with my dick inside of you. I want to know what it'd be like if you were mine. But I can't do that or have that."

All I can do is stare and attempt to breathe as my world is tipped on its axis. Cole, the man that I swore hates me...likes me? Wants to kiss and fuck me?

My stomach feels hollow, and bones carved out at his confession. Because it's everything I've wanted too.

"But I want you to—" before I can even finish my sentence his mouth crashes down on mine. His hand weaves into my hair and his mouth is gentle but firm, coaxing me to open my mouth as his tongue slips in. We're both hungry, ravenous, for each other. His body presses into mine, and I can't help but moan against his mouth when I feel him hard in his jeans.

"I've wanted you since the first day I saw you," he admits as he picks me up, my legs naturally wrapping around his trim waist.

I kiss him wherever I can reach—his neck, dimples, mouth. As I take my sweet time enjoying every inch of him, his eyes close with a gravelly groan.

His erection presses into my pelvis, provoking an overwhelming need for him to be inside of me. "Please, fuck me. I need you."

He sets me down and kisses me again with the intensity of every word he's never said aloud. "Laney—" his hand trembles as he slides it up my neck. His nose runs alongside my jaw, slowly taking his time inhaling me. His voice is a rough whisper. "Fuck, I can't. You know I can't."

"Why? It sure seems like you *could*." I grope his dick through his pants, grabbing and dragging my fingers up and down it, as air hisses through his teeth.

Grabbing my wrist, he corners me against the wall, and pins my hand above my head, pressing himself flush against me, grinding his cock against my stomach. "You're a little cock tease. Do you know that?"

My mouth falls open to argue why it's not a good idea, it's a great idea, but his thumb brushes my lips. Before I fully comprehend what I'm doing, I move my head so his thumb slips inside my mouth.

His eyes track the movement, as they grow darker and more dangerous than ever. Wanting to put on a show for him, I do my best representation of what it would be like if he let his guard down and put his dick in my mouth instead. My mouth is watering for him as I suck on his thumb; swirling my tongue around it and moaning with pleasure.

He removes his finger and kisses me deeply again. I'm squirming under him, needing more. There's nowhere to go since I'm sandwiched between the smooth, cold wall and his hard, warm body.

Suddenly, in one swift motion, he drops my wrist and backs away, tugging on his hair and pain in his expression. "Shit. I'm so sorry. We can't do this."

He walks down the hall, far away from me, as I'm left there still under his spell, chest heaving and body trembling from the memory of his mouth on mine. His boots echo on the hardwood floors, as my heart beats precariously in my chest. I'm so insanely turned on, and he is too.

So why is he running away?

What the hell happened?

21

COLE

I'm screwed. Completely, and utterly, screwed.

First, I went off spewing all those thoughts in my head at the bar. How Delaney is pure sunshine and unbelievably sexy. Those were things I was supposed to keep locked away in the safe corner of my mind.

She just looked so happy, so free, when she was on stage. Then when she came back to me and hesitancy was written all over her—the words fell out of me.

Making a move on her once we got home wasn't supposed to happen either, it was the exact *opposite* of what I was trying to convince myself not to do. I'm forever changed now that I know how it feels to kiss her, the way she wriggled beneath my touch.

This wasn't the plan, to fall for the nanny.

But now I'm so far gone, I'm lost.

After Isabel, I swore I'd never let myself get attached

to someone again. It hurts too damn much to have the person you love leave. That's exactly what will happen with Delaney. We have an agreement of three months. That's it, and it's not enough.

How long would she really want to stay with a grumpy old man like me?

That's why I had to walk away. Because she deserves more than I can offer. She deserves the whole world, someone vibrant and adventurous like her.

I'm not on her level, and I never will be.

Leaving her breathless against the wall nearly killed me. I wanted to get myself off in the shower after touching her, but all I could picture was the confusion on her face when I left her there—lips swollen and eyes full of questions.

I'm grateful for the distraction of picking up Ava from my mom's house the next morning, even if I am dead tired from tossing and turning all night. Delaney was still in her room when I left and I thought of knocking, but decided against it. I'm sure she's not happy with the abrupt way I left things. Communication isn't my strong suit.

The best I hope we can do is keep it professional and civil for the remainder of the summer. Distance will give me the space to let my feelings for her fade...if that's even possible.

Approaching my mother's house, two miles down the road from mine, I try to get myself into check. When I walk through my mother's front door, Ava runs to me, hands and mouth sticky with pink frosting. "Guess what? Grandma let me eat cake for breakfast."

"Is that so?" I say, kissing the top of her head while I glare at my mother. Mom bats her lashes and smiles wide. She knows I'd never do or say anything, even if I don't think cake is an adequate breakfast for a five year old.

"How was your night? You look awfully tired," Mom comments, suggestively.

"It was fine. Uneventful," I reply, dismissing her bizarre hopes and dreams.

"Hm. I figured Delaney would've kept you busy last night."

"We went to The Tavern for a drink. That's it."

Mom walks up and points at my neck. "You sure about that? That's not what your hickey suggests."

My hand flies to my neck, trying to cover and rub away the proof of kissing Delaney. I didn't notice it earlier. I should be embarrassed about my mom calling me out on it, but I can't decide if I'm happy or mortified that there's a reminder of last night bruised into my skin.

Ava assesses the hickey with a serious face. "What is that? Did you get an ouchie?"

"Something like that. I'm okay though."

My mom hides her laughter behind her hand. "Yes, I'm sure you are *very okay*."

I narrow my eyes at her, telepathically telling her to

stop the shenanigans. My mom shouldn't even be so invested in this.

She's greedy to see me settled down and happy, probably wants another grandkid or two. Her and my father were married for thirty years before he died of a sudden heart attack seven years ago. She's of the belief that everyone has a love story out there for them waiting to be found.

Ava pats my cheek. "I want to go home and see Laney now. She told me we could go see the dogs soon. I want to today."

"I'm not sure what she's doing today, baby. But what's this about dogs?"

"The animal shelter. She called and they said we could help there. I'll get to walk a dog!"

"Hm." That's not a bad idea. Ava begs me daily for a dog. I'm against it, but volunteering at an animal shelter seems like a good way to channel that energy.

When we arrive home, Delaney isn't there. I'm simultaneously relieved and disappointed. I'm actively talking myself out of sticking my head into her room, to double check that she didn't move out after my asshole antic last night.

Ava and I kick a ball around in the field behind the house, read a minimum of ten books about a talking dog, and cook her favorite lunch of unicorn-shaped noodles. Now she's thrilled I've caved and am letting her style my hair for her beauty salon game. My hair falls right past my ears now, I'm in need of a haircut, but she says it's perfect for a 'baby ponytail.'

So that's my life now, hair in an updo while eating leftover unicorn noodles straight from the pot, and trying to not look out the front window toward the driveway every five minutes. How often I actually do tells me how far gone I am on Delaney.

The worry sets in once Ava is asleep at 8 p.m., and there's still no sign of her. The house is suddenly too empty, too quiet.

Usually around this time, our nightly routine consists of Delaney watching a murder documentary series, punctuating the air with gasps every few minutes. I make us a bowl of fresh-popped popcorn and sit across the couch from her, trying to stay awake a minute longer so I can be near her.

I'm sure I'm the last person she wants to text her, but the need to know she's safe overrides my hesitation.

COLE:

Hey. Are you okay?

DELANEY:

Yeah, I'm good. Why?

COLE:

You're not home and I wanted to make sure you're okay after last night.

DELANEY:

I'm fine, we're fine. (And when I say
fine, it really is).

COLE:

Ok. Good.

DELANEY:

I'll be back later tonight, don't wait up.

WHERE THE HELL IS SHE? I'm not going to be possessive over her and order her back to the house like a controlling lunatic, but the thought of her out with another man threatens to topple me over the edge of worry. She never said she was out on a date, but telling me not to wait up immediately puts my guards up.

For the next two hours, I'm a complete wreck. My mind is spinning, heart racing. Every single muscle in my body is tense with the torturous thought of another man touching and kissing her.

I want to be the only one that feels her full lips pressed to mine. The only one to hear her tiny moans when I touch her exactly how she likes.

There's no use in even trying to sleep at this point. All I feel capable of doing is pacing back and forth until she's back here. Home. With me.

A beer only amplifies the dizzy worry swirling

inside my brain. I settle on a soak in the hot tub, leaning back onto the cool concrete to get a view of the moon.

The hot tub does nothing to relax me, I'm more wound up than ever. Everywhere I look, all I see are tiny reminders of Delaney engraved into my life. Her sun hat on the gazebo. The Tupperware of leftovers with a note she scribbled on top for me. The hickey bruised on my neck when I stare at my reflection in the bathroom mirror when washing my hands.

My possessiveness only grows stronger every passing minute she's gone. I've never felt this way. Even with Isabel, when I found out about her affair with my best friend. I detached because she broke my trust. But jealous? Possessive? Never.

Looking for a distraction, I impulsively plunge into the pool. Yet another reminder of my nights with Delaney. The abrupt cold water provides a stark contrast to my inner turmoil.

I sit under the water for as long as I can hold my breath. An attempt to clear my mind and convince myself to get a grip. As if submerging myself can wash away the growing feelings I have for her.

When I come up for air, I push the hair out of my face, slicking it back with my hand. I freeze when I see her there, standing on the pool's edge.

Delaney. In a tiny red sundress that barely covers her ass. Long golden hair that I want to run my hands through. Big glossy lips and playful blue eyes that I could stare into all damn day.

I'm suddenly furious. Not at her, but at myself. Because I'm at odds with the way I want to hunt down the man that got to be with her tonight while she looks like this—so goddamn beautiful.

With her arms crossed against her chest, she asks, "What are you doing out here?"

"Swimming."

"You always go swimming at II p.m. after drinking three beers?" She nods her head toward the trio of empty beer bottles.

"Just tonight." I swim closer.

She sits down, slipping her feet into the water and leaning back on her hands, watching me with inquisitive eyes. "Tell me why."

"Because I didn't want to think about you out with another man tonight, touching you." The beer has diminished my filter. I'm kicking myself for admitting that out loud to her.

She doesn't say anything as she peels off that tiny dress, exposing herself in a black lacy bra and thong. Inches and inches of smooth creamy skin. Golden waves of hair tumbling over her narrow shoulders. The sight of her almost naked, every curve illuminated in the moonlight. Everything about her drives me wild and makes me instantly hard.

Sliding into the water, she asks, "Why would you not want to think about that?"

I don't respond, instead swiping a wet hand down

my face, willing myself to gather an ounce of control before I do something I can't take back.

"Would it bother you if another man kissed me? Touched me? Fucked me?" She swims up to me, trying to play some sort of game to make me jealous. "As far as I know, I'm not yours. I can do what I want."

"Fuck, I know that. Okay? I fucking know that," I snap. "That's the problem. I want you more than I've ever wanted anything in my life. But I can't have you. I'm not good for you. I'm ten years older than you. I'd bore the hell out of you. And on top of everything else, you leave in two months."

She gazes at me, truly seeing me, her big blue eyes taking me in. Pausing with a sharp inhale, she considers her next words carefully. "What if I told you most of those things weren't true?"

"How—"

Holding up a hand, she cuts me off. "Do you want to know what I think?"

"Tell me."

Her arms wrap around my neck, as she pulls her body through the water until it's flush to mine. Her expression turns satisfied when her leg brushes against my swim trunks and she feels how turned on I already am. "Be selfish for once in your life. You deserve it, you deserve *me*. You're not *that* much older than me. And yes, I'm leaving in two months. But what's the point in fighting whatever's going on between us? Give in to it and...I don't know. Be free. Be free with me, please."

This is a bad idea. The worst. I'm looking at this through lenses stained with want, but she has a point. Maybe it's better to be with her for two months than not at all. There's no chance in hell I'll be able to stop my attraction to her at this point anyways.

My reasoning and flimsy excuses snap like a twig as our mouths collide, lips still wet and salty from the chlorinated pool water. Her legs wrap around my waist, as she pushes her pelvis into my hardness. I press up into her, eliciting a small moan from her. My swim trunks and her thong are the only thin barriers between us, and it feels like too much.

"We need rules," I mumble against her mouth.

She pulls her face back and gives me a pointed look. "Rules don't sound very free."

"I can't fuck you. We can do everything else, but not that." Because once I do, she's mine. And I won't be able to let her leave in two months.

"Okay, yeah. If that's what you want," she nods, not fully understanding but being considerate nonetheless.

"Good," I say, as I dive into kissing her neck.

Her hands run through my wet hair, and god it feels good. Being touched like this...by her. She gives the ends of my hair a tug, coaxing me to take it a step further as I pull down one side of her bra and take her pebbled nipple into my mouth.

"Oh my god," she breathes.

I switch to her other breast, switching between licking and sucking. She goes wild beneath me, grinding herself against my dick, trying to get more. I swim to the pool's edge and lift her up and out of it, setting her on the poolside mat for cushion from the hard cement.

As I pull down her thong, she watches me still standing in the pool, eye level with her pussy, waiting for my next move. I can see it in her face, she's not sure if I'll run away again like last time.

"Spread those legs, Emerson."

She does as I ask, and then my head disappears between them. Licking her slowly at first, then sticking my tongue inside of her as she gasps.

"Cole, *oh my god.*"

I pick up the speed, spreading her wetness and flicking my tongue against her clit. It lights her up like the stars in the sky above us.

I slip a finger inside of her. "So fucking wet for me already."

Inserting a second finger, I curl them up as I work her back and forth, giving her exactly what she wants. "Is this what you wanted, Delaney? You've been wanting me to touch this pretty pussy?"

She's too far gone in the daze of my fingers and mouth on her, unable to answer between her breathy moans.

I flick her swollen clit once with my tongue before stopping, keeping my two fingers deep inside of her but unmoving. "I asked you a question, sunshine. Is this what you've been wanting from me?" I kiss the inside of each of her spread thighs, leaving a soft trail of affection along her damp skin.

Her body arches from the cement in response to my lack of movement, in desperate need for more. "Yesss," she says on an exhale. "Oh god, please just don't stop."

Hovering between her legs, I mumble against her pussy. "There's my good girl." Then I go in, with everything I've got. Mouth kissing and sucking her clit, my fingers hitting the sensitive spot within at a furious speed. It's all the perfect storm for her as writhes and moans beneath my touch.

"I'm going to come..." she murmurs, breathless.

She rocks into my hand as I finger her, licking her the way I've already learned she loves based on her reactions. Before I know it, I hear her crying out my name as she peaks. Keeping my fingers inside of her, I help her ride that wave as she crashes back to reality.

Sitting up on her forearms, she tries to catch her breath as she stares at me with wide, dazed eyes. "Holy shit. Wow." After a few moments, she regains her composure, coming back down to earth as if she had an out-of-body experience. She sits up on her elbows, tired from her post-orgasm daze, but with a devilish smile. "Your turn."

I lift myself out of the pool, and throw her over my shoulder again, like the first night we were out here. I'm hard as a rock, dick tenting my shorts. As much as I want her to get me off, tonight's about her.

I wrap a towel around her shivering shoulders,

hugging her small body against mine to give her warmth. "Don't worry about me."

She nestles her face against my bare chest. "Someone has to." Sneaking a look up at me, she tacks on, "And I was at Madi's house tonight by the way."

I know it's none of my goddamn business—she didn't need to tell me jack shit. But I'd be lying if I didn't say I'm relieved. Relieved to be the only man who gets to hold her like this.

My stupid rule better be worth it. But deep down I know the truth.

My connection with Delaney is already solidifying at a dangerous rate. One that I don't anticipate ever fading—sex or not.

22

DELANEY

Cole motherfucking Campbell.

My head's been in outer space for the last twelve hours due to the mind blowing orgasm he gave me—without even being inside of me. He must have a magic mouth and fingers because I was in a daze when I went to sleep, and woke up still under that post-orgasm spell.

I'm baffled he didn't want me to return the favor, as well as with his no penis-in-vagina rule. As much as I want him to fuck me, it's not my job to try and change his mind. He has his reasons, and I'll respect that.

I do have to admit I'm ashamed I was vague in my texts last night to him for the sole purpose of seeing if he'd be jealous. It's childish, I know. We all have our faults though, mine being that I enjoy poking the bear —which I did a lot yesterday.

I woke up to a text from Kenneth, *My offer still stands*

if you change your mind and want to show me how much you want your old job back, it read. Attached was some lewd picture of him grabbing his erection through his navy briefs.

Despite the eye burning image, that scumbag's text was fantastic news for me, because now I had some sort of proof of his sexual harassment. My next call was to an old friend, Marissa, who also conveniently works in the HR department at JunoTec. I met her at the office, told her the story about our dear colleague Kenneth, along with the texts. Her lack of surprise when she heard was reassuring because my worst fear was that no one would believe me.

The blonde, airheaded CPA, whose boyfriend was caught embezzling is now also the center of a scandal with a supervisor? There are many people in this office that will call me a liar. My mama may have raised an outspoken wild child, but I ain't no liar.

There was no way in hell I was going to let Kenneth have the opportunity to do this to someone else, to someone that may have not felt comfortable telling him to fuck off.

Marissa ensured that Monday morning, an official investigation would be opened, most likely resulting in the disciplinary action of termination. Those fancy HR words were like music to my ears.

After my morning of 'Operation Take Down Kenneth,' I went to Madi's house to catch her up on my life's current events, with Ella on speaker phone a whole state away. It should have been a PowerPoint presentation with as many key points we needed to discuss—Kenneth, my meeting with Marissa at Juno-Tec, and my insane crush on my DILF boss.

Madi informed me I better keep her and Ella updated from now on, or else she'd revoke my best friend title. Which I know is a load of bull, because we all know we're stuck together until we're old ladies with dentures and seven cats.

Now I'm knee deep in shelter dogs with Ava, brainstorming how we can convince her dad to adopt one. The fawn senior pug with the bug eyes, in particular.

"She's just so cute. I *need* her," Ava pleads.

There is nothing cute about this dog besides her stellar personality. "I know, Betsy is...adorable, in her own fabulous way. But your dad said no and we have to respect that. Best we can do is take her on a walk and play with her in the pen on the days we volunteer."

Ava sits criss-cross on the cement shelter floor, affectionately stroking Betsy's head while showering her with compliments. I snap a picture, and send it straight to her dad.

DELANEY:

Soulmates, don't you think?

COLE:

Cute. But we're not getting a dog.

DELANEY:

C'mon, look how adorable they are. Betsy is old anyways, it'd be a max of four years responsibility.

COLE:

So Ava's heart will be broken within the next four years? It went from a no to a hell no.

DELANEY:

You have a hard, cold heart. You know that?

COLE:

Huh. I seem to remember you liking something hard about me last night.

DELANEY:

Oh, I remember. I remember a little too well actually. Haven't stopped thinking about it.

DELANEY:

P.S. Can we do a repeat of last night again? And again? And then maybe again?

COLE:

I'm counting on it.

Ava gets to hang out with Betsy while I finish cleaning numerous shelter kennels, cleaning food dishes, and scooping litter boxes. I'm a sweaty, filthy mess and couldn't be happier.

Growing up, my mom never let us own a pet. I even won a goldfish at a school carnival and she gave it away to our neighbor, lecturing me how pets are a waste of money. Financial struggles made it clear—feed a pet or feed the family. We counted pennies, I got it. It didn't stop me from fantasizing about rescuing a pet of my own someday though.

Shelter pets and I have a lot in common with our abandonment issues and all. Getting the opportunity to volunteer here this summer is a dream come true. One I don't foresee discontinuing, even after I go back to an accounting job.

The whole ride home, Ava tells me in extreme detail all the ideas she has to try and talk her dad into getting a dog. Drawing a picture of Betsy and herself, begging and crying at his feet, an elaborate plan to dognap Betsy and sneak her into the guest room to live out her days without Cole ever knowing.

The girl is creative, I'll give her that.

When we get back, Cole's already home and cooking dinner, looking entirely too sexy in his backwards hat while he grills marbled steaks on the barbecue. When he catches me staring at him, he grins, dimples gracing me with a rare appearance.

It's obvious we both are thinking about last night, the way he laid me out poolside beneath the stars and gave me the best orgasm of my life.

While Ava goes into a long-winded story about how

she taught Betsy how to fetch today (she didn't), I go take a shower and change into a fresh outfit. When I come back out, he is still patiently listening, nodding, and acting interested enough that it's not rude, but not excited enough to get her hopes up that she'll get to bring home the dog tomorrow.

"Go wash up, baby. Dinner will be ready soon," he tells her.

She runs away, energy restored solely by the hopes and dreams of being a future dog owner.

He takes the thick steaks off the barbecue, setting them down on a large wooden cutting board so they can rest.

"Wow, you really know how to handle meat," I quip, leaning on the patio kitchen's counters with my forearms.

Coming up behind me, he spins me around and cradles my face in his hands. He smells like charcoal and the faint scent of cologne.

"I thought about you all damn day," he murmurs, lips inches from mine.

Then he kisses me, deeply and thoroughly, like I've never been kissed before. I lose myself in him, melting into his touch, getting caught up in the way he unapologetically takes control.

"And what is it you thought of, specifically?" I ask.

He nibbles my ear, and whispers, "How I want those perfect lips wrapped around my cock."

"We might be able to make that very thing happen. Tonight."

I squirm against him as he rocks his erection into me. "Tell me, Emerson. If I were to touch you right now, how wet would you be for me?"

The sound of Ava's singing growing closer breaks our trance like an unexpected alarm clock, snapping us back to reality. We take wide steps apart, staring at each other with lust as thick as heavy fog.

We eat the steak, mashed potatoes, and vegetables that Cole made, followed by a swim in the pool. Ava is starting to get the hang of swimming without her floaties. She swims a short distance between us, back and forth countless times into our outstretched arms before she declares she's exhausted.

Being here with the two of them, doing normal family things, stirs up a range of emotions I'd rather ignore. Staying in this house and living with them makes me feel like a fraud. I don't know how a healthy family operates. My mom worked two jobs and was absent on her rare days off, while my sister and I scrounged our way through life together. We never had a fancy house, family time in a pool, barbecued dinners on the patio while swapping funny stories about our day.

I'm out of place in this world. Feeling awfully similar to an alien in a human disguise, fumbling my way through a completely normal routine, pretending like I know what to do when I have absolutely no idea.

Then there's the half of my thoughts that need to be locked up, never exposed to the light of day, because it's too good to be true. Knowing that a life like this *can* exist. Knowing that life with a family *can* be so damn fulfilling.

I can't want that. Certainly not with this family. And I already feel myself spiraling, losing control like threadbare tires on a rain slick highway.

It feels too easy to picture a life with Cole and Ava. Staying here, being with them, loving them with every single bone in my body.

It's a dangerous thought.

Ava's down for the night, I have the dishes loaded, and Cole has folded the last article of clothing from the dryer —because of course his laundry never even touches a laundry basket. It's straight from the dryer to the drawer. Something I thought was an impossible task until now.

Walking up behind him, I pinch his ass through his jeans. "Goddamn. You have a nicer ass than me. I want to bite it."

"Quit lying. No one has a nicer ass than you, not even me." He walks up and grabs a handful of my backside, giving it a firm squeeze as if he's reveling in the realization that he gets to touch me like this now.

I press my ear to his chest, feeling the steady rhythm

of his heart against my temple. "Do I get to see your bedroom? Or is it your one little secret you're keeping up your sleeve?"

"I figured you'd have snuck in there by now to snoop."

"You know me too well. But no, I actually haven't looked, I was worried maybe you had cameras so you'd know."

"This isn't Big Brother, no cameras."

"Well then, let's go. I can't wait to see if you're secretly a hoarder, or have an array of embarrassing posters with half naked women in there."

He laughs as we walk down the hall towards his room. "How do you even think of these things?"

"Is that a yes, then?"

"I'm afraid you're about to be very disappointed."

When he opens the door I can confirm I'm not disappointed. Not in the very least.

His bedroom is luxurious masculinity. There's a floor-to-ceiling window with breathtaking views of the hills and trees that surround his home, a low-profile bed with a channel tufted headboard, and a fireplace with a cozy sitting area in the corner.

"What the fuck? I should have snooped way sooner. I can't believe all *this* was hiding behind the door." I point around to all of the modern touches throughout the room. "How did you do all this?"

Embarrassed by my flattery, he admits, "I don't

know. I've built and been around enough model homes that I knew what I wanted."

I stroll through the room, brushing my finger along the mantle. "You must do a lot of fucking in here. I'd certainly drop my panties in a quick minute with a view like this."

"I don't bring women to the house...not that there's many to bring home anyway."

I'm surprised, yet relieved, to hear him say it. "That's not entirely true. You brought me to your house."

He takes a seat in the mid-century chair near the fireplace, and shrugs. "You're the exception."

Leaning forward, he rests his elbows on his knees as he tracks my every moment. Watching me marvel at the handcrafted wainscoting and the expansive sea of tall trees out the window. After I've finished inspecting every modern art piece and light fixture in the room, I stride over to him. Dropping to my knees and looking up at him from the ground. I'm certain he knows what I want to do by the confident way he leans back in the chair—ready for me.

My nails glide up his leg as I crawl into his lap, kissing his neck, feeling his rough stubble scrape my cheek, as I unbutton and unzip his jeans. As I go back down to my knees, he looks as serious as ever, but in a different way.

A dangerous, carnal way.

My fingers curl into the waistband of his briefs, as I pull them down to release him. He's long and thick and hard. Intimidatingly so, to where I'm wondering how the hell I'm about to fit this in my mouth.

"Not as small as you thought, is it?" he teases, referring to when I tried to insinuate that he must have a small penis since he drives a huge truck.

"Shut up, and let me suck your big dick."

He smirks, but the smile is wiped clean off his face the first time I swirl my tongue around him. A string of cuss words leave his mouth as I tease him slowly. His fingers lace through my hair, pushing himself deep into my mouth. I take him as far as I can go before gagging on his length.

He sits forward suddenly, cradling my head, thumbs swiping over my cheekbones. "Shit, I got carried away. You okay?"

"Do that again," I breathe.

"What—"

"Fuck my mouth and let me gag on you. Don't be fragile with me. I'm not breakable."

He stares at me for a beat, before grabbing a rough handful of my breast, and then shoving my head back down to continue getting him off.

Taking him in my mouth again, he begins to pump into me, gently at first, and his pace increases. My mouth waters for him, and I can feel him swell, growing closer to that edge of release. Every second longer he's inside my mouth, he relaxes, losing himself in the moment—exactly as I hoped.

One of his hands is still threaded through my

blonde hair, while his other hand grips the armrest of the chair.

"Touch yourself." He nods toward me. "Show me how much you love sucking my dick."

Without even hesitating, I remove my panties and spread my legs as my dress rides up to my hips. He begins to fuck my mouth while I dip my fingers into my wetness, spreading it, and rubbing gentle circles on my clit.

I'm already right there with him, insanely turned on from watching him lose himself in what I'm doing to him. Then in one fell swoop, he grabs me beneath my shoulders to lift me up, placing me directly on his lap facing him.

Tilting his head back, I drag my nails up his neck, my mouth right behind as I kiss and nip a trail from his neck to his temples. He's not a words guy, so instead I show him with my actions exactly how much I'm into him.

I'm slick against his hard dick and I can't help but begin to rub myself along it. Grabbing my hips, he presses me down harder into him. "That's right, get yourself off on me, sunshine. Make yourself come on my dick."

At this moment, all I want is for him to tilt his hips up a little more and enter me. To put me out of my aching agony for him. We're so dangerously close to doing it that if either of us angled ourselves differently, he could slip right in. It goes against his one rule he's adamant about though, so I don't mention it as much as I want to.

He pulls down the top of my dress, bringing one of my nipples into his mouth, pinching the other between two fingers. I cry out, reaching that peak of elation with his name on my lips as I rub my clit against the length of his dick.

Sensing that he's close, I wrap my fingers around his swollen cock. Jerking him off until I feel the hot spurts of come running between my hand and body. He kisses my neck with a groan, his breath hot against my flushed skin. It's a sound I want to commit to memory for the rest of my life.

If I could bottle up this moment with him, I would. The feel of his lips on my skin, eager to taste every bit of me. His muscular legs beneath mine and the possessive grip he has on my hips, holding me into place. But especially the way we relax into each other after it's all said and done, as if we're fusing into one. And how it hits me that there's no place I'd rather be than here—a happy puddle in his arms.

"I think you killed me," he huffs, breath brushing across my neck.

I sit up and pretend to check his pulse on either side of his neck. "Still alive. All the blood probably went to your dick for a minute. It'd take a *lot* of blood with the size of that thing."

"So we've moved on from small dick jokes to big dick ones, I see."

"Do you expect any less from me?"

"I never know what to expect from you. It's one of the things I like best about you."

As I lay curled up in his lap with his arms slung across me, my heart thumps rapidly in my chest. Not because of the superb orgasm I had. No. It's all because every time he breaks down another wall of himself, letting me inside, it is one step further I fall for him.

"I can't believe I sucked my boss's dick," I tease.

"Do you...regret it at all?"

Sitting up, I grab his face and look right into his eyes. Vulnerability is there, tinged with a hint of apprehension. "Of course not. I had two of the best orgasms of my life within the last twenty-four hours."

He snorts, shaking his head like I'm full of it.

"What?" I ask.

"I know you've had it better than me. You're so far out of my league, Delaney."

His self-deprecation throws me off, because he is easily the most attractive man I've ever seen. Not only on the outside, but every single bit and piece he has let me see on the inside too. Everything about him blows me away.

Whoever planted that seed of doubt in his brain is on my shit list—and I highly suspect it's his ex who did a number on him.

My fingers play with the buttons on his shirt. "Why would you think that?"

"Because you're drop dead gorgeous. Not only that,

you're single handedly the happiest, brightest, person I've ever met. Someone who captivates other people's attention without even trying. And I'm...you know."

"What's wrong with being you?" I question further, hoping he'll continue to open up.

"I don't know...grumpy. Boring."

"That couldn't be further from the truth."

He gives me a disbelieving look, and I laugh. "Okay, maybe a *tiny* bit grumpy sometimes. But I like it."

I straddle his lap again, forcing him to make eye contact. "You're the greatest man I've ever met. You're dependable, you're consistent. Hardworking. The best father. Look at you, you're sexy as fuck. You let people be exactly who they are, with zero judgment or comments. You have all the pieces in you that I've wished for my entire life."

He doesn't reply, just stares at me, searching my face like I'm a Sunday morning crossword puzzle. Then he pulls me down, hugging me tight into his body. With our chests pressed together, I can feel his heart beating with ferocity.

We lie there, tangled together, until the night sky deepens into darkness. I'm beginning to drift to sleep when he rises, carrying me in his strong arms. The room dims as he switches off the light, and he gently lays me on his plush bed. He settles beside me, tucking the covers around my shoulders before pulling me close. My back against his chest, his chin resting atop my head, and his arm slung across my body.

I've never felt more at peace, more complete, than I do right now, lying in his bed and wrapped in his arms.

And when he leans over and whispers, "I'm not sure what I did right to have you in my life. All I know is I'm happy you're in it," I realize I've completely fallen for Cole Campbell.

23

COLE

Delaney sneaks out of my bed before the sun is up the next morning. She kisses my cheek and whispers something about leaving before Ava is awake.

After everything she said to me last night, easing those invasive doubts, I couldn't stand to have her separated from me.

Having her there next to me sleeping all night in my bed felt too natural, too right. Now the idea of her sleeping in her own room seems foreign, after experiencing what it felt like to hold her in my arms all night. She stole the covers, and slept as restless as a kid on caffeine, but despite it all I slept better than I have in months.

That pit of loneliness being filled every time she laid her head on my chest, or reached out for me from across the bed. Like she needed me. Like I've always been meant to sleep next to her.

I didn't flat out tell her, but it was the first time I've been intimate with a woman since Isabel. I'm not one for casual hookups, and am too busy for a meaningless relationship as a single, business owning father. Without even knowing, Delaney healed some fractured part of me that had been taking up residence, festering, for the last several years.

Now I'm back at work, trying to keep my mind off all the different ways I'd want to fuck her if she was mine. It's been a hellish day of babysitting a bunch of adults. Everyone is grumpy from the near triple digit temperature, counting the hours to go home.

One of the contractors, Luke, walks into the office trailer I'm holed up in. "Someone's here for you."

He looks too excited, and I want to ask what got into him. No one here is happy today.

It's at that moment I look through the window of the trailer, to see at least half my crew gathered round a pretty blonde. Not just any pretty blonde—Delaney. With my daughter holding her hand.

All of the guys are eating out of the palm of her hand. She's passing out bottles of sports drinks and snacks, a playful smile on her face that she always has when she cracks a joke. The crowd of men are hanging on her every word, and the roar of laughter from outside pisses me off.

I have men, on the roofs of houses, looking her way.

The sight of her smooth tan legs in those denim shorts is going to make someone fall off and kill them, I swear.

Opening my office door, I call out, "Girls, get on in here." It comes out more serious than I intend it to.

Delaney's eyes widen, as she whispers to the crew. "I think I'm in trouble. See you boys later."

Ava and Delaney snicker their whole walk up, surely making a joke about me. I count at least ten sets of eyes glued to Delaney's backside. Internally, I vow to personally tear each one of their eyes out if they keep looking at her like she's their next meal.

"Get back to work," I shout at them, as they jump, breaking out of their spell.

I know how they feel. But the whistle I hear as Delaney enters the office irks me, prompting a silent vow to track down whoever is responsible.

"I think you have a few fans," I grumble.

She looks back out at the crew and waves coyly at the last few bystanders. "You mean my new best friends? Harmless. One of them even offered to change my oil for me. Isn't that nice?"

"I can change your oil."

Grabbing my bicep, she gives it a squeeze with a wink. "Okay, thanks."

I can't tell if she's completely oblivious to the chaos she's stirred or deliberately toying with me. Regardless, I find myself in a primitive state, a boneheaded caveman wanting to sling her over my shoulder, shouting, "Mine!" to every man who dares to believe they stand a chance with her.

"What are you both doing here?" I ask, not used to getting visitors at work.

Ava holds my brown leather wallet out in her small hand. "You forgot this at home, Daddy."

I pat my back pocket where I normally keep it, remembering I did leave it on the kitchen counter this morning. My head was in such a fog from the previous night that I didn't even realize until now.

"Thanks, I needed that. Plus I'm happy I get to see you, baby girl," I say, picking her up and hugging her.

"And you too, sunshine," I say to Delaney, as her wide smile mirrors my own.

We need to keep things discreet between us in front of Ava. She can't even suspect a hint of affection between Delaney and I. But there's no harm in saying I'm happy to see someone, right?

"I told you it would be boring here," Ava remarks to Delaney.

We all laugh at my daughter's bluntness, as Delaney glances around, not ashamed to be snooping at my desk. "You were totally right, banana. Maybe we can get your dad a picture of you for his desk. That would brighten the whole place right up since he loves you and would get to look at your cute face all day."

Ava shouts her agreement while bouncing up and down, like it's the best idea on earth. I'm pretty sure she thinks every thought out of Delaney's head is top tier.

Walking up to me, she tugs on my hand. "Dad, maybe you can get a picture of Laney for your desk too. You love her, right? That's what you told me the other day."

I choke on my daughter's revelation, and start coughing. Damn, five year olds are brutal. You can't tell them anything without getting busted out later. Three days ago, Ava told me she loves Delaney and I agreed she was awesome. The word *love* never fell out of my mouth. The possibility may be spewed frequently in my brain, but I've never said those words out loud. Certainly not to my five year old daughter.

"You okay there?" Delaney looks at me, knowingly. "It's okay, don't be embarrassed. I'm very lovable. Best personality was my yearbook superlative."

"I agreed that you were nice. It wasn't...I'm not..." My brain is scrambling to find the right words. I don't want to fully outright deny it, because hell, I *am* falling for her. But that's not something I plan to confess to the woman that's leaving in six weeks.

"Don't worry, I won't get a big head. Promise." She's beaming, clearly getting a kick out of this. Hiking her thumb over her shoulder, she gestures to the construction going on outside the office. "I'm sure all my new best friends think I'm *nice* too. Huh?"

I groan and roll my eyes, muttering, "I'm going to fire them all."

My daughter has a shit-eating grin pasted on her face as she listens to mine and Delaney's back and forth. I'm scared to even know what thoughts are running rampant in that imaginative brain of hers.

The girls leave the bag full of snacks and drinks on my desk as they head out the door, on the way to gymnastics class. I walk them back out to the car, unsure if my crew will swarm her again. This time I'm glaring at any one who dares look in the general vicinity of her. It works to a degree, but I know the bastards are still undressing her with their horndog eyes from a distance.

After buckling the three point harness of Ava's car seat, I kiss her sweaty forehead before closing the door. Then I gesture to Delaney to follow me round the back of the vehicle, away from nosey five year old eyes.

Leaning into her, my senses are overwhelmed. She smells as sunny as she looks, a happy, floral scent dancing around me as I bury my nose into her golden hair. "I better see that smart-ass mouth on my dick again tonight."

Then before she can say a word back with that fiery little mouth, I kiss her in front of everyone. It's quick, but heated; light, but greedy. It's my modern day caveman version of marking my territory.

Because Delaney is mine.

As much as she doesn't know it, and as much as I don't admit it to myself—deep down there's no doubt that she only belongs with me.

24

DELANEY

MADI:

I saw you like a video of one of those cringe flash mob proposals. Have anything you want to tell us? Any specific employers you may be in love with?

DELANEY:

It was cute, okay?! Stop stalking me!

ELLA:

I think it was you who founded and coined the term F.B.I—Friends Bureau of Investigation.

MADI:

Yeah, remember that time you found Noah's streaming platform, and pre-loaded some of his favorite songs into my car so he'd be impressed.

ELLA:

> And that other time, you tracked down a guy I was talking to's address so we could see if he was still living with his parents...

MADI:

> I don't think she's going to reply back. She's probably too busy watching more proposal videos.

DELANEY:

> More like I'm too busy hating you both!

DELANEY:

> Kidding—love you, crazies.

The summer days fly by in one giant, blissful blur.

Last week, Marissa contacted me to inform me of Kenneth's official termination. I maintained a composed facade, expressing gratitude for the update while silently celebrating with victorious fist pumps on my end of the line.

Simultaneously, JunoTec presented me with an official job offer for the same position I previously held. During extensive conversations with HR and the CEO of JunoTec, they all understood my abrupt reason for leaving. I tamped down the dread in my chest at the thought of leaving Ava with another nanny, as I verbally accepted the offer with a tentative start date in August.

I need to tell Cole. Soon. But every time I picture how the conversation will go, I imagine it will be similar to how a dumpster can catch on fire with a flick of a match. Once I say it out loud, shit gets real. And half of me wants to play house for a little while longer with them. When I tell him, I know he'll pull away even more. And the thought of that makes my stomach drop like an amusement park roller coaster.

The three of us effortlessly settle into a comfortable routine over the weeks. During Cole's long work hours, stretching from sunup to sundown, Ava and I go on a spree of all the fun activities I have planned. From library events and zoo outings to messy art projects, splash pads, and playdates with my niece, our days are filled with laughter. Evenings, when he returns, we eat dinner on the covered patio as we swap random stories from our day.

Ava cherishes every moment with her father when he's home. But it does rattle him that she prefers me to read her a story and tuck her in most nights now. I pretend to not see him peeking around the door frame, that flicker of affection dancing in his eyes as he watches us.

Tonight as I lay Ava down, tucking her favorite rainbow blanket around her shoulders, she asks, "Laney, do you like my dad?"

I tuck a wayward strand of hair behind her ear. "He's a cool guy, of course I like him."

Her eyes turn hopeful, as she snuggles her stuffed bunny. "Good. Then can you marry him? So you can be my mom."

I freeze, attempting to not show her how thrown for a loop I am. Maybe I should have seen this coming, and mentally prepared a better answer. Unfortunately, foresight has never been my strong point. I'm more of a fly by the seat of your pants kind of gal.

"Hm, well that's tricky because your dad and I are friends, and friends don't usually get married. But you know what? You're my best friend. And always will be."

The disappointment in her big brown eyes slices my heart in half, like an ax splitting wood.

Her eyes well with tears, trying not to let them fall. "Okay, Laney."

I lean down and wrap my arms around her little body. "Banana. I promise I will always, always be a part of your life. Even though I'm not your mom, I still love you like you're my family. And one thing about me is that once I start loving someone, I don't stop. So I hope you're prepared for that. Because you're stuck with me for a *long*, long time."

She smiles up at me, in a way no one has ever looked at me before—all signs of sadness immediately wiped away. That look alone makes me want to be a better person. And I'm left wondering how a parent can walk away from their child who is born ready to love them with every innocent bone in their body.

"I love you, Laney."

"I love you too," I tell her, kissing the top of her hair, and then booping her nose for good measure.

I slink out of her room, closing the door gently behind me and leaning against it, before I finally can breathe again.

That exhale only lets a fresh wave of rage roll in, like a storm cloud slowly gathering strength on the horizon. It starts as a tiny seed of heartache for Ava longing for a mother. Now that pressure is building up, like an atmospheric change before a storm, as anger pours out of me like a deluge of rain.

I march off to Cole's room, discovering him just out of the shower, clad in only a white towel wrapped around his waist. He halts, taken aback by my abrupt entrance, then strides over, his eyes radiating warmth at my unexpected visit. My exasperation momentarily fades, overshadowed by the sight of the half-naked man before me. I'm a weak, easily distracted woman—what can I say?

Grabbing me by the waist, he pulls me into him, as I remember my purpose for storming in. "What's the deal with Ava's mom?"

His large hands freeze on my hips. "It's a long story."

While he typically is a man of few words, right now I need him to fill me in on that one missing piece of their life. I've been patient for over two months, minding my own business for the very first time in my life. My sister wouldn't even believe me if I told her I waited this long to ask about someone's personal business.

When a little girl, who is one of my very best friends, asks me to marry her dad, so I can be her mom...it seems like a justified reason to ask for a smidge of the backstory. At least for context so I can know the best way to answer her if it comes up again.

With a sigh, he scrubs a hand down his stubbled face. "The condensed version is, I walked in on her riding my best friend's dick. Once that went down, she couldn't wait to get out of here, away from me, fast enough. Said I was too boring for someone with needs like hers. That the motherly life was holding her back from her dreams. She signed her parental rights away on her way out of town. Usually comes around once a year, if that."

That stormy anger? It's a fucking tsunami now, swirling in my chest, threatening to destroy anything in its path, as the emotions hit me like a tidal wave.

It didn't even happen to me, it's not my trauma—god knows I have plenty of that all on my own. Abandonment issues in particular, which is maybe why this feels even worse. Because I know how soul-crushing it can be.

I feel their pain, so thoroughly it feels like I'm gut punched. These two incredible humans, rocked by the actions of a heartless woman who should have loved them more than the moon and stars combined.

I'm the least violent person on this planet—avoiding even the squashing of bugs because I feel too guilty thinking of the little bug family and friends they'd leave behind.

But for Ava and Cole, I'll light this whole world on fire without an ounce of remorse. I want to find this woman and shake some sense into her. Ask her what horrible things happened to her that made her not appreciate the two most remarkable people on this planet.

I'm frozen, speechless, heartbroken. The tears falling down my face being the only indicator that I heard him. I swipe them away, upset at this colossal bitch I've never met. Embarrassed that *I'm* the one crying when it didn't even happen to me.

He pulls my head to his chest with one hand, and caresses my hair to soothe me. "Shit. Don't cry, sunshine. We're okay, I swear. But please don't cry, it's killing me."

I wipe my nose on my sleeve. "I'm sorry. I hate her so much. How could she do that to you...to Ava? How's that even humanly possible? And with your best friend? God, I hate him too."

"He was always kind of a douche. I should've seen it coming."

"I want to shove them off a cliff."

His chest rumbles with a deep laugh. "They're not

worth it, trust me. Plus they wouldn't allow your elaborate skin routine in prison."

"I hate it when you're right," I mumble, impressed that he's noticed my extensive skincare lineup in the bathroom. "When's the last time she saw Ava?"

"Ava was just about to turn four...so I guess over a year ago now. Haven't heard from her since. It's hard because I don't want to keep Ava from her mom, but I wish her mom would choose a direction, involved or completely uninvolved, and stick with it."

"I can understand that. My parents chose to be the latter. It...hurts less in a way."

"What the fuck is wrong with people? I'm sorry that happened to you too."

"It's fine. It's not, but it is. You get it." I look up at him. His handsome face, etched with concern, wondering how he'll react to the next thing I'm about to tell him. "When I tucked Ava in, she told me she wanted us to get married so I can be her mom."

He stops breathing. I know, because my arms are wrapped around his waist, and I can tell the moment the oxygen leaves his lungs. "Fuck."

"Yep," is all I manage to get out.

"How did you respond?"

"I told her that you and I are friends, and friends don't usually get married. But she's still like family to me. That I'll always be there for her." Shrugging in his embrace, I add on, "I hope that was okay to say. I was caught off guard and scrambling."

Half-naked with a towel slung across his lower half, he walks us over to the bed, sits down on the edge, and pulls me into his lap. "That was good. Perfect, actually."

I curl up in his arms, drained from the emotions of the night. He remains utterly still, his muscles tense beneath me, like being held by a marble statue. His brows furrow, his head surely swimming with a thousand thoughts and feelings.

Reaching out, my fingers brush over his cheekbones that are tinged pink from his long day outside. "Tell me what's going on in that head of yours."

"I'm wondering how she'll do once you find another job and have to leave."

I'll stay. Please ask me to stay.

The stupid, naive, half of me wants him to tell me to not leave. I've dreamt of the possibility an embarrassing amount of times. How it would feel to be here with them every day, if he asked me to stay. The opportunity to watch Ava grow like a weed, graduate kindergarten, lose her first tooth. Getting to glimpse at Cole's disheveled hair and stubbled jaw in awe every morning, as he rolls out of bed with a groan fit for a man twice his age.

The picture of us together is as clear as the sky on a sunny day. But there's no way I can invite myself to live here permanently.

"Speaking of jobs...I was offered my position back at JunoTec. They said I can start in August."

His body flinches, but his voice doesn't let onto any

hint of surprise or disappointment. "That's good news, right? What you've been wanting?"

What I want is to live in a fantasy world where I can simultaneously be here with them and also go back to my accounting job. But it's not our agreement. I'm not sure if it's what he even wants.

"Yeah. And you know, Ava and I can still see each other any time she wants," I promise. "You can't get rid of me that easily. I'm like herpes. Impossible to get rid of, always making a rude appearance."

"Only you could make a joke about herpes and make it cute."

"You think I'm cute, huh?"

Grabbing me by the waist, he tosses me onto his made bed. "I think you're a lot of things. Cute being one of them."

He's hovering over me, bracing himself on his muscled arms that cage me in. His dick is hard through his towel, the heavy weight of it resting on my abdomen.

My hands run through his dark hair. "And the other things?"

"Resilient. Hilarious. Gorgeous. Loyal." With every word, he kisses a new spot along my body. "You're everything to me."

Cradling his head in my hands, I tip his face to mine, kissing him with the same intensity that matches my spiraling feelings toward him.

Hooking a finger into the waistband of my black

shorts, he slips them off and tosses them onto the floor. "Now sit on my face while you imagine what it'd be like if I could fuck you properly."

He doesn't have to tell me twice. I hop on, eager for every moment of affection I can get from him, before he decides I'm too much and he's had enough of me. Before this whole fling topples over like a fragile house of cards.

While I sleep on Cole's chest that night, feeling the gentle rise and fall of his breath, I dream about an impossible world where I get to stay with them.

About finding a home in each other, fear of abandonment in our rear view mirror, settling into our forever. Together.

25

COLE

DELANEY:

Question time. What's your favorite
food?

COLE:

Steak. Or any kind of meat.

DELANEY:

Mmmm, yes. I love a good, thick piece
of meat in my mouth.

COLE:

Delaney.

DELANEY:

Cole.

COLE:

What's something that makes you
absurdly happy?

DELANEY:

The orgasms you give me.

DELANEY:

And rain. Standing in the middle of the pouring rain makes me feel so damn happy and alive.

COLE:

I want to stand in the rain with you.

DELANEY:

It's a date.

Delaney has been sleeping beside me for three weeks now. At first I thought it was only me that couldn't stand the thought of being apart from her at night. But to my surprise it's her that keeps coming back, without me even having to ask. When I come out of the shower, she's sitting there, laid out on my bed and completely naked—ready for me.

At times, it feels impossible not to have sex with her. It seems I've decided to personally torture myself all for the sake of not getting attached. Which I 100 percent already am.

We do plenty of everything else, things I've never experienced or had knowledge of before. Until this week, I had no idea what a standing sixty-nine and lie back blow job was. Not going all the way is the last thread of hope I have at keeping myself distanced from her. Because if I'm this far gone now, how will it be once I know what it feels like to be inside of her?

Every morning I roll out of bed, I can't help but stare at her, fast asleep with a peace that only angels possess, golden hair fanned out on her pillow. Her small hand splayed out where my own sleeping body once was.

I can't help but know that I'm the luckiest man alive.

As well as how fucked I am at the sheer level of terror I feel, knowing I'll be losing her before I know it.

She has plans with her friends today, so I take Ava on a date to the children's museum she's been begging to go to. It's been featured on some YouTube channel she watches that I don't understand the popularity of.

As we merge onto the deserted country road en route to the kids museum, I spot a modified M3 car idling on the shoulder. It has a view of the gravel road leading to my house, but I dismiss it, assuming the occupants are lost or waiting for someone. The only reason it catches my attention is the rarity of random cars in this area. I reside in the boondocks, with only a few houses, each separated by acres.

The blacked out M3 raises a momentary red flag in my mind, but it's soon forgotten when Ava hollers at me from the backseat to turn on her favorite soundtrack.

Three hours, a hyped up five year old, and one exhausted father later, we leave the children's museum. Ava and I stop to pick up dinner before dropping her off at my mom's house for another sleepover. My daughter has informed me that Grandma is more fun since she buys her toys off Amazon and lets her eat as many cookies as she wants—hence why she constantly begs for more overnights with my mom.

My phone chimes, and the name that pops up on my pickup's display screen makes my stomach fall faster than if I dived head first off a cliff.

Isabel.

At the next stoplight, I tap the screen to read her message.

ISABEL:

In town next week. Can't wait to see my baby girl.

Keeping a cool demeanor feels near impossible with how severely my blood is simmering. Isabel puts on a persona of doting, loving mother whenever she decides to show up for her annual visit. However, her silence the other three hundred and sixty four days of the year say otherwise.

Every year older Ava gets, I wonder how she'll react to her mother's hypocrisy. I suspect it will be sooner than Isabel realizes. Hell, Ava sees the clerk at the grocery store more than her own mother. Isabel is practically a stranger to her.

I swipe the screen, thankful my daughter can't read yet. Typically I don't tell her that her mom will be visiting until the day of. Isabel isn't known for her dependability.

We hop out of my truck and make our way to my mother's home. It's only down the road from my own house. A smaller log cabin style home, with a big red barn sitting on acres of property. An assortment of several farm animals run up to the green gate off to the right of the main house, ready to be pet and showered with love. My mom stays busy by spoiling every type of animal she can get her hands on.

Later, as we sit around the table eating our burgers, the thought of having to deal with my ex again hangs over my head like a raincloud. I know it's about to rain when we see her. But I don't know if it will be a sprinkle or a downpour.

Ava has been talking my mom's ear off, finishing off a story about diving for pool toys with Delaney.

My mom looks over at me. "Speaking of nannies, have you started to look for another one yet?"

I bristle, hating to acknowledge the truth. "It's on my to-do list."

"You better get started, remember how long it took you to find one? Though I doubt any of them will be up to Delaney's par."

I push my plate away, suddenly full. "You don't have to tell me that. I know."

My mom looks at me. A pitiful look that I wish I could hide from. "Maybe if you speak to her..."

"No," I say, cutting her off.

Ava has been too busy peeling bits of cheese off her patty to hear most of our conversation up until this point. "I don't want another nanny. I want Delaney to stay."

"I know, baby. We all want her to stay, but this was always a temporary arrangement."

"I don't know what temporary means," she says, with an eye roll. Yep, definitely my daughter.

"It means, only for a little while. She has another job she has to go back to." I try to explain it with no sugar coated bullshit that will only get her hopes up.

Ava takes a big bite of burger, staring straight at me, ready for her interrogation. "Is she still going to live with us?"

"I...don't know. But I don't think so." It's a damn good question. One that I hope Delaney will consider. At the start of our arrangement, she told me she'd only live at the house for three months. I've never wanted anyone to go against their word so badly in my life.

Chewing, she mulls over what I've just said. "Well, maybe if we buy her something good off Amazon and let her eat a lot of cookies she'll want to stay."

"We'll see, kid," I tell her, as I stand to clear our plates, kissing her on the cheek as I pass by. She looks disappointed, yet determined to find a way to make Delaney stay.

I want to tell her I understand better than anyone. That before Delaney arrived it had felt like a cold, miserable winter for months on end. Then one day, the sun of summer hit. So suddenly you don't see it coming.

But the warmth makes you feel human again, it thaws you. It's Delaney.

I don't want it to be winter again. I want summer to stay. Forever.

AVA INFORMS me it's time to get the hell out so she can have fun. Even my own daughter thinks I'm an old stick in the mud. As I'm getting into my truck, my phone rings, catching me off guard since no one usually calls me on my personal phone.

I sigh, as I dig it out of my pocket. Hoping and praying that it's not Isabel since she sent me that text an hour ago.

My shoulders relax when I see Delaney's name flashing on my screen, and I hate myself for the way my mouth unintentionally tips up into a smile. That is until I answer the call and hear a male yelling.

The sound is garbled because of the volume he's shouting. The hair on the back of my neck stands up as I buckle in and slam the gear into drive, racing to I have no idea where. All I know is that she needs me.

Her pleading voice comes through the line. She isn't speaking directly to me though, she's begging the other person there to calm down. *Please, stop. Don't yell. Please, get out of my house.*

House. She's at home.

I turn right onto the main road that's a straight shot

from my mother's house to mine. Instantly grateful that I'm only two miles away. Blood rushes to my ears, my head spinning faster than the cheap carnival rides I hate. Those two minutes it takes me to get home are the longest minutes of my life. Racing thirty miles per hour over the speed limit, I swear I can't see anything, I can't hear anything...except the voice of the man I soon plan to pummel.

The things he's saying are pure venom. Derogatory names and a list of behaviors and doings he expects from her. I recognize right away that it's her ex-boyfriend, Josh. The one from the bar that I scared off once before.

When I fly into my driveway, I throw open my door to sprint toward the shouting. I feel sick, body tingling, when I see the M3 from this morning haphazardly parked behind Delaney's vehicle. *How did I let this happen?* If only I would have realized that car belonged to him, maybe I could have prevented all of this.

But now it's time he learned his lesson. He doesn't get to talk to her like that anymore. He never should have in the first place.

But Delaney has me now. And I protect the things I love.

26

DELANEY

"Please calm down, Josh. Please stop," I beg for the hundredth time.

Josh is raging. It's not the first time he's done this. But it's the first time he's gone this far by stalking me. Internally, I feel as if I've been flash frozen, that icy panic causing my ears to ring and heart pound. But if he sees me crack it will only bring on a new onslaught. A new round of yelling point blank in my face while throwing random shit around.

I'm suspended in this god awful nightmare, too terrified to even move. That familiar terror creeps up my spine as Josh paces the living room floor, back and forth, ruminating with his hands tugging on the ends of his once perfectly gelled hair.

All I know at this moment is that I need help.

I need Cole.

My phone is still in the back pocket of my jeans.

Which means I just need to make a secret grab for it, and call for help.

As Josh turns his back and starts up into a new slew of expletives, I quickly unlock my phone and press the shortcut I created last month for Cole's number. I have no idea if he picks up, as I hide the phone behind my back, away from my ex's eyes.

Josh is unstable, enraged, entitled.

When I came home from Madi's house, I didn't even see his car following me. He just appeared out of nowhere and blocked me into the driveway. As I ran to the house, he followed faster. Barging his way through the door, demanding I pack my shit up and come back home.

When I refused, it set him off. The shouting began, and as it escalated, no sign of him stopping, I mentally prepared myself for the first blow.

He's never hit me before, but a raised fist while he screams in my face sure feels like it's in the realm of possibilities.

His words are projectiles, vicious and unrelenting—I'm a slut. I'm crazy. I'm a dumb bitch that never listens. That it's my fault I've brought him to this level of anger.

Every passing minute, I'm shrinking, withering away. Like a blossom wilting in a furious storm, my petals falling one by one in the gusts of his insults.

I'm having an out of body experience, like I'm watching this horror from a third person point of view. The tall, lanky man who one minute is crying into his hands claiming I've betrayed him; the next he's back to yelling, getting in my face and pounding the drywall beside my head.

All I can do is keep my back against the wall, not knowing if it's better to shrink myself or stand up taller. Will he stick to words or turn to fists? Will he kill me this time?

Every aspect of this mirrors the night that fueled my resolve to leave.

I grapple with the inescapable decision before me—either leave with Josh or deal with the aftermath of refusing once more. But suddenly, the front door swings open with such force that it slams against the entry wall. A picture frame shatters on the floor in response to the impact, accompanied by the resounding thud of boots sprinting towards me.

A sense of peace rushes through me like a river at the sight of Cole. Those green-gold eyes swiftly scan the room taking in the chaotic scene—Josh in my face, a scattered mess of broken glass from the lamp thrown in my direction, dining chairs upturned.

When Cole's eyes lock onto mine, a storm of panic brews within him as he takes in my tear-stained face. In that moment, I sense the shift—the exact second he sees red, transforming his energy into a torrential downpour of vengeance aimed at my ex.

Time turns to slow motion as I watch it all unfold. Cole's jaw grinding, outrage rushing out of his every pore as his hands curl into tight fists. No hesitation, all action like he's a Navy SEAL and NFL linebacker rolled into one.

Josh, lost in his fit of rage, remains oblivious, as Cole strides up behind him. My boss locks eyes with me before forcefully pulling Josh away. The momentum propels my ex across the room, his stunned body flying several feet, reminiscent of Ava tossing her stuffed animal into the air and watching it descend.

"What the hell," Josh snaps, caught off guard as he stumbles, losing his footing. Josh attempts to swing at Cole, but it doesn't land.

"I told you to stay the fuck away from her." Cole's arm snaps back, landing a blow straight to Josh's face.

I'm floating above my own body as I watch it all unfold. How the impact of the punch knocks Josh to the ground—his limbs flailing, a string of cuss words enunciated by a mouthful of blood. How Cole crouches beside him, hitting him again and again. "If you so much as even look at her again, I'll bury you. Do you understand me?"

The man who'd never hurt a soul, fighting for me. Protecting me.

I come back to, and grab Cole's shoulders, tugging him to standing. "Stop! He's not worth it."

Cole's eyes turn to mine, and the emotion in them makes me rear back. He's livid and distressed. Panting, as his eyes scan my body, trying to see if Josh laid a finger on me.

He tugs me to his chest, as the faint sound of sirens

grow closer outside. "He may not be worth it, but you are. I don't know what I'd have done if anything happened to you."

Looking over the crook of his arm, I see Josh groaning on the ground, hands cradling his bruised face as blood drips between his fingers.

I bury my body a few inches deeper into the warmth of Cole's chest. "Are you supposed to run from the cops before they get here? I don't want you to get in trouble."

He huffs out a laugh, a deep rumble in his chest that I feel against my cheek. "I'm the one who called them on my way here. I'll talk to them, own up to everything I did. I'm not the one at fault—made sure to let that asshole swing first so I'd be in the clear."

Reality is settling in, the events of the last twenty minutes crashing into me like an unexpected car wreck. My body is shaking beneath his, and I wonder if this time was the last straw. If this time I'll be broken beyond repair. Maybe this particular episode is the one that will penetrate my usually strong layers of protection.

He runs his hand along the column of my spine, chin resting atop my head. "I've got you, sunshine. I always got you."

The next hours become a blur as I try to hold back my tears long enough to speak with the police as they take their report—telling them how Josh followed me home, barged his way in, screamed and threatened me.

They speak with Cole too, and minutes later he's

released back to me. Tucking me securely under his arm again, as I'm frozen inside and out. Together, we see Josh handcuffed and put into the back of a cop car—a sight that brings both relief and nightmares wrapped into one.

The police mention something about an emergency protective order against my ex. I stare at them, nodding and agreeing, the words never fully comprehending in the current shock state of my brain. Some part of me can hear Cole ask a few more questions, and I'm thankful he's here. Thankful he's paying attention while I stand here disconnected, an empty shell of myself.

Once the police leave, Cole's hand laces into mine as he leads me to his bed. I sit on the edge, a complete zombie, as he takes off each of my shoes with the utmost caution, as if I might break at any moment. He pulls down my light wash jeans, folding and placing them on the nightstand. I don't say it out loud, but somewhere deep in my consciousness I feel the utmost relief that he knows how much I hate wearing jeans while I'm home and relaxing. Only psychopaths wear jeans to relax.

My body falls limp onto the white pillows, suddenly feeling like I'm weighted down, too heavy to stay upright for even a minute longer. He gently brings the covers up to my shoulders, tucking me in with care before slipping out of his own jeans and joining me in bed. As he settles behind me, he pulls me close, enfolding me in his strong arms, where I feel sheltered and safe from the outside world. From Josh. From my own darkness that has slowly been creeping over for the last two hours.

It's there, in the safety of his arms, and with his hand caressing my hair, that I finally break down. There's no gentle tears falling down my face. I'm sobbing, chest heaving, blotchy-faced. I can't seem to stop crying, no matter how hard I try. It's like a dam has burst inside of me, and all of my emotions and issues from the last thirty years are pouring out.

He wraps his arms around me as he pulls me closer, and I bury my face in his chest, soaking his shirt as I let it out. I let it all fucking out.

The harder I cry the closer he holds me, as if he thinks maybe he can hold together all of my broken pieces so I don't shatter completely. "You're safe. I'm here. I've got you," he whispers, repeatedly.

My head is throbbing, as the tears begin to slow after what feels like a lifetime. Hollowness replaces anguish as exhaustion settles in. I drift off to sleep terrified of what dreams or nightmares may find me there.

WHEN I WAKE, I'm still in his arms, my head foregoing the expensive pillows on the bed and resting in the crook of his arm instead. My head feels like someone is taking a hammer to it, my mouth is dry, stomach grumbling.

As I scoot the covers down, his eyes snap open, going straight to mine. "You're awake," he says, voice rough from sleep.

"I'm awake," I repeat.

"How are you feeling?"

"I feel...I'm not sure. Bad? Weird?" I sit up, rubbing my eyes, most likely smearing the remnants of my mascara that are left after crying.

Looking over at the small analog clock on the nightstand, I see it's four in the morning. We slept for almost ten hours.

I roll out of bed, limbs stiff from the long hours of lying down. Making my way to his bathroom, I turn on the shower, peeling the rest of my clothes off and stepping in before the water even has a chance to warm. The cold temperature is shocking at first yet brings me relief in a glacial tormenting way.

After the mess with Josh yesterday, I still feel empty. The cold water reminds me I'm still alive, as goose bumps freckle my skin. There are too many *what ifs* swirling in my head, and my mind isn't even fully conscious yet.

What if Ava had been home? What if Cole hadn't shown up? What if it's like this forever, always looking over my shoulder wondering if Josh is following me? What if I feel this heaviness every single day for the rest of my life?

When Cole steps into the bathroom, he freezes when he sees me. My face is buried in my hands, shower water spraying down on me, as another wave of trauma hits.

There's no way he'll ever like me now that he's seen my broken half. What else lies beneath the surface of my happy disposition.

It's a side no one has seen. One that I try to shove down and ignore as much as possible. Like I'm cramming that darkness into a jar and spinning the lid on before it can haunt me. But right now it's too much to shove down. It's bursting out of me before I have a chance to hide it.

The shower door opens and closes, and then I feel Cole's bare chest against my forehead. His arms snake around my shoulders, hands gripping me closer as if I'll slip right out from under him.

"I'm sorry, I don't know what's wrong with me," I say, my cheek to his tanned skin, the spray of water soaking us both.

"Don't apologize. Yesterday was a lot." His voice is gentle, soothing. So opposite from the deep grumbles I'm accustomed to.

"I shouldn't still be upset. I want to be back to normal...happy."

His fingertips gently lift my chin, guiding my gaze to meet his. "Even the sun doesn't shine all damn day. No one expects you to either." His calloused thumb sweeps across my cheek, wiping away the falling tears. "It gets dark sometimes. It's okay to not be okay. Before you know it, the sun will rise again. You won't feel bad forever, I promise."

I nod once so he knows I heard him, absorbing his words and willing them to penetrate me to my core. *It's okay to not be okay.*

He's right. But at the moment, in the thick of it, this feels eerily similar to drowning. Dark emotions bury me every time Josh's words run through my head without my permission. Only a pinhole of light shines through that offers any hope. Cole is my pinhole. He's the only thing grounding me, like the unyielding anchor of a ship amidst a storm.

Tears continue to fall without my permission. I bury my face deeper into the crook of his arm to mask the fact that my eyes have turned into a perpetual leaky faucet. The cold water sprays down on us as Cole cradles my head in his hands, tilting it up to meet his eyeline. My face is puffy. Eyes red and swollen as the tears continue to brim over and spill out. The look on his face as he watches me is a mixture of pain and scorched earth. He doesn't have to say it—I know he wants to kill Josh. And honestly, I wish in some way that he was able to make Josh disappear for good. Though, the scars would remain forever.

His thumbs swipe the apples of my cheeks, brushing away the tears as they fall one by one. With gentle care, he tucks the wet strands of my hair behind my ears, causing my eyes to flutter shut. Those warm lips of his leave a trail of kisses, from my temples, to jaw, to the corners of my mouth. The act temporarily parts the clouds of my thoughts, and all I can do is sigh my thanks as I melt further into his touch.

Throughout the rest of the day, I choose to revel in the darkness. Reminding myself that happiness doesn't have to be a constant. Because as he said, *the sun will rise again.*

It's what I repeat to myself habitually for the rest of the day. It's okay to feel this way. And it's okay, to not be okay.

LATER THAT MORNING, my sister and niece arrive. I have a hunch that Cole played a role in calling them to support me through this ordeal. As I round the corner in my emotional support sweatpants and worn band shirt, Hazel rushes towards me, her embrace so tight that her arms tremble as they wrap around my knee.

"Nini, here." Her tiny hand holds up a half-weathered bouquet of bright yellow mustard flowers. The gesture brings a fresh wave of tears to my eyes. Despite Hazel having no understanding of the situation, she somehow has the intuition to shower me in affection.

Jess walks over and gives me the biggest mother bear hug, her hand swiping my back as if she could erase my pain. "I'm going to fucking kill him," she whispers into my ear.

Her statement causes a watery laugh to escape from my chest. "I'll help you hide the body," I murmur back.

"No need. Your boss already said he'd do that."

From the corner of the living room, Cole watches us. Ever since he came to my rescue yesterday, he hasn't left my side. He's striving to appear composed, yet the trembling of his hands betrays a blend of concern and rage. I sense that his worry for my well-being is the only thing keeping his emotions in check. It's a new experience for me, having someone care about me to the extent that they put my welfare above their own feelings.

It's dark in the days that follow, and I gradually come back to feeling a bit more like myself. I'm not entirely the same as before—but a new version of myself. I've learned to embrace this current state where happiness coexists with the acceptance of having endured trauma.

When I talk to my best friend Ella, she gives me the number for a therapist she's seen before and highly recommends. The thought of therapy seems foreign to me—I never thought I needed help. I've always prided myself on being resilient and made it a core part of my personality. If I've weathered my parent's abandonment, surely I can live through an abusive, stalking ex right? I have to.

Not bouncing back like I normally do though, that lingering heaviness in my chest pushes me to dial the therapy office's number come Monday morning.

As the appointment is confirmed, a wave of panic crashes over me. What if I'm so messed up that they bolt for the back door? Maybe my brand of chaos is beyond help. Ella tries to reassure me it's not like that, but her therapist has also never spoken to a Delaney Emerson before. I'm a thirty year old who has been dubbed *too much* since my very first breath as a fussy newborn.

Over the weekend, Cole suggests taking the next few days off to recuperate. I refuse, half out of not wanting pity, half knowing hanging out with Ava will be a good, healthy distraction.

When Monday arrives, he sets up shop with his laptop in the living room, discreetly keeping an eye on me as we come and go. It's sweet he's protective. It's not suffocating, but rather a silent assurance that he's there if needed. He seems to understand just how to handle me. Allowing me the freedom I crave, yet subtly offering his support—a balance that keeps me from feeling tied down.

Ava and I swim in the backyard, as we work through her swim lesson exercises. Every day she gets better, stronger, and more confident in the water.

She swims to the pool's edge and back to me, her sun-kissed legs kicking big splashes of water as she swims my way. When she reaches me, I lend a hand to keep her afloat, supporting her in the water as she breathes heavily from exertion. "Look at you go! Maybe I should call you fish instead of banana now."

"No, I like banana. But maybe when I'm in the pool I can be a banana fish."

To mimic a fish, she purses her lips and sucks in her cheeks. I do the same back at her, and it sparks a round of laughter.

When we come back inside hours later, Cole closes his laptop, and stretches his arms out wide, muscles flexing and looking far too delicious at one in the afternoon.

"You two hungry?" he asks.

Ava pats her tummy. "I'm *so* hungry I could eat a giraffe. Or a cow."

His smile tips up, lop-sided and dimple popping. "You mean you're so hungry you could eat a horse?"

Her face twists in disgust. "Yuck. I love horses, I'd never eat one of those."

"But you'd eat a giraffe?"

"Yep. They're not as cute. Kind of freaky with those long necks."

His lips twitch as he tries to contain his amusement. "I see. Well, go get ready so I can take my girls out."

My girls.

My heart stutters at the thought of it. Of being his. Of being a part of them, their little family. It's a dream that seems so close I can almost reach out and grasp it, take it as my own. But he has made it clear he wants to maintain a certain distance. I'm convinced it's why he won't have sex with me. As much as he cares for me, he can't settle down with the wild, shit-show nanny.

After dressing in a comfy white sundress and braiding my hair, I open my door to find Ava feeding a baby doll in the hallway.

With a baby strapped to her chest, looking far too old and eloquent, she looks up at me with big, wondrous eyes. "Wow, your hair looks *so* pretty."

"Well thank you, banana fish. I can do your hair like this too. Want me to braid it for you?"

"Yes!" She bounces up and down as if I've announced a Disneyland trip. If only things like French braids and bananas could bring so much joy to adults, the world would be a brighter place.

She sits more patiently than I expect her to while I part her hair straight down the middle, styling her long chestnut brown hair into two French braids.

As we walk into the Mexican food restaurant an hour later, I'm hand-in-hand with Ava as Cole trails closely behind us. The friendly redhead host leads us to our table, us girls slide into one side of the brown vinyl booth with Cole across from us.

When the bubbly worker places crayons and a coloring page down on the table, she points to Ava's styled hair. "I love the matching braids with your mom. You both look like princesses."

My eyes shift between Cole and Ava, gauging their reaction to the awkward *mom* bomb the lady dropped. Cole remains focused on the menu, and Ava carefully colors a dolphin purple. None of us correct her as she tells us someone will be by shortly to take our order.

Is it wrong that I feel proud to be seen with them, as if I'm a part of a real, normal functioning family unit?

When I think no one else notices the hostess's mistake, Ava puts her hand over her mouth and giggles as soon as we're alone. "Did you hear that? She thought you were my mom."

We join in the laughter, but both Cole's and my laughs sound strained. His jaw clenches, and shoulders tighten, creating a stifling air of tension. As he seems suddenly tense, I'm left pondering how he feels about the assumption. We continue to peruse the unusually large plastic menus, deliberately avoiding eye contact across the table.

The comment sparks a want so deeply within that I douse it with a healthy dose of realism. That Cole would never see me as someone serious to settle down with. And honestly, who would?

When I picture his wife, I see a dainty fairy goddess. Tall, whimsical, quiet, charming. Perhaps a nurse or preschool teacher. Someone that you could trust with your life, and that would without a doubt make a wonderful stepmom.

Not the unfiltered, mini hurricane that once knocked down a small child to catch the bouquet at her friend's wedding. The kid was in the way to be fair.

"We should go visit Betsy after this," Ava announces.

Cole's brow furrows in confusion. "Betsy? Who is that, a friend of yours?"

Ava and I exchange a glance, breaking into big, knowing smiles. "Yep, my best friend," she responds, without giving away that the friend in question is actually the dog at the shelter.

"She's so cute, with those big eyes. Isn't she?"

"Oh my gosh, yes. And her long tongue is my *favorite.*"

He looks back and forth between us, trying to put two and two together to figure out what the hell we're talking about. "Her...tongue?"

"She's missing some teeth, dad. So her tongue hangs out like this sometimes," Ava replies, matter-of-factly, sticking her tongue out the side of her mouth.

After a few beats of silence, before his eyes narrow at us. "You're talking about that one ugly as hell dog. Aren't you?"

She rolls her eyes, clearly five going on fifteen. "Duh. Who'd you think we were talking about? And she's cute, not ugly. So can we? See her after this?"

Cole's phone chimes, interrupting his answer. He takes it out of his pocket and when he glances at the message on the screen, I don't miss the way his jaw works back and forth, irritation seeping from him like smoke through a crack.

"Everything okay? Did someone at work use the wrong grit of sandpaper?" I'm curious who has the power to crack his otherwise composed exterior.

Shoving the phone back into his pocket, he replies, "I'm fine. And what the hell...let's go. Why not."

Ava cheers so loud that I jump and spill the rest of my water, soaking the basket of chips and Cole's pants across the table. The whole restaurant turns to look at the commotion going down in our loud corner booth.

We're our own little shit show, and I wouldn't have it any other way.

When we head out of the busy restaurant a short while later, an older woman with coiffed silver hair sitting in the booth behind ours, grabs onto Cole's forearm to stop him as we pass by. Her frail fingers dig into his burly arm and I can spot the glint of appreciation in her eyes. I want to say *Get it, grandma. Sexiest arms ever, am I right?* But I hold my tongue for the sake of not embarrassing them both.

"You got your hands full with those two, don't you?" The older woman chuckles, still hanging onto him.

Cole nods in agreement as they turn to look at Ava and me, who are standing a few feet in front of them.

"You've got that right," he says, rubbing at his neck like we're the sole cause of his neck tension.

"Well, you're one lucky man. Treat them well and do everything you can to keep them, alright?" The woman remarks before waving goodbye to all three of us.

He looks right at me as he replies, "I plan on it."

27

COLE

I'm still picking dog hairs out of my jacket the next morning. Seeing Ava and Delaney's faces while an old smelly dog jumped all over them was worth it however.

Isabel texted me again at dinner, telling me she wasn't sure when she'd be by this weekend anymore. Apparently her other plans trump seeing her own daughter. Same story, different year.

Seven years ago, Isabel and I met at a bar downtown. She wasn't shy about pursuing me—flirting at the bar, asking for my number, texting me constantly throughout the day in the coming weeks. As a quiet, shy guy I liked the attention. Enjoyed an attractive woman not being nervous about how much she wanted me.

Isabel was always on the hunt for the next party, a night at the club, a weekend on the coast with the girls. At the time I hadn't thought twice about it. Hell, I liked the space and the fact that I didn't have to keep her entertained. But then one day we found out she was pregnant. Not able to drink. Feet suddenly too swollen to go out dancing until the sun rose. She became bored —with me, and life in general.

While I prepared the nursery and bought baby essentials, she began to become more distant. Drifting further and further away from me and the impending fate of motherhood. I tried to whisk her away on vacations and sign us up for various activities to keep her mind occupied. But it was never enough. Isabel wanted the high life—booze, men at her heels, and the freedom to go whenever she wanted.

That guilt of giving my child a deadbeat mom is why I said yes to go see the damn dog. Which we're definitely not getting. Even if I can see the allure.

While Betsy was quite possibly the ugliest dog I have ever seen, I appreciate the way she just chilled, soaking up the love from my daughter and Delaney. I guess we have that in common, appreciating the love those two give. Knowing we're lucky bastards because they're from another world, far too good for us.

Ava slips another picture she drew under my door this morning before I leave for work. The folded up construction paper has a picture of Ava, between Delaney and myself—all three of us smiling and holding hands with abnormally long arms. I'm as tall as the house we're standing beside, and Delaney is as short as Ava. Betsy the dog even got a cameo, standing inside the tall rectangular home. It's messy, it's perfect, it's us.

Impressed with her artistic capabilities, despite the ulterior motive to talk me into a dog, I walk to the fridge to hang it there before taking off for the day. I want her to be proud of her work and know I'm proud too. Seeing the three of us there together in that crayon drawn world feels right. We feel like a family.

Fuck. Delaney without a doubt feels like a part of our family now. Ava feels it, I feel it...it's undeniable.

The unexpected thought sends a jolt of panic through me. I shouldn't feel like this. Not with her. Not so soon.

The thought of living without her makes my stomach sick. Which is why I need to talk with her, and discuss if she plans to move out or stay.

No matter what, I'm reminded that I need to put out another ad for a new nanny. It's the absolute last thing I want to do, but is completely necessary.

As I rush out the door to work, I make sure to leave my daily note next to the freshly brewed macadamia nut coffee.

It's become our ritual. A note and a fresh pot waiting for her in the morning. I'd be lying if I didn't say I get a kick out of spoiling her. Which is why I leave the information for the spa day I booked for her after her therapy appointment.

Last night in bed after we both gave each other mind blowing orgasms, she told me she had scheduled a therapy session. I didn't miss the way her voice shook when she cracked a joke about scaring off the therapist. For as tough as she is, I can tell she's fragile too. So first thing this morning, I called in a favor with my cousin, whose wife owns a fancy spa in town. They were able to squeeze Delaney in a time slot that works perfectly, right after her therapy appointment.

The thought of her worrying makes my heart ache, knowing I won't be able to be there for her since I have to work. Luckily, my mom is coming to take over for the afternoon until I'm off, so Delaney can take all the time she needs after the appointment to decompress.

An hour later, knee deep in writing a bid proposal, my phone buzzes.

DELANEY:

I can't believe you.

COLE:

Why's that?

DELANEY:

You bought me a whole freaking spa day? Like the whole shebang with a massage and facial and pedicure.

COLE:

What do you think? You like it?

DELANEY:

I think…that I'm going to deepthroat your dick tonight to show you how much I love it.

COLE:

I'm not mad at that...

DELANEY:

Then you can give me another type of facial. :)

COLE:

Good god, I'm hard already. Are you trying to kill me or something?

DELANEY:

Nah. I'm not into necrophilia.

WHEN I COME HOME after having to work a fourteen hour day, Ava is already tucked into bed fast asleep while Delaney is swimming laps in the pool. I slide the back door open and slip out into the dark night.

Standing at the edge of the pool, I watch her glide through the water with effortless grace. The moonlight illuminates every movement, casting a shimmering glow across the surface of the pool. My heart races as I stand there watching her.

When she stops at the far side of the pool's edge, she finally notices me watching. She swims over, panting from the laps she swam, hair fanned out behind her like an honest-to-god real life mermaid.

"Hi," I get out, my mind numb with the awareness that I want her as much as I want my next breath.

She smiles so bright it rivals the glow of the moon. "I'm happy you're home. I've been waiting for you."

Besides my daughter who was born with the instinct to love me, no other woman has told me she's been happy to see me. I'm not that type of guy—the one people look forward to seeing, easy to love. I'm moody and rough around the edges.

I stand there, staring at her like a goddamn fool. Even though she sleeps in my bed every night, I still feel like a lovesick teenager who's out of his depth around her.

I'm pretty positive Delaney is aware of the effect she has on me. Especially when she says, "Take off all your clothes and come join me."

"You want me to go skinny dipping?"

"Yes, skinny dipping, swimming naked, whatever you want to call it," she says as she peels a blue bikini top over her head, throwing it onto the cement.

"I shouldn't." My willpower is currently low from the thought of finishing on her face all day. Swimming naked with her might push me over the edge, do things I promised the both of us I wouldn't do.

"It's not like you haven't seen my ass before. And if you're worried about Ava, she's sleeping hard. I wore her out earlier by playing tag and swimming, so there's no chance she'll wake up."

"Fine," I reply, stepping on the heels of my dirty old boots to kick them off.

As she watches me strip down, her eyes are eating

me up. And I swear to god she licks her lips when I pull down my jeans and she sees the hard-on straining against my briefs. When I pull those down too, my final layer, my dick springs free, already rock hard for her.

Her gaze is fixed on my cock when she says, "Cole Campbell. You are the sexiest man I've ever seen."

At a loss for words, I dive in, before swimming over to her. Delaney's tan shoulders peek out of the pool, the water hitting barely above the swells of her breasts, far enough to drive me even more wild. The water sloshes between our bodies as her legs wrap around my waist, bare pussy on my torso.

I kiss her neck, tasting the sweetness of her skin mixed with the salty chlorine. "How are you so fucking beautiful?" I mumble against her neck. Her nails drag up my shoulders until her hands tangle in my hair. I resist the urge to let out a groan in response to her touch. "How was therapy?" I ask when my lips break apart from her. I've been wondering all day how she was doing.

"Terrifying. But good, really good. I'm going to keep going." Her forehead drops to mine as we breathe the same air, chests heaving as if the oxygen is thin. "And thank you for the spa day. It was exactly what I needed to decompress after."

"Good. That's what I was going for." My mouth goes straight back to her neck, as her head tilts up to the night sky, letting me reach those sensitive spots she loves for me to pay attention to.

Her hands run through my hair as she bears down on my dick, rubbing herself against it. As she grinds herself against me, her pouty lips fall open with a sigh. With my hands on her ass, holding her up, I press her into me, working us into a steady rhythm like waves in the ocean, that toes us close to the line. I'm right there, lined up at her entrance, wanting to push in. But I shouldn't...I vowed to myself I wouldn't since this thing between us isn't supposed to be permanent. But damn it, her wriggling beneath me, the head of my dick slipping in an inch drives me more wild than I ever thought possible.

She rocks that inch of my length in and out of herself, hungry for more. "Fuck me. Please."

"There's nothing I want more than to be inside you right now. But fuck...I shouldn't. I can't." My voice holds a note of desperation. We both can see every last bit of my willpower crumbling by the day, by the minute.

"Tell me why," she whispers, as she continues to rub on me, and press her breasts into my chest.

Her actions obliterate any last chance I have at coming up with a vague answer. "Because I'll be so far gone on you if I do, there'll be no going back. Once we do that you're mine and only mine."

"And if I want to be yours?"

"The day that happens I'm going to bend you over and fuck you so hard you'll have no choice but to want to stay here with me forever."

Her nose brushes against mine, tender and sweet,

but she doesn't respond back. Doesn't tell me if that's what she wants too. Our mouths crash together, desperate to relieve the hunger growing. When I reach between us, dipping my fingers into her, she whimpers against my mouth.

Everything about her is captivating. The way she arches and writhes against my hand, wanting more. The small sounds and gasps that escape from her swollen lips. The way her fingernails drag and dig into my back, marking me with her eagerness to come. And especially the way *my* name falls from her mouth when she comes with my two fingers deep inside her and a thumb rubbing her clit.

I don't take any of it for granted.

Once she's finished, Delaney holds true to her earlier comment about giving me a blow job. She walks me to the gazebo, and gets down on her knees. Looking up at me with a coy smile, she gets straight to business. Sucking me off, taking every inch she can, as she works me up and down. It's not long before I feel my length swell with the need to come.

My hand is fisting her golden hair. "Fuck Emerson, I'm gonna come."

She pulls my painfully erect dick out of her mouth, swiping it along her full lips. "On my face. Just like we talked about."

Those words are all I need to topple over that edge, marking her gorgeous face with streaks of my hot come. She looks like a goddamn masterpiece when she's covered in it. The ultimate marking of my territory.

After getting a clean cloth and wiping her up, we find our clothes before heading inside.

She jumps up onto my back, peppering my face with several quick kisses. "Save an excavator, ride a contractor?"

"You can ride me any day." I carry her on my back like a koala, all the way to my room. Standing beside my bed, I gracefully fall sideways onto the mattress to avoid squishing her with my larger frame. She giggles as I flip around, hovering over her, encasing her body between my arms. I take in the freckles dusting her sloped nose, those big blue doe eyes, and sun-kissed cheeks.

I'm a goner. One hundred percent infatuated. She's already mine as much as I try to deny it.

Yet I'm too chicken shit to admit it to her.

"How is everything about you so goddamn perfect?" I ask.

"I really am the best, huh?" Delaney teases as she scrunches her nose. I pinch her butt at her cheeky tone, causing her to belly laugh.

Grabbing me by the shoulders, she slides out from beneath me. My eyes track her every movement, like a hunter and a deer, as she walks to the open area of the room, extending her hand out. "Dance with me."

In any other realm or lifetime, I'd have refused. I don't dance. But as my legs pick me right up to cross the room, I realize there's no way in hell I'd ever say no to her. Grabbing her hand, I pull her flush against my body. "But there's no music."

"You don't need music to dance."

My arm gently slides down to her lower back, while my other hand holds hers. With her head resting against my chest, we stand there swaying side-to-side, moving to some imaginary music and the euphoria swirling in our minds. Surprising her, I spin her out with one arm and twirl her back in. Her body collides with mine, forcing out an exhale, as a smile bursts onto her face.

If four months ago you'd have told me that a gorgeous blonde woman, with the personality the size of the Pacific Ocean, would be in my arms right now—smiling at me like *that*—I'd have said they were a goddamn liar.

There's not an ounce of me that feels worthy of her affection. I'm not a good man. I'm not nice, charming, funny. But hell, she makes me feel like all those things. For her, I want to be a better man. I want to be her everything.

I rest my chin atop her hair, as we continue dancing with our bodies intertwined like vines of ivy.

"You make me feel so damn alive."

Looking up at me, those bright sapphire eyes see right through me.

She has to see it. She has to know I'm so insanely in love with her that I can barely breathe.

Staring up at me as if I hung the moon, she

murmurs, "You make me feel normal."

Delaney must see my brain stutter, unsure if her comment is a positive or negative. Then she presses her cheek against my chest and says, "All my life, I've been called too much. When I took my first breath in the hospital, my mom said I cried for so long they thought something was wrong with me. That I began life like a bull in a China shop. Then all throughout school, I got in trouble for being too loud, too talkative, too distracted. Each step of life, I'd think I'd finally have a clean slate and find my place where I'd be accepted for being fully myself. With college, with work, with dating...I've always felt like a kooky peg trying to fit in a sensible-sized hole."

She takes a deep breath in, her arms looping around my neck as she continues, "Yet when I'm with you, I don't feel that way. You don't judge me or tell me I should tone it down or act differently. Around you, I feel like I belong. Like suddenly, I'm not a mismatched puzzle piece, but instead, I've found my spot where I click in effortlessly. So thank you. Thank you for making me feel like I'm good enough the way I am."

My hands find their way to her face. My nose brushes her cheek as I whisper into her ear, "Never change. Because I love you just the way you are."

Maybe I'm a fool for partially professing my love to her.

But for Delaney Emerson, I'd be a fool for the rest of my life if it meant I got to spend it with her.

28

DELANEY

The next morning, the doorbell rings, and Cole and I spring up in bed like two jack-in-the-boxes. Wide-eyed and overly alert for an hour when the sun hasn't even made an appearance yet. My life mantra is that if the sun is asleep, then so am I. So who the hell is ringing the doorbell before 6 a.m.?

We look at each other before he jumps out of bed on high alert. Through the app on his phone he checks the front door camera.

"Shit," he mumbles, before pulling up his jeans and grabbing a fresh T-shirt from the drawer.

"Who is it?" I ask, still cocooned in the duvet.

"My mom."

"What's she doing here at this hour? Is she okay? Is there an emergency?"

"Yeah, she's fine. I wish it was for an emergency…"

From the open security app on his phone, I hear his

mom start to sing *happy birthday* while looking at the front door camera. Glancing at his phone, I see her holding a pink box of donuts as she stands there looking far too awake as she hums to herself.

I gasp when it all clicks in my brain. If it's not Ava's birthday, which I know happened months ago, then it must be Cole's.

"It's your birthday! Why didn't you tell me?" I throw my half-naked body at him, kissing his stubbled cheek.

"Because I hate any kind of attention on my birthday. It's just another day to me."

"Okay, Ron Swanson. But still...happy birthday! I'm so excited."

"Thank you. Also I have no idea who Ron Swanson is."

"Don't worry, I'll educate you later on your personality doppelgänger." I spank his ass. "But for now, go let that superstar of a woman who birthed you inside the house."

He kisses me once softly on the forehead. "I'm going to be forced to celebrate today, aren't I?"

"Oh you have no idea," I say, winking and making inappropriate gestures with my hand and mouth to him. Letting him know what he's in store for later.

Looking up at the ceiling, with a hand swiping down his face, he sighs, "Lord, help me."

As he takes long strides out of the room, I rush to throw on presentable clothes and comb through my hair that currently resembles a rat's nest. Waltzing into the kitchen a few minutes later, I see him prepping the coffee maker, while his mom lounges in a kitchen chair taking a big bite out of a maple bar.

I take the seat beside her. "Good morning, Susan. Also thank you for birthing this man forty-one years ago. You're a true hero."

"Good morning, dear. And you're most welcome. You know it wasn't easy. Look at the size of that head. My vag—"

"Don't finish that sentence, mom. If you give me one present today, let it be that." He's clearly in a great mood to celebrate.

Susan glances my way, cupping a hand to the side of her mouth like it will block her voice from her son hearing. "Like I said, my vagina decided against it, and they had to cut me right open for a c-section."

"Oh gosh. Yeah, he does kind of have a big head, doesn't he? Never really noticed until you said it."

Cole sets down two cups of steaming coffee in front of us with narrowed eyes. "Enjoying yourselves over here?"

Susan gives both her son and I a sly look before taking a sip of coffee. "You two were clearly the ones *enjoying* yourselves."

"Mom," he warns.

"What? Can't a mother be happy for her son? On his birthday nonetheless."

Susan pats my hand, as I choke on my own laughter. "I'll leave it at this. For years, I've hoped for someone that could make my son smile. Let's just say I've never seen him smile as much in the last forty-one years as he has in these last couple months."

He stands there tensed, shoulders halfway to his ears, looking like he's about to faint from embarrassment.

"It's probably because of all the org—" I clap a hand over my mouth, realizing who I'm speaking to. My eyes dart from Cole, who is pinching the bridge of his nose, to his mom who is smiling from ear-to-ear.

Susan laughs, amused. "From the orgasms? Yeah, I figured that was part of the equation."

Cole throws some leftovers in his lunch bag before turning to us. "You two are going to put me into an early death. This may be my last birthday at this rate."

Susan stands from the table, grabbing her satchel purse before hugging Cole goodbye. "Stop being so dramatic, son. You know you love us."

Love. That damn word saturates the air around us, floating around like it's wondering if anyone will claim it.

As he embraces his mom, his eyes find mine, brimming with warmth, silently affirming what we both feel.

The notion of loving, and being loved by him, is terrifying.

It's also everything I've ever wanted.

"Banana, since it's your dad's birthday today, we get to be super special party planners. So what do you think we should do for him? I'm thinking maybe a fancy steak dinner and his favorite dessert?"

Her eyes light up, as she jumps into the air, her arms waving around not being able to contain her excitement. "A party. A big one. With a unicorn and a magician!"

"Oh wow. Okay. I see what you're going for and I like it. Problem is, it's a weekday and I'm also not sure if your dad is much of a unicorn-magician kind of guy."

She clasps her hands in front of her, begging. "Please, Laney. He's never *ever* had a birthday party before. Also he would want a chocolate cake. A huge one, with extra sprinkles. And definitely a magician."

Damn it, I can't say no. It's physically impossible with her big brown puppy dog eyes staring up at me like I'll crush her entire world if I say no. I think it goes against human nature to be able to resist those eyes.

I whip out my phone, searching for local magicians. Scrolling through, there are more options than I expected. One name in particular I recognize. I'm fairly certain he was one grade above me, and we had pre-calculus together.

"Your father is going to kill me," I mumble, as I hit the call button.

"Ella, I think I made a bad decision."

My friend's reassuring voice comes through the line. Ella is the rational one in our friend group, so she'll tell it like it is. "On a scale of one to ten, are we talking about trying to save that lost dog and getting lost in Cabo at 2 a.m. level of bad decision? Or more like you chose the wrong hue of foundation again level?"

"Where does hiring a local magician and inviting a bunch of people over on a Tuesday for Cole's birthday fall on that scale?"

The line goes silent for a moment. "Oh...yeah. You fucked up."

I groan. "Don't tell me that. He'll be home any minute and Linus from high school is coming in a half hour."

"Linus. As in, the Linus that was not ashamed of picking his nose and wiping it under the desk Linus?"

"Yep, that's him."

"Please don't tell me he's the magician."

I'm silent, because she said not to tell her. And nose-picking Linus is definitely the magician I hired.

"Blame the five year old with the adorable puppy dog eyes, okay? They're a force to be reckoned with." A knock at the door makes me jump. "That's probably Madi, Noah, and Jude. I've got to go."

"Jude's there?" Ella's voice comes out in a strained tone. I'm not oblivious to the way she occasionally mentions him and then pretends to not be interested.

"He is. I have no idea how to grill a steak, so I enlisted Noah and Jude's help."

"Well, tell them all I said hi. And have fun."

"Thanks, and don't worry. I'll try to sneak a picture of Jude for your spank bank."

Ella's voice raises a whole octave in panic. "Don't you dare, it's not like that."

"Mhm, whatever you say," I sing-song back to her, before hanging up.

Pulling open the door, Madi, her handsome brother Jude, and lumberjack of a fiancé Noah, walk straight inside. They take in mine and Ava's busy work that took us a solid two hours. Pink and green streamers accent the walls. Herds of balloons are scattered across the floor. The gigantic, neon happy birthday sign hangs in the dead center of the entryway to the main living area.

"Perfect timing. I just got done talking to Ella, by the way, she says hi."

The mere mention of Ella's name instantly grabs Jude's attention, as if he's been eagerly anticipating someone saying it, and now that it has happened, he's fully engaged. In a matter of seconds, he transitions from taking in the architecture of Cole's house to being fully locked and loaded on the conversation.

"How is she?" Jude asks.

"She's okay. Recently out of a relationship with an asshole. So you know...single again, but it's for the best." I waggle my eyebrows at him, trying to convey my message. But Jude glances away, pretending he has no idea what I'm hinting at. Those two have a history that's clearly unfinished.

I guide the guys to the barbecue, where they can take charge of grilling the tomahawk steaks that I bought today. If I had tried to tackle the grill myself, the party could have ended in two ways—either a house fire or food poisoning. It's in everyone's best interest for them to handle it instead of me.

Madi, Jessica, and I clink glass bottles of beers together as the men set up. Ava, Hazel, and a few other kids are running around the deck growling, pretending to be bears.

Madi looks around with a smirk on her face. "Cole is either going to kick you out or hate fuck you tonight."

"Don't get my hopes up with the latter," I sigh.

My sister nearly chokes on her sip of beer. "Um, excuse me, what have I missed?"

"Nothing much. That's the problem."

"Guess I should've seen this coming. He's hot, you're hot, you live together." She waves her hand in the air like she's swatting every reason why the two of us would like each other. "But isn't he...a little old for you?"

"It's not *that* bad. Only eleven years. It's more like ten and a half, technically." I look at my nails, pretending to be nonchalant, but internally worried my protective sister will blow a gasket.

Jessica's body rocks forward as if I've gut punched her with shocking information. "*Eleven* years? Are you crazy?"

Madi shrugs her shoulders, pointing a finger with the rest of her hand wrapped around her sweaty beer bottle. "You know, I think it works. I've always pictured Delaney with an older guy. He can probably...handle her better." She turns to me, on the verge of being apologetic, but also not ashamed. "No offense. These younger men don't always know what to do with a firecracker like you."

Jessica purses her lips, considering. "Yeah, you've got a point."

"Thanks for the insight, ladies. I didn't hear a word of it though since I'm shitting myself that Cole will see this wild party any minute now."

Madi and Jess look around at the small crowd. There's us, Susan, and a few of their family friends, strewn across the spacious backyard.

"There's under fifteen people here, Delaney. I just counted them all. I'd hardly use the word wild."

"Yeah, but I'm talking about *Cole* here. The man thinks going grocery shopping counts as a night out." I never stress, because I typically don't care enough. But at this moment, I care. And I'm definitely stressed.

Who springs a whole party on a man that despises surprises and undoubtedly treasures his alone time? Maybe I'm pushing him too far this time. What if he takes one look around, steam flowing from his ears like one of those cartoon characters? What if he suddenly realizes that I'm a lunatic?

I'm surprised he hasn't come to that conclusion yet

actually. Or maybe he has, and he's counting the days until my gig is up. I'd bet good money he has a secret calendar stashed somewhere, crossing out the days until I'm gone.

Hearing the doorbell ring insistently, I make my way back through the house, wondering who else could be here since everyone seems to be accounted for.

Ava is at my heels, excited to greet more party guests. Cole may have a horrible day, but at least I'll go to sleep knowing Ava had the rager she wanted.

Swinging open the front door, I freeze. A woman stands there, twirling her dark hair around one finger, scrutinizing me from head to toe. Her red lips snarl in disgust as she observes Ava hugging my leg. Though she terrifies me, there's no denying her beauty. She's somewhere around forty, tall and waifish, with curly dark hair and legs for days. Standing side-by-side, this woman is the exact opposite of me.

"Mom?" Ava asks from behind my legs.

My soul leaves my body at the word.

Ava's mom. Isabel.

The woman I always imagined throat punching is standing four feet away from us.

"Come here, baby. Give your mom a hug." Isabel extends her arms, expecting her daughter to run and jump into them.

Ava's usual uninhibited self is suddenly replaced with tentativeness, and she looks to me for reassurance. Against every instinct, I muster a half-hearted encouraging smile. Then, with painstaking care, she takes slow steps towards her mother. As she leans her stiff body forward, Isabel reaches out for the hug. Their embrace feels awkward and mechanical—like two department store mannequins attempting a hug.

She runs back to me, worry tracing her features, as her arms reach out to me. "Hold me, Laney."

I hoist her up, aware of the fact that we probably look comical since I'm pint-sized and she is tall for her age. But there's nothing I wouldn't do to comfort her right now. If my head is reeling, I can only imagine how she feels at seeing her mom for the first time in over a year.

"Is Cole home?" Isabel snaps. Her eyes are icy, arms crossed in front of her chest. She doesn't like the fact that Ava wants me to hold her.

As if Isabel summoned him by name, Cole sprints up the grass-lined path to the house. He's out of breath from his mad dash from his truck, his face serious and haunted, as if he's seen a ghost of times past.

Isabel gazes at him, her grin unsettling. It's not a typical smile; rather, it mirrors the expressions worn by Disney villains who believe they're miles ahead of everyone, harboring some hidden agenda up their sleeve.

She surveys him from head to toe, as if sizing him up for her next conquest. I notice the appreciative glint in her eyes, which makes her next words catch me off guard. "Your hair could really use a cut," she remarks, running her manicured hand through his hair. "I've always preferred it short."

He stiffens under her unexpected touch before stepping back, deliberately putting distance between them.

Ava observes the whole exchange, quiet as can be. Come to think of it, I don't think she's ever not talked or made a random noise for this long.

Grinding his teeth, he replies, "You should have told me you were stopping by today."

"I texted you last week that I was in town. That's enough of a heads up."

"Come on in, I guess," he sighs, defeated.

Isabel strides past the three of us, as if this is her own home. Her designer heels click on the hard floor as she scans the room before heading straight to the bar cart to fix herself a drink. I want to ask her to make me one too, preferably a double to endure this party turned nightmare.

Cole cautiously approaches my side, gently lifting Ava from my arms. The sight of them melting into each other for reassurance from the unexpected visit melts my heart in countless ways.

When he turns to head to the living room, he stops dead in his tracks at the sight of the gigantic birthday sign. Through the view of the tall windows, he spots the dozen or so people hanging out in the backyard. Everyone outside is in their own little world, oblivious to the Isabel-sized bomb that was dropped on us. His eyebrows raise in surprise, before landing in their final destination of their normal grumpy furrow.

"Emerson...what is all this?"

"Surprise?" My hands nervously commit to doing jazz hands in tandem with the word surprise. Fucking jazz hands. Now is not the moment for ten celebratory fingers.

"Care to explain yourselves, ladies?"

I tread carefully. "It's a birthday party...for you."

At the mention of the birthday party, Ava's little head pops straight up. "It's the best birthday party in the whole world! We planned the whole thing."

Right then the doorbell rings again. I groan as the timing couldn't be worse. This time I know who most likely stands on the other side of the door.

Cole answers it before I have the chance to, and I hold my breath.

"Can I help you?" he grumbles in a deep voice.

"Hi. My name is Linus. I'm here as the magician for the party today."

Swiveling on the heel of his worn out work boots, Cole glowers at me. "The *magician* is here."

Hauling in a large black duffel, presumably filled with magic supplies, I finally spot Linus. And holy shit, he's attractive. Booger-picking, gangly Linus has transformed into a beautiful fucking butterfly.

Who knew hot magicians were a thing?

Rearranging my astonished expression back into a mask of professionalism, I risk a glance at Cole.

He looks upset. Very upset.

Question is, what is he mad about?

The party, ex-wife, or magician?

Only me, Delaney Emerson, could end up in a situation like this.

I'd planned for a memorable day, but I had no idea it would be *this* type of memorable.

29

COLE

On my ride home from work, I envisioned walking into my house and spending the rest of the day relaxing with my girls. Maybe eating a cake that I know was most likely prepared by my daughter's sticky, licked fingers. Ending the night with my head between Delaney's legs and her mouth on my cock.

In all honesty, I shouldn't be surprised at the recent developments.

But a surprise birthday party and Isabel all on the same day? No, I wouldn't have seen any of this coming from a mile away.

"C'mon, come to your mom. I want to see how much you've grown," Isabel beckons, waving Ava over. She's pushy, and I want to remind her that she wouldn't need to see the several inches Ava's grown if she was actually here consistently.

I keep my lips sealed for my daughter's sake. I won't inject negative thoughts into her mind about her mother—Isabel is fully capable of doing that on her own.

Her arms cinch tighter around my neck, as if bracing for an imminent tsunami about to sweep us from the shore.

I whisper through her long hair. "You can go if you feel comfortable. I'll be right here, baby girl."

Pulling back, she looks at me in a way that cuts me down at the knees. How could someone not want to be a part of her life?

"Laney too, right? She'll be right there?" she asks, eyes darting around the room with indecision.

I look over at Delaney, who is walking back inside after showing Linus where he can set up out back. A tense smile is plastered on her face while she twists her hands in nervousness. I've never seen her worried before and it makes me do a double take.

"Of course, her too. We're both here."

Isabel chimes in, with an eye roll. "I'm not a monster. She's fine. C'mon, baby. Get over here."

Walking in her mom's direction, Ava's pink light-up sneakers shuffle with hesitancy. Isabel grabs her hand, balancing a red cup in the other.

"Let's go out here. A little privacy would be nice, don't you think?" Isabel practically drags her away, and it feels like she's taking a fraction of my heart with her. I'm suddenly glad for the handful of people in the backyard, so they're not completely alone together.

Ava's apprehension cuts through me like a knife. She's my free spirit, usually chatting nonstop with a crooked smile glued to her face. It fills me with guilt to witness her energy drown in overwhelm at the sight of her mother.

Beside me, Delaney clears her throat. "Wow. I didn't see that coming."

"Yeah, me either."

Delaney inhales, ready to say something else, but her friend's fiancé that I recognize from the bar walks in through the slider with a pile of steaming meat on a blue serving plate. "Steaks are ready."

It smells good, and makes me remember I'm not just stuck in my annual worst nightmare of Isabel. I'm also in my second worst nightmare of having a surprise party thrown for me.

Jude walks over, slapping me on the back. "Hey, happy birthday. Nice to see you again."

"Hey, thanks," I reply. We make conversation as Delaney and Madi pull a few side dishes from the refrigerator. My gaze remains fixed on Delaney as she moves about, a bundle of nervous energy. She steals glances at me, quickly looking away when our eyes meet, as if she believes I'm angry with her. But I'm not.

Surprised and a bit uncomfortable? Definitely.

Angry? No. At least not at her.

If it wasn't for Noah and Jude talking my ear off, I'd

go pull her into my chest and tell her it's okay and that I'm not upset. Tell her that the fact that she even cares enough about me to pull off something like this warms me up like a hot summer night. And I'd definitely tell her that her ass looks incredible in those shorts.

Moving outside to eat, I get stuck talking to one of the dads about the new residential homes my crew has been working on. I'm half-assing the entire conversation since my eyes never leave Ava.

She's deserted hanging out with her mother, to play tag with Hazel. Isabel sits in an Adirondack chair, scrolling on her phone and occasionally taking selfies against the backdrop of the rolling green hills surrounding the house. Apart from dragging Ava out here, I haven't seen Isabel try to play or interact with her daughter. It feels more like she's here to fulfill her yearly quota of minutes before riding off and not speaking to us for another three hundred and sixty-five days.

The sound of a speaker playing some shitty mystical music begins to blare. My eyes scan the backyard to find the source, thinking maybe someone connected to the outdoor bluetooth speaker by accident.

It's the damn magician though. He's set up on the wooden deck, and waving the crowd over to his display —a red velvet curtain on a background stand. Tacky silver stars dangle in front of the curtain, and a black podium stands in front of it with several items. This Linus guy pulls on his black suit jacket and it makes me hate him even more, because it's tailored to fit his buff frame perfectly.

Aren't magicians supposed to be dorky and awkward? Because this guy isn't. In fact he looks like an actor pretending to be a magician.

The second he saw Delaney look him up and down in shock, he thought he had her in the bag. His expression turned cocky as his eyes took her in too. Now I've had to stand here with one eye supervising my ex and daughter, and another eye on Delaney and the goddamn magician talking all night. I'm out of my mind with jealousy. And I shouldn't care, but I definitely do.

I hope his tricks fall flat or someone chooses the wrong card during his little show. Not that I'm bitter or anything.

Guests gather round as the show starts. First, Linus shows off a newspaper to everyone, shaking it, holding it out slowly for us to inspect its authenticity. Then he begins to tear it to shreds. But in the next instant, the torn pieces are whole again.

What the hell. That was kind of impressive.

Throughout the rest of the show, there are claps and cheers, and ooh'ing and aah'ing as the blond man puts on a damn good show. He flips cards through the air, juggles glasses of water, cuts rope and reconnects it again. His offhand jokes actually make me crack a smile, and I'm a tough critic. Maybe I've judged the whole magic thing too quickly. This would definitely be a five star review.

As the show concludes, the crowd begins to disperse. Delaney continues avoiding me, and Isabel remains glued to her chair, oblivious to her daughter running amuck.

As I say bye to a few families I notice charismatic, smug ass Linus walk up to Delaney. She tips her head back and laughs at a joke he makes. I can't rip my eyes away from them as I'm stuck in nightmare number three of the day—someone asking her out.

She's not even mine. I'm an asshole and have unfortunately drawn that line in the sand for us both. But fuck, she *feels* like mine.

My entire body screams at me to go do something about it when I hear him ask if he can take her out this weekend. My heart is pounding, ears ringing. I hate myself for how I'm about to cockblock. I'm not normally this guy. I don't get jealous. I don't get attached. And I definitely never give a shit unless it's about me or my daughter.

But I can't stop my legs from moving toward them. I can't stop myself from putting one arm around Delaney's narrow shoulders and pulling her against my body. I can't stop the kiss I plant on the top of her head and the way I say, "Hey, sunshine. Everything okay over here?"

I make a mental note to donate money to a gender equality charity later to counteract my current state of douchery. I'm not too proud to admit I'm out of control and that I'd kill any asshole that would pull this with my daughter.

She stiffens under my arm, looking up at me like I've got two heads. "Um, yeah...everything is okay."

Linus's eyebrows shoot up as he points to us. "Sorry, didn't know you two were together."

Her mouth drops open as she tries to piece together what the hell my problem is.

Pulling her closer against me, I extend my free hand out for Linus to shake. "No worries, man. Good show by the way."

See, I'm not a total asshole. I can still be polite.

Linus shakes my hand and then turns away, cheeks pink from his foiled plan. I walk a few yards away with her body still tucked into me. It feels good to hold her like this. In front of everyone.

She elbows me. Hard. "What the hell are you doing?"

"What do you mean?"

"Don't play stupid. What was with that whole caveman act over there?" Her eyebrows are knit together, arms crossed in front of her chest. It dawns on me that I've never seen angry Delaney before. She's adorable and terrifying and it makes me want to kiss her dizzy.

I decide to come clean, because I know I fucked up. Maybe she is into magicians and wanted a date with that guy. Or maybe she's mad I'm being affectionate in front of our friends and family. It's something we've never talked about since we're technically not official. Which I'm quickly realizing needs to change.

I take my arm off of her to give her space, and scratch at my stubble. "Look, I'm sorry. I messed up."

"Yeah, you did. I'm not your territory. I wasn't even going to say yes to him. But I'm capable of telling him all on my own. You know I'm not shy." Her eyes flutter shut for a moment as she takes a deep breath, centering herself. "You don't even want me like that anyway, so stop pretending like you do."

My mouth falls open, ready to rebuttal the hell out of that statement. To tell her I've never wanted anyone more than I want her. That I had come to terms with being alone for the rest of my life, until I laid eyes on her for the first time. That my heart ran away from me the more I got to know her. That my love runs so deep for her that I can feel it coursing through my veins every second we're together.

"A word, Cole?" Isabel marches up to us, and I instantly know it's not going to be good. She's got that look on her face like I tossed her phone into the pool on purpose. Not that I've wanted to do that this entire time (I have).

I bury my face in Delaney's hair, whispering into her ear, "You've got it all wrong, Emerson."

She lets out a shaky exhale that makes it difficult to walk away. I feel sick to my stomach with the need to hash things out with her, and let her know how I feel.

I'm done burying my feelings. I'm done being scared

of rejection. And I'm definitely done with trying to stop whatever is going on between us.

While I follow Isabel into the house, I scan the yard, making sure Ava is okay. Luckily, she seems oblivious to any drama with her mother as she barrel rolls down the gigantic inflatable water slide...that I had no idea existed until today. A purchase that has Delaney written all over it.

Isabel slams the screen door with so much force it bounces back open. As I close it with more ease, the silence is so thick you could cut it with a knife.

That's when I know I'm in for it. Despite her infidelity and parental abandonment, I'm still the villain in her eyes. And I'll take that role with the acknowledgment that perhaps I played an unknowing part in her downfall. Because every villain is a hero in their own story.

Isabel picks a piece of imaginary lint off of her black dress. "What the hell did I witness out there? Care to explain yourself?"

"I'm not sure what you're getting at."

Isabel points a long fingernail at me. "That you've been fucking the help?"

"The help?" Who the hell says *the help*?

"The nanny, Cole. Catch up for fucksake."

"I don't need to explain myself to you." I grind my teeth so hard that I may no longer have teeth by the end of this conversation.

But I'm trying hard to stay calm, not for her sake, but for my daughter's.

"You look ridiculous being all over her like that. Isn't she a little too young for you? Aren't you embarrassed by how that reflects on you?"

"It's none of your goddamn business. Is there anything you want to talk about that's related to our daughter?"

I've hit the spot she's sensitive about. Ava. I'd almost feel sorry for her, but I don't. Not when she actively tries to stay away all on her own accord.

"I don't want that woman to be her step mom."

"And why's that? Enlighten me about what's so wrong with her." This should be good. Isabel has zero right to an opinion about who spends time with her daughter.

"It's not about what's wrong with her. It's about what's wrong with you." Isabel's smile turns tight and I know I won't like what she's about to say. "It'll hurt Ava when you drive that woman away. Exactly like you drove me away. You have a way of sucking the life out of people. Don't you think someone like her, young and pretty, will get bored of someone like you? You're unexciting and irritable. If you really love her, and if you love your daughter, you'll spare everyone the heartbreak and not get involved."

I'm silent, because it hurts. Because I know she's fucking right.

Isabel has a skill for hitting where it hurts. It's as if

she instinctively finds that vulnerable spot and expertly picks at it until it starts to bleed.

I snap, not able to hear another word. "Get the hell away from me and go spend time with your daughter."

She knows she's succeeded, patting my shoulder and eyes squinting with a fake pitying smile. "Think about it. Everyone will be less hurt in the end."

The worst part of it all is that it's true. For the last three months it's been the reason I've convinced myself to distance myself from Delaney.

For the next hour, I walk around with my head miles away, trying to map out how our life can fill a Delaney-shaped hole. I've come to the conclusion it's impossible right as the remainder of the guests leave.

Madi, Noah, and Jude head out, wishing me a happy birthday and winking at Delaney as they go out the front door. I can only imagine what that's all about.

Now it's only Isabel left. She's been in the background for the majority of the party, scrolling social media and most likely pretending to be a doting mother. Her phone rings, and she's laughing obnoxiously loud, telling someone she'll be over in a few minutes and to save her a bottle of wine.

Ava is holding Delaney's finger as Isabel grabs her oversized purse and crouches down in their path. "Baby, come give me a hug before I leave."

My daughter, with the bravery the size of a whole army, stares her mother straight in the eyes. "No. I don't want to."

The moment she says it, I feel all three of us grownups freeze. I knew this would happen someday, but I can tell Isabel didn't.

"Don't be like that. Get over here and hug me."

Right when I'm about to step in and tell my daughter she doesn't have to, Ava stomps her foot. The action causes her bedazzled light-up sneaker to flash. "No. My dad never makes me hug people if I don't want to. And I said I don't want to."

The look on my ex's face is one I've never seen. A mixture of confusion, anger, or perhaps the hurling realization that she's thoroughly fucked up as a parent. She stands and opens the front door, as it squeaks on its hinges. Right before stepping out into the night, Isabel turns around and looks right at me. With a tip of her head toward Delaney, she says, "Do yourself a favor and remember what we talked about Cole."

Then that devil of a woman is gone just as quickly as she arrived.

I feel Delaney's eyes on me, trying to get me to look her way to answer the hundreds of questions she has swirling in her head. She's always the first to make sure everyone is okay.

Ava pipes up first though, lifting her shoulders and dropping them again with a dramatic sigh. "Wow. I *really, really* don't like her."

Her statement catches us so off guard that all we can do is look at each other with wide *how the fuck do we respond to that* eyes.

Then Delaney grabs her hand and gives her a twirl. "How about we dance? Dancing fixes everything."

Minutes later, I sit back with my beer watching my girls dance to some upbeat song I've never heard in my life.

They jump around, arms in the air, spinning across the room like two whirligigs in a windstorm. If it wasn't for the dull ache behind my sternum, I'd be able to soak in this moment. Relish in the fact of how damn good I have it, how lucky of a man I am to be able to watch my two wild girls dance their hearts out.

But it doesn't happen like that. Because I'm pissed about two things.

First, how years ago I got involved with such a vile woman, who turned out to be an even shittier mom to my angel of a daughter.

Second, being that I know this is one of the last nights I'll have with Delaney. That in the process of doing what needs to be done, I'm destroying whatever's left of my heart while simultaneously doing what everyone else in her life has ever done to her—leaving her. Failing her.

And the thought of that wrecks me to my core.

30

DELANEY

Something has gone terribly wrong in the last two hours, and I'm not entirely sure what did. All I know for certain is that the heartless woman is responsible for the current doubt written all over Cole's face.

The surprise party may have not helped either.

He tucks Ava into bed, and my heart melts into a drippy puddle on the floor as I hear them sing "You Are My Sunshine" and recite their daily affirmations through the half cracked door.

For as much of a pessimist as he likes to say and think he is, he sure acts and parents like a positive person.

Gently turning the knob of her bedroom door, he closes it noiselessly. As he pivots, he discovers me seated silently on the floor right outside the door.

"Sorry, I wanted to make sure she was okay without interrupting."

The cartilage of his Adam's apple bobs up and down as he swallows. "Yeah. Yeah, she seems like she's okay." He blows out a big breath. "Damn, kids are crazy resilient, aren't they?"

"They are. Which is good when they have a psycho parent. Trust me, I know."

Like a summer storm rolling in, doubt and pain illuminate his face again. I'm not sure what's going through his head, but I want to get to the bottom of it, if he'll let me. I'd do anything to make him feel better. His heart feels like an extension of my own. One to protect and nurture.

I grab his hand, feeling the rough calluses of his palm scrape against my own smooth one. Leading him down the long hall to his room, I stop at the door. "We need to talk."

The expression on his face shifts, growing even more serious. "You're right, we do."

Last time we talked at the party, we left things on unfinished terms. He acted like I had suddenly sprouted a magician fetish and was practically pissing all over me in front of Linus. I'm not going to say I hated it, but I'm also not a fan of hypothetical golden showers —which is why I snapped. Because how could he act like he cares so much, while behind closed doors he's shuttered off a whole portion of his heart to me? It's not like he plans to keep me around for much longer.

Crossing the threshold of the room, we make our way over to the bed. The covers are still in disarray from being interrupted this morning by his mother at the door. It was just hours ago, but it already feels like another lifetime.

We both sit stiffly at the edge of the bed, neither of us making a move to get comfortable.

With his hands in his front pockets, he bobs his head toward me. "You first."

I look him straight in the eyes, needing to gauge how thoroughly I fucked up. "On a scale of one to ten, how angry are you about the party?"

His smile quirks up on one side, making a dimple pop. "Zero."

"*Zero?* So like, not at all?" I nudge his broad shoulder with my own. "Are you fucking with me?"

"I've never had a birthday party before. Ava loved it. Both of you were happy. What more could I ask for?" He shrugs as he leans forward, bracing himself with his elbows on his knees.

"Hm. You need to act like you're a teeny bit mad or else I'll be out of control." I wave my hands in the air. "You know that saying—give me an inch and I'll go a mile. I'm pretty sure they came up with that with me specifically in mind."

The corner of his mouth tips up again but it doesn't reach his eyes this time. Instead he looks...conflicted. Dread thunders in my stomach, lava hot and alarming.

I swallow. "What did you need to talk about?"

He drops his face into his hands, scrubbing at his eyes as if the friction will ignite his courage. "This is too hard. I...don't know how to say it."

A distressed Cole puts me into immediate caretaker mode. I scoot closer and place my hand on his back, rubbing soothing circles along the columns of muscle on each side of his spine. "Tell me. Whatever it is, it's okay." I say it more to myself than him, because I don't have a good feeling about whatever he's about to tell me.

He looks back up at me. "Fuck, Delaney. We can't do this anymore."

"Do what?" My hand freezes on his back, as the burn of rejection begins to torch my chest.

"This. Us."

The room suddenly feels much too big, the lighting too bright. My heart stops for a moment, in shock at his words.

"Oh." I can't let him see that he's ripping me in two. "Tell me why."

"Because you deserve a life far better than what I can give you."

"That's not true." I tap his foot with my own, as his eyes focus on some distant spot. "Hey, look at me." Those hazel eyes flash to mine. "Everything I want is right here. You, Ava...that's enough for me."

"It seems like enough right now, but in a year? Five years? You'll change your mind."

"I won't," I say, making a point to look right at him. To convince him. "Trust me, I won't."

He doesn't respond, causing my panic to flare hot and bright. Most of the time, I can be optimistic. But currently, all I see is the devastation of the man I love pushing me away. It makes my stomach churn, my skin crawl with desperation.

I need him.

I need *them*.

"I don't understand. Are you sure the party didn't freak you out? Did I go too far?" I can feel my thoughts pouring out, rushing away from me like a fast-moving current before I can convince my brain to shut up. "I can do that sometimes. Go too far. Is that why you don't want this...me, anymore?"

His eyes, previously fixed on the floor, briefly meet mine, a flash of ferocity passing through them. "No. This is not your fault. It's all me," he admits, dropping his head back into his hands.

My world feels thrown off its axis. This can't be happening. The second I get too comfortable with the prospect that I've found my place in life. And now he's doing what everyone else has always done.

Leaving.

Why is it that everyone I believe would love me ends up leaving? What's fundamentally flawed in me that drives people away, especially those I expect to stay?

Cole and Ava are my home. The hope, the possibility of us forever. It felt too real, and now it's slipping between my fingers like sand.

My eyes well with tears, as I stare at the ceiling. Telling those traitorous watery bitches to get back inside the tear duct where they belong because we do *not* cry over men. But my heart aches because I know he isn't any man. He's *the* man I've always wanted.

When he sees the tears rolling down the apples of my cheeks, I swear I see his face mirroring my own—his heart breaking in half.

"Fuck, I'm so sorry. Please don't cry. It's killing me, sunshine."

"I thought you..." I want to say *loved me*, but stop myself. "How can you be over me so quickly?"

Cradling my head, he stares at me, his own eyes filling with tears now, before he pulls me close to his chest. "I'll never get over you," his voice cracks with emotion. "You've changed me. You've changed my life."

The words are meant to be reassuring in some twisted way. Instead, it makes me cry harder than before. Chest heaving sobs racking my body as I cling to him like a raft in a storm, and he clings right back.

How can it all feel so right for us, only to end like this? He holds me fastened against him. The sound of his heartbeat thunders beneath my ear, as if it's trying its best to pound its way out through his ribs.

I can't fall apart right here in front of him.

As if he's contagious, I pull myself from his arms. It unleashes the first trickle of pain, separating myself from him. But if this is truly his desire, then I'd better saddle up and start acclimating. "If this is really your decision, I'm not going to sit here and beg for you to want me."

Standing abruptly, he smooths his hair back with one hand, while looking at the planks of the floor as if it holds all of life's answers. "I want you more than my next breath. That's not the problem."

"If you want me too, then there should be no problem. That's how easy this all can be."

"It's not that easy." He begins to pace the room, a hand tugging at the wavy ends of his hair. "You deserve more. You deserve fun and adventure and everything bright. I'm the night, you're the sun...I'll dim you if you stay."

I stand on wobbly legs, my entire mind and body feeling drained from the ups and downs of the day. His face is full of confusion as I cross the room to wrap my arms around his waist once again. He hugs me back, so naturally, as I melt into him like hot butter.

"I can't stop you from dragging the past into your future." I squeeze him tighter, knowing this might be the last time I feel wrapped up in his warmth and safety. "Remember you have so much to offer exactly as the person you are. Don't sell yourself short, because from where I'm standing? You're everything, Cole Campbell."

His chest vibrates with a shuddery breath as I tear myself away from him. As I walk down the hall to leave his room, I feel his eyes on me as he stands motionless in the middle of his room. I don't risk a glance back, because I know I'll be too weak. My heart will crumble like old clay if I see the pained look on the face of the man I wish could love himself enough, so I can have a chance to love him too.

I glance out the tall windows on the way to my room and see the setting sun glimmering like it didn't get the memo that my heart is in two.

The sky is turning from bright oranges and blues to inky shades of black. Day and night. They blend together so seamlessly, without even trying. People make a point of watching the sunset, to marvel at its beauty. Half of me wants to march back down the hall, grab Cole, and sit him in front of this window. To show him how breathtaking the melding of the day and night can be. To prove how remarkable we could be too.

I don't do it though. As much as I love him, I vowed years ago when my parents left that I would never try to convince a person to stay or love me.

When I slip under the cold sheet of my bed, the imaginary life I built up for the last few months comes crashing down around me. Lying here, alone and cold, sleeping in my own bed for the first time in weeks only magnifies the loneliness of the situation.

Tonight I can't reach out and touch him while he snores softly beside me. I won't feel his breath on my neck when he whispers how damn lucky he is, like he does every night. I won't feel that overwhelming sense of home in my bones as I awake in the soft light of the morning.

Instead, I lie awake staring into the darkness. Wondering how the fuck this all happened. And most of all how I'll survive someone leaving me again.

MY THIRD ALARM blares for me to wake the hell up already. I groan, silencing it and rolling out of bed. Looking into the mirror, I look just as shitty as I feel. Messy hair from tossing and turning, puffy eyes and dark circles from alternating between crying and not sleeping.

Coffee is the first step I need to remedy this. Coffee won't fix a broken heart, but it'll help me not feel like absolute death.

When I walk out of my room and straight to the coffee maker, I stop in my tracks when I see Cole. Bent over the counter, grinding the beans to make a fresh pot of coffee. He can't hear over the sound of the grinder, and hasn't seen me yet either.

The sight of him has me nearly running back to my room to hide out. But I remind myself I'm a big girl and can face this. Even if I don't fully believe it.

He's unfairly gorgeous as always—the type of man who is sexy without being aware of it. Wavy dark hair, muscles flexing as he holds the grinder in place as it obnoxiously whirs. He has matching dark circles under his eyes, and he looks...sad. Shoulders slouched and those long fingers rubbing out the tension knots in his neck.

I should hate him, but I don't. If anything, I think I love him more.

He truly believes he's doing this because he's not enough. If only he understood that he's my world.

The coffee grinder stops, jolting me from my daze.

Not expecting to see me standing in the kitchen, he startles and clears his throat. "Morning. Coffee will be ready soon."

"Thanks. I need it." I half-smile, sad, but attempting to keep it lighthearted. "Looks like you do too."

Messing with the brim of the hat he's wearing, he replies, "Look...I understand if you don't want to finish out the next couple weeks. I wasn't sure..."

"I do. I am," I reply, interrupting him. There's no way I'd bounce out of here and leave Ava because her father and I are in shambles. "I'd like to finish the two weeks if it's okay with you."

"I'm fine with that. Anyways...I'll get out of your hair." When he begins to walk past me, back toward the hallway, my hand shoots out on its own accord, grabbing his bare forearm. We both look down at the contact where my small fingers press into the golden skin of his arm.

"I'll leave it be after this. But first, can you clarify one thing for me?"

He nods once as our eyes meet again.

"Did you ever really care for me or was this all one big made up fantasy in my head?"

His eyes shift from confused to dark within a millisecond. A pause fills the room for so long that I begin to doubt that he'll ever answer. Until he surprises me by taking a step forward, wrapping my loose hair into his fist, and running his other hand up my neck. His mouth brushes my ear as he leans down into me. "Every fucking day I think of what it'd feel like to marry you and know you're mine forever. To fuck you, have babies with you. To grow old with you. To have a life with you. This has been the realest thing I've ever felt."

As I stand there frozen, he backs away. His words echo in my brain, making it seem impossible to fathom a world where he thinks daily about marrying me, having babies and building a life with me.

Heading to the entry way with his work bag, he pauses to lift a tentative hand in goodbye before clicking the front door shut behind him.

I'm obliterated. Short-circuited. Body buzzing, brain spinning to overthink and process every detail of the last two minutes.

I couldn't have come all this way, forcing serendipity's hand to have him choose me as his nanny. Him letting me into his life and home. Falling in love with both Cole and Ava....for it all to end.

I just have no idea what it will take to make him see his worth.

31

COLE

Four years ago, when Isabel left me with a wriggly, screaming, almost one year old in my arms—I thought that was the worst day of my life. Now I see I'm wrong, because *today* may very well be the worst day yet. All because I'm an asshole that's somehow trying to do the right thing in some twisted, screwed up way.

Pushing away Delaney is long term what's worst for me and best for her. If she doesn't see it now, she will sooner than later. Maybe not tomorrow, but in five years she'll realize what a huge six foot four inch bullet she dodged.

Still doesn't help the constant ache in my chest when I think of the confused look on her face as she realized what was happening last night.

Now I'm stuck at my job site, trying to pretend that I'm getting some semblance of work done. Everything's gone to shit and it's not the day for it. I have people on my crew walking off the job, another hundred degree day, and bids to submit to potential clients.

But my head is in a whole other world, trying to cope with the fact that I've broken things off.

Realizing that my inner turmoil isn't going to lessen, I take a break from work to clear my mind and head to Little Elm bakery. I try to tamper down the memories of seeing Delaney here at the table in the corner near the window three months ago. I remember being so completely enthralled with her that I felt sick with hope. The way Ava looked at me with her doe eyes, and we both knew she was the one.

After the boisterous redhead owner, Sherie, rings me up, I turn around and spot Jude grabbing his coffee from the barista. He's in scrubs and staring down at his phone. It's the awkward decision between pretending I never saw him or going over to say hi. The guy radiates golden retriever energy though and I don't want to be a dick.

"Hey man, what's up?"

Jude shakes my hand, and smiles. "Long time no see. Just grabbing a coffee before my shift. How's everything?"

I could lie and say fine. But fuck, I'm bursting at the seams and have no one to talk to. "Not great, actually. I broke things off with Delaney last night."

Jude's eyebrows shoot up. "Well, shit. On your birthday? What happened?"

"Nothing happened which is what makes it even worse." I sigh, and run my hand down the stubble I meant to shave this morning. "You know her...she's incredible. Positive, and sunny. She deserves so much more than being tethered to an asshole like me."

Taking a large gulp from the paper cup, Jude hums in thought. He wipes his mouth on the back of his hand. "I personally don't think you're an asshole, but I know what you're getting at."

"So you think I made the right decision?" The words tumble out of my mouth. So far, this has felt anything but the right decision. I'm desperate for the need to have someone pat me on the back and tell me I did the right thing.

"No offense, but I don't think it was your decision to make." I open my mouth ready to rebuttal, even though the same thought has crossed my own a hundred times. Jude holds up his hand to pause me. "All I'm saying is, you shouldn't have decided for her. Just because you have this idea that she's too good for you, doesn't automatically mean that you can't be together and that you get to be the only one to decide it."

Looking at it from that perspective makes too much damn sense. "Well, shit."

Jude looks at me with amusement, before turning serious again. "If you love her, then go get her. Don't be a fucking idiot and let her walk away. The regret will eat you alive. Trust me, I've been there."

"Wait, did you and..." I begin to wonder if he's referring to Delaney. They have been friends for over a decade.

Jude shakes his head. "No, not her. Someone else."

The barista shouts my name. "Good, because that was about to be really damn awkward," I chuckle. "Thanks for the advice, man. I better get going."

Grabbing the large coffee and box of pastries from the counter, I head back to my truck.

Talking with Jude has made me even more confused. Here I thought I was doing the commendable thing by severing ties with Delaney. But maybe he has a point. Maybe it wasn't my decision to steamroll her with and make.

Using the voice command in my truck, I call up my mom on the drive back to the worksite. Even at the age of forty-one, I still unashamedly seek her advice. Much like Delaney, she's blunt. She's honest. She'll tell me how thoroughly I fucked up, or commend me for doing the right thing.

Her voice comes through the speakers. "Hi, Son."

"Hi, Mom."

My mother doesn't miss a damn thing. "What's wrong?"

I sigh, getting straight to the point. "I broke things off with Delaney last night."

She laughs once—short and disbelieving. "Well, why'd you go and do a thing like that? I thought you two were happy, no?"

"We are...we *were*." Silence stretches on through the

line, and I know she's waiting for me to elaborate. "Shit, I don't know. Isn't it easier to end things right now? And save us both a whole lot of heartache down the line?"

"Hm. Sounds like the chicken shit way out to me."

I smile, expecting nothing less. "We're opposites. She'll get bored with this lifestyle of being tied down."

Mom sighs, a combination of compassion and annoyance that I'm a fucking idiot. "Sure sounds like you've got a lot of reasons why it wouldn't work out. Also sounds like you're doing quite a lot of projecting."

"Projecting?"

"Delaney isn't Isabel. She's not going to take off on you two. And hell, even if she does, at least you can say you tried. That counts for something. It's a whole lot better than purposely trying to sabotage yourself out of happiness."

Happiness. She hit the nail on the head. Delaney is the warmth of a campfire on a cold day. The break in the clouds in the midst of a storm. She's reawakened a dormant piece of my heart that I thought had been lost forever.

My mom continues, "You both deserve happiness. Maybe this *could* all fall apart. Maybe she will run away and break your heart. Maybe you're such an asshole that she'll loathe you after three months—or three years. Because honestly, I wouldn't be too surprised based on this dumb ass decision you've forced upon her and yourself."

I husk out a laugh. "Gee, thanks."

"Listen, love is a risk, always has been and always will be. But it's a damn rewarding one. Despite the worst-case scenario lurking in the corner, it can also be the most beautiful thing. You might love her with everything you've got, and she'll wrap herself up in that and never let go. Perhaps you'll build a happy family and grow old together, sipping coffee together in your pajamas on the front porch swing every morning. Often, if something seems too good to be true, it's worth fighting for. Every potential bad day is worth it, because it also holds the potential for a thousand great ones. So fight, goddamnit."

After ending the call, I take a few minutes to drive around town and collect my thoughts. Like the light of day, I see how thoroughly I've messed up. A trigger reaction based on my insecurities. One part of me screams to still leave things be—self-doubt creeping in that I'm not good enough for her. That this will hurt far less for everyone to end things at present compared to later down the road.

The other, lovesick half of me wants to go right back home and tell Delaney what a dumb idiot I am for trying to run her off. Tell her that even though she's so far out of my league that she's in a whole other dimension, I want to strive to be the man that can possibly be good enough for her someday.

Instead I drive back to work and get my crew in order, submit bids, and stew over the fact that I'm a goddamn coward.

COLE:

Going to be home late tonight. Work problems. Do you mind putting Ava to bed?

DELANEY:

Loads of sugar and spooky stories normally do the trick, right?

COLE:

I think you're joking, but just in case...no.

DELANEY:

I'm teasing. We'll be fine, boss.

COLE:

Haven't heard that nickname in awhile.

DELANEY:

We're back to our "professional" relationship now, so I thought it would be fitting.

COLE:

It's always been more than that.

DELANEY:

You can't keep doing this to me.

COLE:

Doing what?

DELANEY:

> Acting like you care when you've
> already made up your mind about us.

IT'S LATE when I arrive home that night. The sun set a solid hour ago, yet the sky seems abnormally bright for the hour. My meltdown earlier in the day had me doing overtime to catch up. The downside of running your own business is that you can't have any off days. People's livelihoods depend on me. Running numbers for the remainder of the day did prove to be therapeutic in some odd way though.

My mom and Jude's words kept running through my head on repeat like a hamster on a wheel. I bulldozed Delaney with my insecurities and made a decision for both of us, a move I'm far from proud of. I regret not allowing her the chance to make up her own mind about our situation. For not fighting through my hang ups in order to be what she needed.

Which is why I need to see her, talk to her, make things up to her. Beg and cry at her feet if need be. Tell her I'm a damn mess but I'm also madly, stupidly in love with her.

My steel toe work boots thump across the hard-wood mirroring the sound of my heartbeat pounding in my chest. Approaching Delaney's door, I find it closed. The crack beneath is pitch black, indicating that she's probably asleep for the night. I find Ava's door the same and don't want to risk waking her. It kills me that I didn't get to say good night to my daughter like I have for almost every single night of her life.

After checking all the locks on the doors, and scanning one last time for any signs of Delaney being awake, I make my way to my bedroom to attempt the seemingly impossible task of sleeping. I know it won't come easy tonight, like it didn't last night.

I'm not used to this. Caring so much that it consumes every moment of my day and every facet of my brain.

Flipping the light switch near the door, a small table lamp illuminates the room. The wide space is dark and shadowy, but I feel every muscle still when I see them there, illuminated in the soft warm glow of the light.

Ava is spread out on my side of the bed, her tanned arms and legs extending like a starfish. It's a marvel how a small human can occupy so much space in an otherwise vast bed. Her usually wild hair is tamed into a single braid, with a dark strand escaping onto her forehead. A tiny snore, accompanied by a garble of sleep talk makes me want to hold her tight while she's still this little.

Delaney rests on the opposite end, curled up on her side, as compact as possible. It's as if she's folding into herself, shielding whatever vulnerabilities remain. While fast asleep, her angelic face forms a gentle pout.

It's as though she's dreaming about those who have wronged her, teetering on the edge of defeat.

Despite my best effort, I feel like my boots are glued to the floor. I can't stop watching the two girls I love the most in this world, so peaceful and perfect.

Suddenly, Delaney's blue eyes flutter open, and I become aware of how creepy I must look, standing beside the bed, staring with wide eyes as if I've seen two angels. Which, in all honesty, is entirely accurate.

Delaney simply stares right back through her half-closed dark lashes. The weight of it nearly knocks the wind from my chest like a punch to the gut.

She blinks again, clearing the fog. "Shit, sorry. Ava missed you and wanted to sleep in here. Guess I accidentally fell asleep too." She starts to sit up. "I'll go."

"No, it's fine. You stay. I still have to shower anyway. But I do want to talk to you."

With a nod, she looks me up and down, as if she's suspicious about whether I'm a dream or not. "Okay. Go shower first though."

I stand there for a beat before nodding as mechanical as a robot, forcing myself to move back down the hall and away from my two favorite people. The sight of them together confirms the epiphany I've had today.

That I've been reborn into a new version of myself. This version finds myself fighting back tears when I see the way Ava and Delaney's bond—as if they've known each other for their whole lives. This version of myself is aware that a love of this magnitude will completely change the trajectory of our lives. This version of myself will be a better man because the two people in my bed right now are my entire world.

I hurry to the bathroom, in a flurry of the thousand different emotions that have been coursing through my body in the last twenty-four hours. It's more than enough to leave me in an emotional hangover. I'm drained, yet wired, because I know that I need to talk to Delaney.

As I shut the water off in the shower, I hear my bedroom door creak open and close in the hallway, followed by the quiet sound of footsteps padding down the floor. I dry off in a frenzy to catch Delaney before she goes back to sleep. Throwing on gray sweatpants and a black shirt, I take long strides down the hall to find her.

But the sight of her closed door, and ocean sounds of her white noise machine from within, causes a pit in my stomach.

It feels crucial to apologize, to confess, to have her back. I almost can't bring myself to knock on her door at midnight and ruin her sleep for a second night in a row. I'm just selfish enough that I do it anyway, rapping the wood gently with my knuckles. A few seconds pass, and there's no answer. No sounds of her getting up from the bed.

The lack of response fills me with a mishmash of dread and guilt. Is she asleep, or upset with me and not wanting to talk?

Honestly, I wouldn't blame her.

Why should she believe me now? Why should she feel anything for me after the way I ended things? Delaney Emerson doesn't owe me a damn thing.

But fuck, I can't live out the rest of my life without at least trying to fight for her. Without telling her how completely in love I am with every facet of her.

Since I'm due back at work in five hours, we probably won't get the opportunity to talk for another day or two at this rate.

So all I can do is leave her a note and her favorite breakfast in our normal spot, while crossing my fingers that she'll be able to forgive me someday.

Chocolate croissant for you, and a muffin for Ava, in the pink box on the table.

I really need to talk to you later, by the way.

P.S. – I googled Ron Swanson and I'm not sure if I should take it as a compliment or insult that you said we share the same personality.

EVEN THOUGH I'M dead tired and running off of three hours of sleep and four cups of coffee, today has been off to a better start. Today isn't blazing hot, thanks to the cool Delta breeze that has picked up overnight. My crews are also happier because of the breakfast burritos I brought in from the taco truck around the corner.

Food fixes almost everything, so I'm crossing my fingers it can be the first step to mending things at home and at work.

My brain is still in hyperdrive though, wondering if my girls are up. If they've seen the breakfast I left for them and the note I left by the coffee pot.

My phone chimes and I should be ashamed for how fast I drop everything to dig my phone out of my back pocket.

DELANEY:

It's a compliment. Ron Swanson is my favorite.

DELANEY:

And speaking of favorites, thank you for the chocolate croissant. I didn't realize you knew that I love them.

COLE:

You were eating one the first time I saw you at Little Elm.

DELANEY:

Well, well, well. The truth comes out that you were watching me.

COLE:

If I say yes, I'll sound creepy. But yeah, busted. I definitely was.

DELANEY:

Here I thought you hated me in the beginning.

COLE:

The opposite.

COLE:

The first time I saw you I was speechless because of how drop dead gorgeous you are. Then when you opened your mouth and I heard your personality shine through you only got more beautiful. And to be honest, I also wanted to shove my dick into that smart mouth of yours.

DELANEY:

You should've told me, I'd probably have sucked your dick on the very first day.

COLE:

Stop giving me a boner at work.

DELANEY:

Oh sorry, I forgot. Professionalism only now.

COLE:

I need to talk to you tonight.

DELANEY:

I think you've said plenty. Let's forget anything ever happened and be civil until this is all over. Please.

DURING MY LUNCH BREAK, I meet Renee, a retired school teacher and family friend of my mother's, who has the experience to handle looking after my daughter. Once I learned she previously led a classroom of twenty-five kids, I knew a few hours after school would be a breeze for her.

Ava starts kindergarten in less than two weeks, and the thought of her starting her own little life outside of my own scares me to death. Change isn't my forte, and I have a sneaking suspicion that her starting school will be harder on me than her.

I'm relieved it's settled. Relieved there's a plan. But with everything up in the air with Delaney, I'm still a mess.

After sorting out work matters, I rush home, ensuring I'm back in time to put my daughter to bed and speak with Delaney.

While texting her today, I got the sense that I've been put back into the safe box of professionalism. But I know her well enough to sense that beneath her composure, she's tucked the pain away into a hidden corner.

Entering the entryway, Ava lunges into my arms like a pint-sized whirlwind with pigtails, clad in her mermaid swimsuit, drenching my clothes with her wet body and hair. "You're home!"

Delaney stands in the open concept kitchen, watching us with a small smile on her lips and arms crossed over her chest.

I spin Ava around a few times before setting her back on the floor. "Go get changed and then you can help me make asparagus, okay?"

She high-fives me in agreement before galloping to her room.

Standing nearby, Delaney looks stunning in her black one-piece swimsuit that molds to her figure. The cold A/C is blowing, causing her nipples to pebble against the thin fabric. My weakness around her is undeniable; just being near her stirs something inside me—a magnetic pull.

She's watching me, and I know she has something to say by the way she's biting her full bottom lip, working it back and forth with her top teeth.

"How are you?" I ask, closing the gap and leaning my elbows on the sleek countertop.

"I'm perfect. Great." Her eyes catch mine for a millisecond, before darting away. She smiles, but it doesn't reach her eyes. I know she's fibbing.

"Tell me the truth, Emerson."

"What do you expect me to say? Of course I'm not okay." She swipes tears away with a knuckle, looking pissed off as if her own eyes have betrayed her by reflecting how she's feeling internally.

The urge to bridge the gap and hug her close against my body is a battle I have to actively fight against. But after what I've done I don't think I have the privilege to do that anymore.

"Listen, I messed—"

Ava runs back into the room, twirling around in a unicorn costume, singing at the top of her lungs, wet hair still dripping onto the floor.

I shut my mouth, not finishing what I was about to say, so that she doesn't catch onto any tension between us. The conversation will have to wait until later.

Side by side in the kitchen, Ava and I team up to prepare dinner. Perched on a stool, she snaps asparagus spears with determined focus, treating them like brittle twigs. It's the only way I've found to get her into eating asparagus. As I ask about her day, she responds with a succession of stories, flitting from one topic to the next. Her chatter is like a whirlwind, and though my brain struggles to keep up, I could listen to her talk in circles for hours.

"How do you feel about school starting soon?" I ask, taking the asparagus spear from her and adding it to the baking sheet.

"I don't know. Will there be kids there?"

"Lots of them."

Squinting her eyes, she debates her level of excitement. "Then yes, I'm excited. I want to make friends. *So* many friends." She sprays oil on the vegetables while I sprinkle salt. "Dad, is Delaney still going to be my nanny?"

"No, she is going back to her old job soon. Grandma's friend, Renee, will be picking you up from school and staying here until I get home. I met her today, you'll like her. She's nice."

"Probably not as nice as Laney though…"

"No, maybe not that nice. Delaney is special."

She turns to me, her face very serious. "You need to make her stay."

My heart twists. "You love her a lot, huh?"

"The most ever. Do you love her a lot too?"

"Yeah." I pause, unsure if I should be admitting something of this magnitude to my five year old. "Yeah, I do. A lot."

Ava nods, satisfied we agree and are on the same page about our deep love for Delaney. Then she breaks into a long-winded story about a dinosaur dream she had last night that I'm almost certain she's entirely making up on the spot.

Once dinner is in the oven, Ava begs for an episode of the show with the talking dog. I turn it on, grateful for a minute to finally speak with Delaney alone.

Earlier when I asked her if she was okay, I saw her happy facade shatter like broken glass.

If only she knew she didn't have to pretend to be happy. If only she knew I love every part of her, the vivacious parts she thinks are unlovable and the murky portions that she buries deep down.

I need to make this better.

Standing out in the hall, I knock once on the wood of her closed door before entering. What I see is like a knife to my stomach.

Delaney doesn't even look up as she folds her clothes into neat piles and places them in the large gray suitcase. She's sitting with criss-crossed legs in the middle of the room, her belongings grouped in stacks on the cream rug.

In her quiet vulnerability and palpable sadness, she seems lost. I stand frozen, a silent witness to her slipping away even further.

This is all my fucking fault. This is what I said I wanted and knew would happen.

I attempt to clear the panic from my voice. "Going somewhere?"

She keeps folding, one shirt after another, not sparing me a glance. "Yes. It's for the best."

Silence spans across the room, both of us not talking.

"Look at me, Emerson."

My stubborn girl keeps her head held high, eyes down on her task, looking everywhere but me.

I walk to her, crouching down to her level on the floor. Using my forefinger and thumb, I delicately grasp her heart-shaped chin to gently turn her gaze to mine.

Dropping my forehead to hers, she instantly melts into my touch like clay.

"Don't leave. Please. Stay here." Touching her again for the first time in forty-eight hours has reverted me back to sounding like a caveman.

"And why should I do that?" She closes her eyes, her forehead still resting against mine, weary and grief-stricken. "You already made up your mind about us—about me."

My hand slides to the back of her neck as I pull her head to my shoulder. I feel her tears soak my shirt as her body trembles in my arms.

"I want you. You belong here. This is your home."

"But you said—"

"Ignore what I said. I was an insecure coward not thinking straight. I'm so sorry. Please forgive me, sunshine. I want this, I want *you*."

As if a sudden realization of my toxicity has hit her, she rips herself away from my arms. Dropping her face into her trembling hands, it's as though her body is betraying her, shaking uncontrollably. "Leave me alone, please. I need time to think this through."

I'm gutted, but I know I deserve it. This isn't a reverse uno card I can lay out to undo all the damage I've done. If I lose her I have no one to blame but myself.

Standing on heavy legs, I walk to the doorway, leaning against the jamb of the door. She wipes her eyes on the sleeve of her white shirt, the mascara leaving dark streaks on the fabric—still not daring to look in my direction. With a big exhale, she goes right back to work, packing away her belongings into a suitcase far too small for the things she's accumulated in the time she's lived here.

Right on cue, Ava calls my name down the hall to fix the volume for her. It's my signal to get the hell out.

But I'm torn as I stand there watching my free-spirited woman turned inside out.

If Delaney leaves, so does my heart.

She's it for me. She's my endgame.

And now I need to prove that I won't abandon her like everyone else has.

32

DELANEY

Taking the cryo rubber face mask out of its foil package, I stick it onto my face. It's a rubbery looking, bright pink mask that can only be best described as borderline horrifying. Once again, skincare has proven to be my always faithful companion. Firming collagen will never abandon me, so long as I keep purchasing it from the makeup store.

Ever since Cole told me we're over, I've been on autopilot. Fully functioning, while simultaneously having an out of body experience. I smile just the same, make casual small talk and laugh just the same—but inside I'm running on empty, completely drained and tired.

It's easier to pretend to be happy so that no one takes notice of a deeper problem rooted inside—that a piece of me is so dysfunctional and broken that everyone runs away.

He was the only person in years to give me hope. Even though he never 100 percent told me he was in, I felt it like a sixth sense. I *knew*.

There's no denying a connection that's so solid and reliable that you can feel it in the marrow of your bones.

Then he burst the bubble and I felt myself detach, free falling in all the foolish anticipation I let myself dream about.

Last night, I packed the majority of my belongings into suitcases. I didn't even recognize myself when I started stress-folding my clothes into tidy piles. Jessica would have been proud, but it's not me. I don't fold clothes. I shove them in with zero shits and sit on top of the luggage to zip it closed.

After trying my best to act like everything was okay after he ended things, I finally cracked. I'm like Humpty Dumpty. I fell and all my innards came spilling out, and no one can ever put me back together again. At least not like how I was when I thought he would never leave me.

I pour myself a cup of steaming coffee, still in my freaky little face mask, when I hear the high-pitched scream. The unexpected sound makes me jump, causing my mug of coffee to spill all over the counter and the notepad nearby. The scream starts up again and when I turn around, Ava is pointing at me, yelling, "Monster!"

My chest heaves, laughter wanting to spill out, but I hold it together. Peeling the face mask off gets another fresh round of screams—so loud and piercing that I'm surprised it doesn't shatter the tall windows.

"Banana, it's me. It's Delaney." Once I have both sections peeled off, Ava stands there, eyes bugging out from her scare while she inspects me head-to-toe.

"Oh." She walks closer, staring at the pink rubber lookalike material dangling from my fingers. "Did you steal a monster's face?"

"No, silly. It's a face mask. It's good for my skin. I'm sorry it scared you though."

She pokes it with one finger. "Can I wear one? I want to be a scary pink monster too."

"I don't think you can wear this one, it's for grownup skin. But we can make a homemade face mask and have a fancy spa day, what do you say?"

Like a night to day difference, she yells again, happy this time. "That's the best idea ever! Let's do it."

Ava grabs the ingredients I ask her to find—a cucumber, plain yogurt, and honey—while I scoot a stool over to reach the blender from the tall cabinet. After throwing the ingredients into the blender's plastic jar, we cover our ears from the noisy hum of the spinning blades, then proceed to stick our tongues out at each other while our ingredients combine.

My heart concurrently overflows with love and mourning, knowing that times like this exist, but that we won't get to experience them together again. A blissful fleeting moment.

When the grinding is finished, the homemade

product looks white and creamy like mayonnaise. Pouring it all into a bowl, Ava dips her finger in and licks it. "Maybe we can use this to dip carrots in later too."

"Good idea. Now come here, so I can slather some veggie dip on your cute face."

She giggles and squirms like there are a million ants in her pants as I smooth the mixture onto her olive skin. "It feels cold and slimy and I love it." Her pink tongue pokes out, licking the face mask around her mouth. Case in point of making it with edible ingredients.

I smooth the white mixture onto my own face before snapping a picture of the two of us. Big smiles with white teeth, creamy face masks, messy buns, silly expressions. I can't believe a five year old has become my best friend, but my love for her has blossomed naturally throughout the months. We understand each other. Two irrepressible girls in a composed society.

On the acacia poolside table, I place a wooden charcuterie tray filled with strawberries, crackers, and cheese, alongside two pool cups full of orange juice. The morning is gorgeous. Warm, with trees swaying in the cool breeze. The sounds of birds and wildlife in the distant, sprawling hills shining in the fresh sunlight. It's like the day hasn't realized I'm nursing a broken heart. While I'm feeling like a storm is raging on the inside, the outside has decided to be all gorgeous and show off its organic beauty.

Ava bounces up and down with excitement, before she settles into the reclined chair like royalty. I place a cold cucumber on each of her eyes, igniting a round of giggles which make the slices roll off.

I settle into the chair beside her, with a glass of orange juice in one hand, and a ripe strawberry in the other. "So how do you feel? Relaxed?"

"Oh yes. *Very* relaxed." She takes a bite out of the cucumber slice before placing it back on her eyelid with a begrudged sigh. "My dad needs to have a spa day so he can relax too."

The mention of Cole makes my heart stutter. "Hm. Do you think he'd wear a fancy face mask like us though?"

"Dad will do anything we want because he loves me. And you."

"You're right, I do love you, Banana."

Her dimples appear, a spitting image of her father's. "I know you do. That's not what I meant though." She sits there, serene with her eyes closed, like she's well acquainted with the luxurious spa life. "My dad said he loves you. He told me last night."

I feel the blood drain from my face at her innocent confession. Cole loves me? And he told Ava that?

"Is that so?" I reply, pretending to be nonchalant, while really I'm holding back the hoards of questions that I want to, but can't, ask my tiny best friend.

"Yeah. He said he did. *A lot*," she replies, dropping

bombs left and right while the cucumbers slide in opposite directions on her face.

I shove the revelation to the back of my brain, unable to emotionally process it at the moment. Instead I focus on staying in fun nanny-friend mode. It's easy to do with the rate we jump from activity to activity.

After our spa day, we go swimming, drifting around on donut shaped floats in the lukewarm water. A squirt gun fight ensues, that leaves our bellies sore from laughing for a solid hour.

Once we head back inside, we go our separate ways to change for a trip to the mall. Cole asked me last week to take Ava back to school shopping. As I remember the look of pure relief on his face when he saw how excited I was to do the job, it makes my chest pang with ache. *This is how it could be. Spa days and back to school shopping, and coming home to a family everyday.* I let myself imagine it for a fraction of a second.

It feels good. It feels right. It feels scary to open myself back up to the possibility of it.

After changing into a red floral sundress and combing through the knots in my hair, I go grab the credit card he left out to use for the shopping trip. It's next to the stainless steel coffee maker, with a puddle of the spilled brown liquid beside it. As I wipe the mess I'd forgotten about with a paper towel, I see a note covered in splashes of coffee.

An entire page full of Cole's small boxy letters scribbled on the ivory paper of the notepad:

I'm so sorry. I got scared that I wasn't good enough for you. I thought I would be doing you a favor by setting you free.

And while I still believe that you deserve more than a stubborn man like me, I realize it wasn't my decision to make.

I'm yours, if you'll have me.

I can't offer you fun, or adventure, or sunshine and rainbows.

But I can tell you that every day I'll choose you.

I will be dependable, loyal, and supportive every day.

I will tell you that you're so absolutely, unbelievably gorgeous every day.

I will love you to my very core every day.

I'm not a loud person. But I realize now that the loudest way to love someone is by making them feel seen and understood.

I see you and I understand you, Delaney.

Take your time thinking about it. Because

if you decide you want to stay, to be mine,
we have all the time in the world.

I tear the page off the notepad with so much force it's like the paper has personally offended me. Holding the note closer to my face as if I'm plagued by blurry vision, I read it again. And again. And again. The actual number of times I reread those black lines of ink is embarrassing. When I think I've comprehended what he's telling me, I realize I don't. Which causes my eyes to lock onto the words again. To read again.

Being meticulous, I fold the paper into a small square and tuck it into the safety of my pocket.

Maybe I'm a fool, but I know what I need to do.

I've been lost for years, circling around to find my way, seeking out what's right.

This note is my map, turning the bewilderment to certainty.

I know where to go now.

I sit amongst the sea of paper shopping bags, waiting for Cole to come home. He texted me hours ago letting me know he'd be home late again.

Ava was exhausted after our full day of shopping. She was practically begging to go to sleep early so she could wear her new puppy print pajamas.

The highlight of my week was getting to see her face light up as she made important fashion choices—like if she prefers a dinosaur or kitten on her shirt, or if she wants the pink stripe or yellow flower pants.

Spoiler alert, we bought it all.

In my defense, when I had asked Cole what the budget was, he waved me off and told me to not worry about it and have fun. Problem is we may have just had a little *too* much fun.

The key in the lock jolts me awake, my spine straightening like a zipper. Cole opens the door as he scrapes his work boots on the coir bristles of the mat before entering. He strides into the dark house, flipping on the lamp closest to the doorway. He looks dead tired, shoulders slumped forward and another shade darker from working in the hot August sun.

My body feels alive at the sight of him. Every bone, muscle, tendon, and nerve in my body becomes hyper aware of his presence—feeling as if they've been injected with a staggering hit of dopamine. I'm trying to play it cool, anchoring myself to the floor so I don't take off running and jumping into his arms.

The hurt my heart endured days ago, that I thought was irreparable, has been mended and stitched back together with each line he wrote in that damn note. One thing I'm certain of is that no man alive has written a letter so full of unfiltered love and vulnerability like the one Cole left for me today.

I'm sitting on the area rug, out of sight in total darkness. A tall glass of wine is cradled between my hands as I sit here mulling over everything I want to say to him.

My body is buzzing like an electrical current knowing that he will walk in and see me at any minute. It's the anticipation of the last week coming in full force.

The light switches on and Cole startles, grabbing at his chest, when he sees me. "Holyfuckingshit—"

"Welcome home, boss." I take a sip of my white wine, smiling over the rim of the glass and feeling giddy on the kick of spooking him. I get too much amusement over startling grown men and watching their souls temporarily leave their body.

"Why are you sitting in the dark? Are you okay?" His tired eyes look me up and down for any sign of hurt. Once he sees that I'm perfectly fine, his eyes narrow. "Are you going to murder me?"

"Someone's been watching too many true crime docs with me," I tease, standing up from the plush rug to walk over to him.

Time feels like it's at a standstill with every step further I approach. He stands there, with his hands tucked into the front pockets of his jeans. As if he's trying to physically restrain himself from reaching out and touching me. I'm close to him now, the closest we've been in days. Those green-brown irises burning a trail along my skin as we stand there, inches apart, simply staring into each other's eyes without a word spoken.

The weight of our stare only builds the dense tension licking between us. His gaze drags up and down the entirety of me, tortured and hopeful at the proximity.

Unable to hold it in anymore, a slow smile spreads across my face. He must take it as a good sign because his mouth mirrors mine, one dimple indenting his cheek in the process.

I take one last sip of my crisp white wine before placing it on the small end table beside us. "I saw your note."

"Yeah?" His long fingers grasp the back of his neck. "Look, I understand if you don't want..."

My hand wraps around his forearm, one finger stroking the bone in his wrist, causing him to freeze mid-speech. I lift his arm gently to slide his hand out of the safeguard of his pocket and lace my small fingers through his large ones. "I want you. I want us. I want this."

Cole's exhale feels significant, like he'd been holding one giant breath for days and can finally release the oxygen from his lungs. He slams me into the wall of his chest, both arms snaking around my body as his face buries into my hair. "I'm sorry, Delaney. I'm so damn sorry."

"I know. And if you do that again, I swear I'll put fingernail clippings in that box of bran cereal that only you like."

"Once again, I have no idea how you come up with

these things. But I can promise you it'll never happen again. I'm in this for good, if you'll have me."

My heart pounds against his chest, the dust of our fall out settling with an ease I'm not acquainted with. I shouldn't be so trusting, with him or anyone for that matter. Yet for some reason, I can't help but believe every word he says. It's like a sixth sense that washes over me, coaxing the insecurities that have lived deep inside me for years.

Raising our intertwined hands to his full lips, he places a soft kiss on my knuckles. "Come with me. I still want to talk about it."

I nod, as his hand gently squeezes mine before he leads me down the long hallway to his bedroom. As we cross the threshold to the room, it dawns on me that I no longer feel like a stranger in a spare room, or a houseguest for the night. It feels like I'm home.

Cole surprises me by scooping me up, one hand on my back, while his other hooks under my knees. He walks over to the bed in the corner of the room and plops me down into it, as he always does. "No more sleeping in the spare room. I want you back in here with me."

Looking at him, I want nothing more than his mouth on mine, and the warmth of his body pressed against me. It's been too long. Not kissing Cole for three days is three days too many.

He leans down to my eye level, placing one hand on each side of my hips and caging me in against the mattress. My heart is in my throat with the anticipation of him touching me. "Are you going to kiss me now, or do you plan on torturing me?"

His eyes zero in on my lips. "I wasn't sure if I was allowed to quite yet."

"You should know by now you can do anything you want with me."

Before I finish my sentence, his mouth is on mine. I part my lips automatically, inviting him into my mouth. Our tongues swirl together, as he deepens the kiss. It's everything—full of months of need and want, vulnerability and eagerness. Apologies and anticipation.

He murmurs against my lips. "Trust me. There are a lot of things I plan on doing to you." Arching up from the plush of the comforter, I press my breasts against his hard chest. His arm weaves around my waist as he pulls me flush against him.

He's hard, straining against his jeans. I rock my hips into him, grinding against him. His voice is a deep grumble. "I told you that you were trying to kill me."

"Death by sex. If you're going to go, might as well go while getting some dick action." My hands reach for the button of his jeans, but his hand grabs mine, stopping me. My heart slams on its brakes, thinking he's going to deny me. Again.

"Shit. I need to take a shower really fast. I worked outside all day, and the things I plan on doing to you require me...to smell better."

"Are you sure this isn't your way of rejecting me?" I

try to make my comment sound like a light-hearted joke, but my insecurities bleed through my tone.

Standing before me, Cole's intense gaze locks onto mine, his expression turning feral.

He grabs my face, one calloused thumb stroking my temple before he brings his mouth to my ear. "Emerson, I'm planning on fucking ruining you tonight. I promise."

He doesn't even wait for my response before he saunters off with more confidence than I've ever seen from him. The next seven minutes feel like torture. And I know he's gone for exactly seven minutes because I stare at the clock on the wall the entire time he's gone. Contemplating if I should get naked or let him do the honors of undressing me.

When he reappears, his hair is damp and freshly combed. He's shirtless and in nothing but a pair of gray sweats that I'm surprised even come in a size tall enough for him. The substantial outline of his dick bulging through the fabric would make any sane person take a second appreciative glance. Solid and tan, Cole's chest is firm, his stomach smooth. I've never seen him work out once; he's sculpted from the physical labor of his job alone.

I bite my bottom lip as I continue to ogle him. "I've missed this...seeing you shirtless."

Without missing a beat, he lowers himself onto his knees, bringing us to eye level on his low-profile bed. "I've missed everything about you."

My breath hitches as he kisses me, hard, before lifting my flimsy tank up and off me. He grabs a handful of my breast, his thumb stroking the pink nub of my nipple before he lowers his mouth to it. "I've missed these perfect tits." His other hand slips beneath my sleep shorts, sliding right past the fabric of my lace panties. He dips one finger into me. "I've missed this pussy that gets so fucking wet for me."

Everything about him is demanding in the most tender possible manner. The way that he groans into my mouth when I grope his erection through his sweats. How he presses his pelvis against my grasp, egging me on, to keep going. His mouth trailing down my neck, nipping my collar bones, tasting every inch of me that he can.

Cole works my wetness in and out with one finger, and then adds a second. I feel myself winding tighter, getting closer. I'm starved for more of him which has me freeing his cock from the sweatpants that have been torturing me with how they've tented from his erection for the last several minutes. When I finally wrap my hand around him, his head tilts back as he grows impossibly hard.

Suddenly, Cole removes his fingers from me. I moan in complaint about the lack of contact, squirming like it might give me an inch of relief. "Keep touching me. Please."

He hooks a finger into the waistband of my shorts,

pulling them down in one swift motion. "I'm going to fuck you now, Delaney."

I didn't think today could possibly get any better, but apparently I was wrong. Because today will forever go down as the day Cole and I *finally* have sex.

Nodding toward me, he instructs, "Lie on your back and spread your legs." He slides his pants down before stepping out of them. The muscles in his arm bulges as he grabs his erection and begins to fist it. "I want to see your face when you take every inch of my dick for the first time."

I scramble to do as he says, lying back on the mattress and letting my knees fall to the side. My whole body lights up like Christmas has come early. Electrified and magnetized for the man that's looking at me like no one else has before. He slides between my open legs and opens his nightstand drawer, grabbing a small bottle of lube and a condom. Right as his fingers move to rip the foil packet open, I reach out to stop his hand. "I have an IUD and I've been recently tested. If you want to...you know..."

"Are you asking me to fuck you bare?"

"I'm asking to feel as close as possible to you."

The affection blossoms across his face, before his scorching stare replaces it once again. "It's been years for me. But I'm clear too."

With that, he flicks the cap open on the bottle of lube, rubbing a few drops along his length before lining himself up. Brushing the smooth head of his dick against my clit, he spreads the wetness that seems to quickly accumulate every time I'm around him. Reflexively, my hips rock forward greedy to get more.

It's the moment we've both been wanting for months. I'm holding my breath, still not positive if it'll happen. If he'll let that last piece of himself, that he's protected tooth and nail, go. But then Cole looks right into my eyes as he pushes himself inside me, with a slow unmistakable confidence. With every inch deeper, I arch a little further into the mattress. I exhale but it comes out as a moan, flicking on something feral in his expression.

He bottoms out, filling me all the way up, stretching me to a point that's borderline painful, yet intensely pleasurable.

"Cole, oh my god," I gasp. It's almost too much, but he takes it slow, giving me time to adjust to him.

"That's it, sunshine. You take my dick so good."

He braces a forearm on each side of my shoulders and leans forward to kiss me—moving in and out of me at a slow, deliberate pace. As if he's savoring every moment of this as much as I am. As his speed increases, I whimper into his mouth. His reaction turns from gentle to urgent and rough.

"That's my girl. You like it when I fuck you, don't you? Being so full of me you can barely breathe?"

"Yes," I say on an exhale—almost unable to get the words out, let alone have my brain function with an appropriate response.

Tucking me into the curve of his arm, he thrusts into me hard. His mouth is on mine for a moment again, before he pulls back to admire my face while he continues to fuck me.

The tip of his nose drags up my jaw, stubble rough against my cheek. "Fuck, you're gorgeous. You know that?"

Every word he says pulls me that much closer to the edge. Strumming my body in a different sense than just physically. That tension in my belly builds up at a rate faster than I expect. I'm already right there, ready to come. Part of me is ready for that burst of ecstasy, while the other half wants to prolong it.

I try to get the words out, try to let him know I'm so damn close to coming. But I can't speak because I'm being fucked better than I ever have before. Cole must see it, as he always sees everything when it comes to me, because he jumps into action to get me to that finish line.

He hooks my knees over his broad shoulders, and grabs my hips, lifting everything except for my shoulders off of the bed. "That's it. Come for me, Delaney." The new position deepens the penetration of his hard length. That, paired with the unrelenting speed that Cole drives into me and his thumb rubbing circles on my clit, has me crying out his name. I come undone for him in every way. My fingers curl into the white duvet, as my entire body erupts into an euphoric state. I see him watching it all happen with the utmost look of intoxication, as if he's drunk off the sight of how he's perfectly unraveled me. The sounds of his fast thrusts slapping skin-to-skin echo throughout the room.

The rush of finishing hits me like a crescendo—building up to that extravagant impact of bliss. I feel myself tighten around him as he pulses inside of me. We're on cloud nine together, in some far off dreamlike state, with his dick still inside of me as I take every last drop of his come. His face tips to the sky as he finishes with a groan.

Pulling out, he collapses his body onto mine. His nose tucks into the crook between my shoulder and neck as we lay there, breathing like we've ran a high-altitude marathon. Every last bit of our energy expended in the last ten minutes. The brunt of his weight is supported by the side of his body resting on the mattress. One heavy arm is slung across my torso, a beefy leg curling around both of mine, gathering me against him like I'm his security blanket. The weight of his body feels like a private safe haven. Hard, yet soft, and warm. Tangled into a pile of bare skin and deep exhalations.

My brain is attempting to play catch up, on a slow rewind to hash out what the fuck just happened. Cole's magical dick has me stunned speechless for perhaps the first time in my life.

"You okay there?" he mumbles into my neck.

"If I say I'm not, will you fuck me like that again?"

I feel his cheek pulse against my shoulder with a

smile that I can't see. "Don't worry, there's a lot more of that coming for you. I've thought of at least a thousand different ways I plan to make you come with my dick."

"We better get to it then." I make a move to grab his already almost recovered semi.

"Give me a few more minutes. I am old after all," he laughs.

I squeeze him against my palm. "You sure don't *feel* too old."

"How cliche would it be if I said it's because you make me feel young again?"

"Well, you know I love a good cliche."

A beat of silence passes and I can almost hear the sound of the gears turning in Cole's head.

He sighs, the breath of it warm on my skin. "I think we should talk about...you know, everything...before we do it again."

For as much as I prefer to gloss over confrontation and awkward conversations, I know this talk is needed. To move forward we need to clear the debris from the path.

This is why I know Cole might be it for me. That I know maybe I can have a real, healthy, adult relationship with him. Because I want to stay. I want to get messy and hash it out and keep going.

Past Delaney would have been out of here faster than a Formula 1 driver. Present Delaney is ready to communicate in order to come out stronger, together.

I lift the bedsheet to take one more glance at his

bare ass, hoping it will give me the courage and maturity I've been sorely lacking for the last three decades. "Okay, let's do it. Let's talk."

Then I slap his ass cheeks one time for good measure. Because I can only be *so* responsible. And it is a good ass.

33

<h1 style="text-align:center">COLE</h1>

The crack of Delaney smacking my ass rings through the air. My skin tingles where she spanks me, a red handprint already splotching into view. I nip the soft tissue of her earlobe with my teeth. "You're going to pay for that later."

"Yes, sir," she says, in that breathy voice that always makes me instantly hard.

The blood rushes to my dick just as I expected, making me hard again as I try to order it to stand down. From the first time I saw Delaney, I knew having sex with her would be earth shattering with the potential to ruin me forever.

What I didn't expect is to feel resuscitated. That broken part of me healing and coming to life as I came buried deep inside of her. This feeling of being completely consumed in one another could never get old.

She pushes herself up onto one elbow, and rests her head onto her hand, as long blonde tresses fall angelically around her face. Reaching out, I grab her free hand with my own. Touching her at all times only feels right, particularly in a moment like this.

My thumb swipes over the smooth skin of her hand. "Basically what I want to say is I'm a coward. I thought it'd be easier to leave you now than have you leave me later, once you decided you're bored with this life. We're...different from one another. We both can admit that."

She smiles. "Yeah, there may be some truth to that. But it's not a bad thing. In my eyes at least."

"Last week I thought there was no chance in hell someone as perfect as you could be happy and satisfied long term, with some boring, grumpy asshole like me. But then I realized being with you is worth the risk of getting my heart broken. As long as I get the chance to give this, and give you my best shot, then that's what counts."

"I hope you know I'm not as perfect as you may think."

"Faults and all, you're perfect to me."

She won't meet my eyes. Instead, she becomes extremely interested in picking at a loose thread on the knit blanket.

I kiss the skin of her bare shoulder. "Tell me what's on your mind."

Delaney pauses picking at the thread and stares

straight at me. The look in her eyes is serious and vulnerable and tender. "There's a reason everyone leaves me."

Her self-deprecating vulnerability stabs me in the heart like an arrow. She believes that something is wrong with *her* and not with the assholes who have abandoned her in the past. And I won't have that.

"You're not the problem, Delaney. It's them. Because *you* are an angel...to me, you're a literal angel who's transformed my life from the first second I spoke to you. You love as deep as the ocean, and laugh as loud as a bell. You inject happiness into everything you're a part of. I wish you could see yourself how I see you. How everyone sees you. Because every bit of you is magic."

She blinks those dark lashes, fighting back the tears that are pooling in the corners of her eyes. "And if I'm too broken?"

"Look at me, sunshine." Those blue eyes lift to mine, this rare side of her cracked open and raw for me to see. I run my hand through her honey locks as I bring my forehead to rest on hers. We both close our eyes and breathe in one another. "Everyone, in some way or another, is broken. Every single person on this earth is a mess in their own special kind of fucked up way. I think it comes down to finding the person that can grow something beautiful in those darkest parts of ourselves. You're exactly like that for me, and I want to be for you too. Together we make each other whole again."

Delaney makes a contemplative noise before she lets out a shaky exhale. "So this is for real then? You aren't going to try and leave me again?"

I grab her hand and rest it on my heart so she can feel the way it's pounding out of my chest, rhythmically steady. Just like my personality...anxious, but reliable. So she knows that even though I'm scared as hell, I'm here, and I'm trying. I'm putting it all out there for her to see and take.

"I'm yours...I think I always have been, from that first moment I ever laid eyes on you. I tried to keep my distance, tried to not love you. But it's impossible. Because I love you to my core. Every facet of you. The bright, the dark, the everything in between. You're it for me."

In one swift motion her plush lips land on mine. She kisses me, pouring every feeling she has running through her into the kiss. I match her, going in for it with zero inhibitions. My hand grips the back of her neck, pulling her into me. The softness of her body pressed against mine sends a jolt of electricity through me, her faint moan mingling with the warmth of our entwined breaths.

"I love you so goddamn much," I mumble against her mouth.

She pulls back and looks at me. So stunning it knocks the wind from my lungs. Bee stung lips, and big ocean eyes, and messy hair. A cheeky smile blooms on her face. "Tell me that again."

My hands grab her by her waist as I drag her body into me, setting her round ass on my lap. Wrapping my arms around her small frame, I hug her close. Her shoulders shake with a pleased giggle as I leave a trail of delicate kisses along her neck. My mouth lands close to her ear, and I feel the goosebumps rise from her skin. "I love you, Delaney."

She turns around to face me now. Her legs straddle my thighs, surely feeling how much I'm getting off on telling her that I love her. The tips of her fingers run through my hair, caressing me with so much affection it nearly does me in. Her touch alone makes my eyes want to roll to the back of my head. I could sit here, just like this all day, and it would never get old.

With her fingers still tangled in my hair, she tilts my face down causing our eyes to lock. "I love you too. So goddamn much."

When Delaney says it, repeating my same words back, she can't help but smile. Not any small, coy smile. No, it's the one that beats the rest of them. A smile that makes her eyes sparkle like the ocean at sunset. So fucking beautiful it makes my chest hurt.

The way it rolls off her tongue, as if she's never been more confident about a statement coming out of her mouth. My chest hums in response to her words. A warmth coiling in my belly, creeping up my body and springing a new awareness that we're crossing into new territory.

It strikes me that I'm not even nervous. Instead, I

can't wait to see how our future unfolds. In some sense, I know this is it. Some would say it's too early to call it. But I've never been more sure that this is my forever. With her, with Ava—all of us together as a family.

Delaney wiggles her shoulders to scoot deeper into the nook of my arms. She rests her head against my chest with a satisfied sigh. "Now that we're all in love and having sex...is it too soon to ask you to do me while you wear your backwards hat?"

A laugh bubbles up and out of me, surprised at her request. My hats are worn to keep the sun or my hair out of my eyes—practical. Yet to her, it's like porn. I can see the way her eyes go all warm and dark when she sees me in a hat that I've turned around. It's why I love wearing one around her so often. I get off on seeing her all hot and bothered for me. "You should know by now that I'll do anything you want, Emerson. Especially when it comes to fucking you."

"Cole Campbell. You're such a softie." She kisses my cheek, then my nose, then the corner of my jaw. "You're so lovable it pains me."

"Most people say I'm a pain in their ass."

She winks. "Don't sell yourself short, you're also that. A very sexy and lovable pain in my ass."

I tickle her ribs, as the sound of her full on belly laugh echo in the room. "I should stick my dick in that smart ass mouth of yours," I growl into her ear.

Pushing me onto my back, she drags her head down near my crotch. I'm harder than a rock watching her ass in the air, wiggling around like a lion on the prowl. Her lips trace a line along my length. The warm air of her breath and pressure of her plush lips make the air hiss through my teeth.

We have sex, multiple times throughout the night—my hand tugging her ponytail and spanking her ass. Delaney riding my dick and taking control. Taking our time, enveloped and savoring every moment.

There's an infinite depth of desire for each other, fueled by the pent up lust of the last three months.

You'd think we'd get physically exhausted, but that spark that's been kindling for months has us all over each other as if the world is ending and this is our horny send-off.

We relish every iota of each other throughout the dark, starlit hours. She lies down telling me stories of her wild child days that have me smiling until my cheeks hurt. Her cold feet curl under my legs, her hands staying wedged between her cheek and the pillow.

For us both, the realization that this isn't temporary is setting in. Our summer fling has ended, having morphed into a deeper relationship that hopefully lasts until my dying breath.

It's not missed on me that I have the honor of loving her and being loved by her. Delaney Emerson is a rarity. She's the gorgeous human equivalent to winning the lottery or a rare astronomical event.

Somewhere in the chaos of the last week, I've

learned that insecurities have the power to take root and alter reality. Twisting it into some ugly, distorted doubt that threatens all the good things in your life.

But I've found that you don't have to listen to those doubts. You can actively choose to tune them out and dive headfirst into the good that you're still not quite sure you deserve. It will feel terrifying, and risky, and unnatural embracing it. But with a bit of luck, and a lot of love, it will yield something so extraordinary that it's beyond your wildest dreams.

And that's what Delaney is.

My wildest dream come to life.

34

DELANEY

"When are we going to be there?" Ava asks for the tenth time. "I *hate* long car rides."

Cole's hands clasp and unclasp the steering wheel before glancing at his daughter in the rearview mirror. "We've only been in the car for eleven minutes. Besides...this'll be worth it. Trust me."

"I don't think anything will be worth a long car ride. I want out already. *Please.*" Ava groans, rolling her head back dramatically. She locks eyes with me as I smile at her from the front passenger seat. "Tell me where we're going, Laney."

"I have no clue. Your dad is being super duper secretive. Where do you think he's taking us? To the bank? To go watch golf? To go in search of some type of new drill?"

"Wow, am I really that boring?" Cole's eyes crinkle

with a smile that makes his dimples pop. He's sporting his classic navy backwards hat, that holds wisps of dark hair away from his face. His skin glows golden under the sunlight radiating through the windshield. He's a total smokeshow that makes me want to drop my panties for him.

"Good thing Laney is your *girlfriend* now, Dad. She can teach you how to be fun." An excited smile showing all of Ava's pearly white teeth takes over her face.

Cole wasted no time in telling her the good news. He took her out for a father-daughter doughnut date this morning and told her that her father and I are dating. That I'll be staying and living in the house with them. But most importantly that nothing will change for Ava. She will always be the number one priority, no matter what.

Her reaction was described as the equivalent to someone's favorite team winning the Super Bowl. Apparently, all of the fellow customers inside Lawson's Donuts also heard the good news via Ava jumping up and down and shouting her approval at the top of her lungs.

When we discussed how to tell Ava, we suspected her reaction would be happy. We just didn't know she'd be so thoroughly invested that as soon as she came home, she'd set to work making pictures of stick figure Cole and Delaney's wedding.

To be honest, the thought of marrying Cole makes me giddy. I'll never admit it in a million years since I do have a very important badass image to uphold after all. Word can't spread that Delaney the man-eater has gone soft. So soft, I'm basically mush at this point.

When I group text Madi and Ella about the recent developments today they could see through the *but we're not rushing anything* bullshit from a mile away. *Bet you'll be engaged within the year,* Ella had text. Madi responded with, *More like married within the year.*

We plan to take our time enjoying each other and dating. But this morning after Cole made me come twice within ten minutes, I jokingly said *marry me* in my dazed post-orgasm state. He arched his eyebrow and said in that confident, no bullshit voice of his *I'm planning on it.* Then his mouth twitched with amusement while his eyes ate up how my face turned a deep shade of pink in embarrassment and let's be honest...a healthy dose of hopefulness.

When another five minutes of driving passes and we pull off on the next exit, I begin to recognize our surroundings in the rural countryside. There are rows and rows of tall yellow sunflowers. The orchard of sunny blooms blur together as we pass by them. If we take a right on the road up ahead it will only take us to two places. My favorite plant nursery or the beloved animal shelter that we volunteer at. An inkling has my head whipping in Cole's direction. His head is turned dutifully toward the road, but his eyes take a quick glance at my sudden reaction.

"Um...are we going where I think we're going?" I

whisper. Ava is distracted in the backseat, singing a song she made up about the ridiculously long fifteen minute drive she's had to endure.

With our hands intertwined, he brushes the back of my hand with his thumb. "You'll have to wait and see," he replies, a smug smile playing on his lips.

"Ugh, I hate surprises."

"Says the woman who loves surprising people."

My eyes narrow at him. "Is this payback for your surprise party?"

"No." He pulls into the parking lot of Lawson SPCA, tires crunching under the loose gravel. "This is the start of a new chapter. For all *four* of us."

Mentally doing the math to double check that there are in fact only three of us in this car, I make a squeal that I should be very embarrassed by, but am not. We're here to adopt a motherfucking dog and I could not be more in love with Cole than I am at this moment.

Realizing that we've come to a stop, Ava glances up and out of her window. "Dad...is this the surprise?! Please tell me this is the surprise. And *please* do not let it be cleaning up poop like Laney always has to do here."

"It's not cleaning up poop, baby girl." Cole tries to mask his husky laugh behind his hand. "Now that Delaney is officially living with us, I thought why the hell not one more to really round us off?"

She unbuckles her booster seat and flings her door

open with the strength of one hundred bodybuilders. "Betsy, my baby! I'm coming for you!"

Cole and I scramble to catch up to her, the energetic five-year-old now transformed into a miniature road-runner. He swiftly tucks his worn leather wallet into his back pocket, while I sling the strap of my crossbody purse over my shoulder. The three of us power walk to the front door of the shelter, passing rows and rows of the dogs housed in their tiny outdoor cement cells.

I can feel the weight of their sad puppy eyes like a boulder on my consciousness. There are shivering chihuahuas, handsome pit bulls, and countless hyper mutts. Loud dogs and depressed dogs, black and brown and orange. Every single one of them is as cute as the next. Their alerted barks reverberate from within their kennels, pulling at every single one of my tens of thousands of heart strings.

I wish I could take them all home, chuck ball after ball to each one, and cuddle them into a warm bed with a kiss every evening.

For now, Betsy suffices—but I'd be lying if I didn't admit that someday I have plans to have a small herd of rescue dogs running rampant in the sprawling acres of Cole's property.

We tear open the lobby door like we're here to rob the joint. Brittany, the adoption facilitator, walks to the front desk with a giant mischievous smile on her face. She's short and curvy with long black hair, her colorful tattoos peek out from her blue Lawson SPCA shirt. Ava and I have grown close to her over our weeks of volunteering, and she knows our deep love for Betsy.

Brittany waggles her eyebrows up and down. "Well, well, well...can't say I'm surprised, ladies."

"You know I'd take them all home if you let me," I reply, with a wink.

"You did mention before that there's plenty of space in that back field of yours..." Brittany nudges my arm, before turning to Cole who is shaking his head, probably wondering what he got himself into bringing us here.

"Nope. Only one. We're leaving with one dog, everyone," Cole says, side-eyeing me and Ava as we smile at each other conspiratorially.

He runs his hand along the dark stubble of his jaw, a nervous tick of his that I feel honored to be aware of. It makes me love him tenfold and simultaneously want to help ground him. Which is why I reach out and grab his hand, looping my fingers through his much longer ones.

His tense shoulders automatically relax, as his hazel eyes crinkle in the corners as he smiles down at me. There's nothing like being under the gaze of this man. Someone who thinks he's cold and rigid, but actually has a bigger heart than anyone I know.

Ava runs over to us standing in front of the solid oak desk and grabs my free hand. I squeeze her tiny warm palm in rapid gentle succession, and she mirrors the compressions. We're channeling our excitement into our hands since I know internally we're both screaming with happiness and performing a full out cheer routine.

With Cole holding my left hand and Ava clasping my right, I don't see how life could get any better.

Brittany leads us down the hall to Betsy's kennel, filling us in on the adoption process. I really hope Cole is listening because I'm far too distracted by the shelter mayhem.

Who knew all of my life's dreams would come true in the course of twenty-four hours? A loving family. A stable home. And now the most beautiful, crotchety old dog.

"Oh my gosh. Look at her. My little baby." Ava's hands squish her own cheeks together, with major hearts in her eyes, as she stares down at Betsy. The fawn-colored senior sits on her worn dog bed, licking her behind.

I lean into Cole and whisper, "No turning back now. Ready for Betsy to give you a big wet kiss on the lips with that mouth?"

"That dog's mouth will come nowhere near my face."

"At least we know where the source of her bad breath is from now."

His only response is a hand dragging down his face as his body shakes with silent laughter. When Brittany unlocks the chain link fence door, Betsy ceases her butt licking and pops her head up in alert at the gaggle of us staring and crowding into her small space.

Ava crouches down on the cold cement floor with no inhibitions. "Betsy! You're going home. With us! Can you believe it?"

As if the dog actually understands every single word said to her, Betsy slowly stands on her arthritic legs before stiffly trotting over and into Ava's outstretched arms.

Betsy's curled tail wags with such ferocity it seems like her entire body is vibrating. Cole and I kneel on the ground beside our newest family member, saying our hellos.

My heart is bursting with such contentment from the time we sign the adoption paperwork to the car ride home. Even when I clean the puddle of Betsy's urine in the entryway from her excited leaky bladder—all I feel is happiness. Pure, raw happiness.

Cole walks over and hugs me from behind, pulling my back snug to his chest that could double as a brick wall. We stand there watching Ava dote over her new senior dog.

Betsy lies fast asleep, front paws in the air, on her boujee new dog bed. Ava lies parallel beside the bed, looking at her new pet as if she's seen the seventh wonder of the world in the form of a potential world's ugliest dog contestant.

I sigh, happy and content and complete on so many different levels.

"Was that a happy sigh?" he whispers into my ear.

"Yeah, it was. Really damn happy."

Cole kisses the top of my head. "Good. Because that's my goal everyday for the rest of my life. To make my girls happy."

"Think you'll be sick of me within a month?"

"Never." His teeth nibble the cartilage of my ear as my body melts into a happy puddle in his arms. "You're stuck with me now, Emerson. Forever."

EPILOGUE

COLE

One year later

"Dad, are you okay?"

I gaze down into Ava's brown doe eyes. A look of concern has her face inching closer to inspect me. Swiping a hand across my forehead to catch a bead of sweat, I let out a deep sigh. Internally I'm freaking the hell out. Although I pride myself on maintaining an exterior that reads calm, cool, and collected—or at least I thought. Turns out I can't get anything past my intuitive six year old. "Yeah. How come?"

"Well, you look...constipated," she replies, tapping her chipped fingernail polish finger to her chin. "And a little sweaty."

Busted. I'm not constipated, but I am stressed. And definitely a little sweaty. Since I don't want my daughter thinking grown men need to conceal their feelings, I poke a hole in this masked confidence and let it all out instead. "Well, to be honest I am worrying a bit. I also have a question for you."

She perks right up at the mention of my inquiry. "Okay, hit me with it."

"How would you feel if I asked Delaney to marry me?"

"Are you *kidding* me right now?" She jumps up and down, her little fists raised in the air triumphantly. "She's going to be my *mom*?"

I nod to confirm, igniting a round of whooping and hollering combined with a sequence of dance moves that I swear I've seen Elaine execute on *Seinfeld*.

That's it. That's the reaction I was hoping for. Ava's victory dance has me smiling bigger than ever. I figured she'd be thrilled with the news, but her through-the-roof excitement of having Delaney become a permanent fixture in our family fills my chest with warmth like a hot summer's day.

Delaney has been in our lives for a little over a year. Having witnessed Ava flourish in kindergarten, and even volunteering in her class amidst her busy schedule at JunoTec, she has already been more of a mother to her than Ava's biological one.

Ever since my birthday last year, there's been no word from Isabel. Out of politeness, I text Isabel a picture of Ava on her first day of kindergarten. No reply.

No *happy birthday* messages on Ava's birthday. No Christmas card in the mail.

At this point, I'm thinking Isabel may have decided to permanently step out of the picture. Which is fine by me. Ava has expressed zero interest in her mother ever since Delaney has been in our lives. She has filled and healed that maternal want that Ava always longed for.

We would never force Ava to call her any specific title, but I already can picture the sparkle in her bright blue eyes when she hears Ava call her *mom* for the first time.

I smile. "So I take that as a yes?"

Ava throws her body into mine, wrapping her arms around my neck and squeezing me so tightly that the blood rushes to my face. "Duh, of course yes!"

We pull back to look at each other, and the sight of the happy tears in her eyes causes my heart to grow to unimaginable levels. My eyes fill up, matching my daughters. The tears escaping from our eyes are the definitive evidence of how much Delaney has changed our lives for the better, in every single way.

"I hope you have a plan, Dad. And a ring...a big, sparkly one."

"A ring, yes. A plan? Kind of."

Ava raises one eyebrow at me, signaling that she's not impressed with my uncreative ass. "It's *Delaney*, Dad. She's the best person on the whole entire planet, so you better make it good." She crosses her arms in front of her, all full of dark wild hair and attitude the size of a small army. "I'm talking *extra* amazing, okay?"

Geez, kid. No pressure or anything. But she's right. Delaney deserves the best, because she is the best. Delaney and Ava aren't like everyone else. They're special. They're mine. And if one thing is promised in this world, it's that I'll die knowing I've given my girls a good, happy life.

"Well if that's the case, I'm gonna need your assistance. Think you can help an old man out? Maybe help me plan a party?"

Her eyes light up with pride. "I thought you'd never ask."

~

Delaney

The sound of hushed voices through the bedroom door wakes me up bright and early. Opening my blinds I discover it's one of those rare dreary summer days— what people here call earthquake weather. The sky hangs dark and ominous, waiting to pour down and ruin someone's hair. Hot and muggy, with not an ounce of wind. The forecast didn't prepare me for this.

It's Cole's birthday today. For years, *my* birthday was my favorite day of the year. But now I know celebrating someone you love—in my case, Cole and Ava—is just as, if not more, fun to celebrate. Their birthdays are my new favorite.

Now I'm crossing all my fingers and toes that the weather will cooperate. Because in five hours we have forty people coming over for a "small" intimate party.

To my surprise, when I brought up his birthday to him last month, he was all over the idea of a birthday party. He's been very involved with the planning and even suggested inviting our closest friends and family which had me almost fainting from shock. The only rule he laid out was no magicians—can't blame him on that one.

I saw an inch and took a mile with the opportunity to help plan a rager of a birthday party. When I started dishing out invites to people like Ava's kindergarten teacher, his eyes widened only by one impressive millimeter. I know he was thinking *Miss Keely is a close friend?* But I know the woman's coffee order and we gossip about the *Golden Bachelor* so she basically is family now. Plus, in total honesty, I wanted to see exactly how relaxed this version of Birthday Cole is—my suspicions are on high alert.

As I walk down the hall, my furry slippers pad along the hardwood as I simultaneously hear voices shush each other. Standing in the kitchen, I find Cole, Ava, and my best friends Ella and Madi. All in various awkward positions, feigning the picture of calm, cool, and collected.

My jaw drops, a mixture of confusion and excitement. "Um, what the hell is going on here?" I say, as I pull my best friends into a group hug, smooshing their bodies together in my animated embrace.

"Surprise?" Ella wheezes from under my arm.

"I feel like it's *my* birthday, waking up to my favorite people in one room. What are you all doing here?"

"Nothing." Cole looks uneasy, as he fidgets with the edge of his coffee cup.

Suspicious. Very suspicious. Must be a classic case of birthday nerves.

Stepping closer, I rise on tiptoes to meet his lips, savoring the blend of coffee and the alluring scent of cedarwood from his body wash. "Happy birthday, handsome," I murmur, my words as warm as the affection in his gaze.

One arm snakes around my waist, pulling my body flush to his as he nuzzles my neck. "Thanks, gorgeous." Over the last year, Cole has surprised me. For an introverted, shy man, I expected him to not want to partake in PDA. To my surprise however, he initiates it more often than I do.

"Okay, gross. You're in love, we get it." Ella pretends to gag, but turns to wink at me over her shoulder. She's single, and loves to pretend like she hates romance—but we all know she secretly fucking thrives off of it.

Madi chimes in, "We thought we'd get here early to help you get ready. Didn't want you to be stressed on your—his big day." My friend tosses her brunette hair out of her face with a pageant queen smile too big for seven in the morning.

Madi loathes mornings as much as I hate not talking for a full ten minutes. Something is going on and I can't put my finger on what. But I have a laundry list of tasks longer than a *CVS* receipt to complete before everyone arrives. I'll take any help I can get.

COLE TAKES Ava out for an errand, while my best friends and I transform the backyard into an adventure zone with bristle ax throwing and paintball targets. We pick up six dozen birria tacos and an array of sides from our favorite Mexican spot, and arrange kegs and whiskey flights on the back deck.

When Cole had brought up having a party, he said he would handle setting everything up. But I told him this is my Super Bowl—let me have this speck of party madness chaos to look forward to. He was more than happy, and a smidge reluctant, to let me take the reins.

Between orchestrating the party logistics and shouldering a full load of accounts at JunoTec, this month has been nothing short of hectic. Yet, diving back into work has not only kept my mind occupied but also keeps my extroverted social battery charged. Initially, I was nervous of the side eyes and gossip I'd surely be subjected to when I went back to work. But people were nicer than I anticipated, with many offering congratulations and high-fives for helping to get those two douchebags Kenneth and Josh out of there.

The most challenging aspect of my day is being away from Ava for a full eight hours. However, knowing that she's thriving and enjoying her own little social world at school brings me some comfort. She recently mentioned that Renee is *almost* as fun as me. While I appreciate the sentiment, I suspect she might have been sparing my feelings. I've seen the array of intricate art projects and adorable dog outfits they've crafted together—it's a level of creativity that's beyond my skill set, but undeniably right up Ava's alley.

There's been no word from Josh ever since that day, either due to Cole's fists, or the final restraining order the judge approved. The last I heard, Josh's parents whisked him away to one of their old money estates on the opposite side of the country to escape the fallout. While I'm grateful for the distance, I can't help but hope he won't inflict similar harm on anyone else in the future. But for the first time in a long time, I feel safe.

Returning from his daddy-daughter date, Cole's face lights up with a wide smile as he spots his closest friends and family eagerly awaiting him in the backyard. For as much of a loner as he claims to be, there are a lot of people who love and want to celebrate him.

The party rages for a solid three hours. His co-workers challenge him to an ax throwing beer pong mash up game that Cole, of course, wins—because he's unfairly good at everything he tries.

We indulge in and sample a variety of five fancy sounding whiskeys that all taste harsh and the same to my unrefined palate.The kids perform an interpretive dance to an ABBA song that all the grown, tipsy party guests over-the-top applaud to—thank goodness we don't have neighbors closeby.

All in all, the day is intimate, and perfect, and everything I had hoped it would be for him.

That is until the rain starts. And damn, does it start with a fury—as if it wants to show off for the big celebration. The dark ominous clouds that have been lingering for hours, finally decide to pour down on us with a vengeance. A harsh, frosty bite penetrates the air as thick droplets pelt the ground, instantly soaking us head to toe.

Everyone screams in surprise from the rain, shielding themselves from the wet onslaught, with anything they can instantly get their hands on—jackets, paper plates, outdoor furniture cushions. They make a run for it indoors, while I stay right where I am in the middle of the grass, face tilted to the sky, soaking it all in. A perfect mixture of elation, tipsiness, and wonder. A turbulent rainstorm, surrounded by my favorite people on my gorgeous boyfriend's birthday?

A little over a year ago, I could never have predicted being so immeasurably happy. Not superficial happiness. But a joy that runs so deep it has nowhere to go but overflow.

"Delaney." Cole's deep voice growling in my ear makes me jump a foot in the air. He wraps his arms around my waist, the warmth of him penetrating the cold wet fabric of my shirt.

"Damn it. You scared the hell out of me. I thought you ran inside with the others."

"Without you? Never." His cheeky smile lights up his face, making me want to jump him and fuck him right here in the grass.

His hand wraps around my hips as he pulls me against him. A shiver runs down my spine, not from the chilly summer storm, but from the way his eyes eat up the sight of me.

In response, I grind myself against his pelvis, feeling him grow hard through the denim of jeans. This intense connection and hunger between us will never get old. Kissing his stubbled jaw, I whisper into his ear. "I want nothing more than your dick inside me right now."

"Trust me. I want that more than anything too." He pulls back a few inches, staring down into my eyes as he tucks a wet strand of hair behind my ear. "There's one thing I need to do first."

Heavy droplets of rain begin to pour down even harder now, their force so powerful they seem to bounce off the ground. Drenching us to the bone within seconds as goosebumps break out across my skin.

Then he does the last thing I ever expected from him today. He drops down in the sopping wet grass onto one knee. My hands fly up to my cheeks in disbelief as my heart begins to race. Either he dropped a birria taco into the mud or he's about to propose. Every nerve in my body is frozen with the hope that's been coursing through my veins for the last year.

"From the moment I met you I became unraveled and rebuilt with the hope of a future infinitely brighter. And it's all because of you. Because you're my sun. Nothing in this world is perfect. But days filled with belly laughs over ridiculous jokes. Watching you and Ava dance like a couple of maniacs to some song you two can't believe I've never heard before. Getting to hold you on the best of days, and kissing away your tears on the worst of days. Seeing the way your mouth tilts up when a good joke or comeback pops into your head. Being with you, around you," he takes his voice down to a whisper, "and in you." When I laugh through my happy tears, he smiles back with a new confidence. "Messy, raw, love and acceptance is my idea of perfection. And that's what we have." His voice breaks, causing my own happy tears to start falling from my eyes. Clearing his voice he continues, "Seeing your smile alone makes me want to be a better man. I love you. Ava loves you. We just love you so damn much and want to have you as a permanent part of our family, for the rest of our lives. So Delaney Emerson, will you please marry me?"

Tugging his arm to pull him to his feet and out of the mud, I jump into his arms and hug him, squeezing him as close as humanly possible—wrapping myself up into his warm body. "Are you kidding me right now? Yes! Absolutely, one hundred percent yes."

Our noses graze each other's, then slide downward until our lips meet in a gentle collision. His mouth parts, drawing me into a kiss that overflows with every new hope and promise. So sure, and steady, and loving.

We stand there, making out in the muddy field, for far too long, before he places me down, my feet squishing into the rain-soaked earth.

Grabbing my left hand, he slips on the most dreamy diamond solitaire. My hand shakes as he brings my knuckles to his soft lips, kissing each of them with the utmost gentleness.

Before I even realize what's happening, Cole scoops me up and spins me around. Burying my face into his plaid shirt as I laugh, I breathe him in. Committing this memory to heart.

This isn't the end for us. Not even close.

It's only the beginning. Of belonging. Of safety. Of true, messy, out of this world love.

And now something that once seemed intangible has come true. True acceptance—every flaw included.

He's mine. They're mine. I'm theirs.

We are a family—forever.

THE END

ACKNOWLEDGMENTS

Hi. Wow. I'm still in disbelief that I wrote a book *and* had the courage to publish it.

I've always loved writing but never saw it getting to this point. Starting in the third grade, my class was given an assignment to write a short story. Leave it to me to write a whole freaking chapter book...my poor teacher. But that teacher encouraged me to explore my passion and to keep on writing. So thank you to Mr. DiMichelle for sparking that fire in me to explore a craft I so thoroughly love.

The biggest thank you to my two daughters. I didn't know what true love was until I held you both in my arms and felt that immediate unbreakable bond between us. Thank you for loving me more than I've ever been loved before, and allowing me to do the same back. Being your mother is the greatest honor I'll ever have. I hope I can make you proud and give you everything you deserve—because you both are worthy of the entire world and more. My deepest hope is that you discover what you love in life and chase it with ferocity.

Thank you to my parents. For allowing me to follow my passions, even though I tended to flit from activity to activity with the attention span of a squirrel. Tap, ice skating, ballet, guitar, piano, drums, writing. You let me find my path and supported me every step of the way.

Thank you to Melissa Smith Editing for alpha reading this story. You were my very first set of eyes on this book, as well as the first person to read my writing. If it wasn't for you and your enthusiasm for Cole and Delaney's love story, this would still probably be hidden away and floating in a sea of icons on my desktop. You believed in me, which made me believe in myself. So thank you times one thousand.

Thank you to my copy editor and proofreader, Kristen Hamilton. You were one of the first Bookstagram accounts I followed when I began my author journey. Right away, I knew that you'd be the person I'd hire to be my editor if the day ever came that I had the guts to publish my book. You supported me every step of the way, screamed The Way You Shine from the rooftops, and were such a vital part of this journey. I cannot thank you enough for being my safe person to send my manuscript to, and for polishing it up to be the best version it could possibly be. Your encouragement and expertise have truly elevated my work beyond what I could have imagined.

To my readers, I hope you enjoyed Cole and Delaney's love story. Thank you for reading this far and immersing yourself into their crazy little world. The support I've already received has been mind-blowing. To think people actually want to read some silly little story I've written is a concept I'm still attempting to grasp.

Two years ago, I didn't think I was capable of writing a book. Then, I wrote two. I was terrified of sending these stories into the world, but here we are. We did it.

Remember you can do whatever you put your mind to. It's scary, and daunting, and vulnerable. But you can do hard things—because you're capable, and what you want matters.

ABOUT THE AUTHOR

Amelia's passion for writing began in the third grade when her teacher praised her story about hidden treasure as "phenomenal." Pair that with obsessively rewatching classics like "You've Got Mail" and "Notting Hill" as a child, and it's no wonder she now writes romance novels.

When she's not immersed in writing or lost in a book, she's busy raising her two fierce daughters or enjoying pizza dates with her husband.

Keep up-to-date with Amelia at her website, AmeliaChasenBooks.com, and at all the sites below: